SURVIVING REAGAN

SURVIVING REAGAN

ISABELLA

SAPPHIRE BOOKS

SALINAS, CALIFORNIA

Cover Design by Christine Svendsen
Editor - Kaycee Hawn
Book Design- LJ Reynolds

Sapphire Books
Salinas, CA 93912
www.sapphirebooks.com

Printed in the United States of America
First edition – June 2014

This and other Sapphire Books titles can be found at
www.sapphirebooks.com

Dedication

My life has a finite number of days, and I hope to spend
all of them with you, Schileen.

Thomas, Eric and Alex, forever in my heart.

Acknowledgements

Sometimes we are lucky to find friends who become family. I am lucky to have found that with all of those who have come on this journey with me.

Thank you,

~I~

Chapter One

C hadwell Morgan here," she said reluctantly. Chad had been off the grid for the last two weeks. It was the payoff for a long job she had taken protecting an executive traveling in the United Arab Emirates. It had been a tough gig, one where she and her team put in long hours with little sleep and spent countless hours doing surveillance. She'd been glued to the pompous ass day and night. Jack Clark had hit on her more times than she cared to count and the results had been the same each time for the stupid bastard, *no*. She should've just told him outright that she was a lesbian, but somehow she suspected he would see it as a challenge and pursue her even more relentlessly.

Chad tossed the jump rope on her bag and slid her arm across her forehead, wiping the perspiration off.

"Hey buddy. What're you doing?"

"Marco. I'm still on vacation. This better be good." She'd left strict orders to be left alone for three weeks. She couldn't resist packing her *crackberry*, but it had been turned off to the world outside. As soon as she had turned it on it went off instantly. It was one thing to be off the grid, another to be completely out of the loop. The past two weeks had been bliss, no technology, no email, no internet. Sure, there had been plenty of opportunity. The hotel lobby had a business center that she had to ignore each time she passed it. It was chock full of people who couldn't be on vacation without their technology tether.

She'd spent quiet time relaxing by the pool reading sappy lesbian romance books her team had bought her when they found out she was going tech free. Who knew lesbians wrote such racy novels? The main characters had better sex lives than she did, dressed better, and were always fit and trim. They were ready to kick someone's ass, had all the answers to life's questions, and she found herself envious. Where were all the over-forty, hardworking shmucks like her in the novels? It didn't matter; they were good for a quick escape to somewhere else, where women loved women. Her kind of world.

"I know, boss, I'm sorry. I got a sweet deal that I couldn't pass on. I thought I would run it by you and see who you want to push it to. I was thinking Thomas and Meme."

Thomas had worked with Chad on the Reagan Reynolds case and was proving to be a great asset to the company. Meme, on the other hand - *who names themselves Meme*, she thought, having a shiny object moment. Focusing back on the question, she wondered if *Maryann* had enough training and was ready to work a case.

"Why don't you send the details over to my hotel and I'll check them out? When do you need an answer?"

Chad had decided to do more of her work via paper, lately. Electronic trails had been creating issues for high government officials, which made her job easier, but left her business vulnerable from the government snoops.

"Can't I just send you an email with the details? You can look it over and then call me and give me an answer."

"Marco…"

"I know, I know. You're instituting new policies concerning electronic communication, but seriously, this is like taking two steps backwards, boss."

"You remember that when the government comes sniffing up your ass because they got your texts, emails, your tax records, and other electronic shit. Damn Marco, someone was just snooping through our files last month and we still don't know who it was. Obviously, the firewall didn't protect us from someone that high up in the government. The more government contracts we take, the more shit we have to cover-up and I'm sick of burying someone else's garbage." Chad stroked her temples, trying to stave off the killer headache she knew was coming. It always did when she argued with Marco.

"Well, the good news is this isn't a government job."

"Goody, goody. Send me the file and I'll look it over." Looking up at the clock, she continued, "If you get it out to the messenger service, I should get it tomorrow. So if you want me to look at it, get a move on."

"All right, all right. I'll drop it in the mail now. Call me when you get it."

"Now that you've got me working, I'm adding days to my vacation, so don't expect me back until next Wednesday."

"What?"

"You heard me. If you keep talking to me I'll tack on another day, so hang up and let me get back to my women," she said, picking up one of the romance novels she had started that day.

"Women?"

"Marco?"

"Okay, okay. You'll have the brief tomorrow."

"Bye." Chad didn't give Marco time to answer. Turning the phone off, she tossed it on the bed, hoping it would eat the damn device.

Slipping on her swim trunks and tank top, she grabbed her towel, water, and her book. Somewhere by the pool was a chaise lounge, a bikini-clad waitress waiting to take her order, and the beating sun.

Chapter Two

Reagan struggled through the piles of papers on her desk. Leafing through a stack, she was looking for one document in particular. *Grunt work. It was just grunt work*, she thought to herself. She'd been exiled to the documentation section of the R&D factory. Her job was to document the research and development phases of new equipment. She knew everything there was to know about their new 3D printers that would revolutionize small part exchange in the war theater. The military could set up small metals parts shops in the field and fix equipment on the fly. They could make parts for everything from copiers to weapons. It put the military back in control of the supply side of the war and not have to rely on contracting companies who charged exorbitant rates for shipping and fulfillment.

Reagan had brought the idea to R&D and she was spearheading its inception on a small scale. She'd rolled it out in small test markets and the feedback had been fantastic. She wouldn't break her arm patting herself on the back, but she would do everything she could to get the word out. Her marketing idea was to let the supply side of the Navy set up shop in the Asia Theater and try it out. Reynolds Holdings had sent trainers to train the staff on its use, run it through its paces, and report back. Her orders to her team were to push it past its limits. Get tough with the equipment and make it break. So far, they hadn't been able to do anything past gum up the works using the wrong metallic hardening substance in the pressure jets.

"Hey, boss, you got a minute?" A worker walking by Reagan's office flagged her down.

"Sure, what's up?" she said, slipping on a coverall jacket.

"It's the new CNC machine. We spit out about sixteen hundred parts in the last three days and it's taken a dump. I think it's the cutting fluid."

She'd picked up engineering terminology quick. Her on the job training was via the "sink-or-swim" method of learning. She'd decided to be a grunt on the floor, sweeping up the metal shavings, learning how to make her own cutting tool for the metal lathe and then she'd machined a couple hundred feet of metal stock. She was pretty proud of the fact that she could get an almost a mirror finish on her stock and she cut a mean screw thread. While that probably wouldn't get her a job, she was much closer to understanding those women known as *rough trade*. She discovered she liked to work with her hands; it was hell on her manicure, but it was rewarding in a way she hadn't expected.

"Well, Jimbo, when you're using the machine non-stop for the past three days, what do you expect from your equipment?"

"Yeah, but we gotta have these parts out of the 3D printer and in the field within the week. So, she's gotta do double time."

"She?"

"Oh, my machine, I call her a she." He smiled at her and then rolled his eyes as he explained, "You know. Don't you call your car *baby* or *girl*? Well, I call the CNC Bessie. I had a cow growing up that gave so much milk my family had to sell it or waste it. She was a work horse."

"A cow that was a horse, now that's different," Reagan said, pulling off the cover where the gears and belts were located.

"Here, I don't want you to get greasy," Jimbo said, handing Reagan a pair of latex gloves.

"Thanks."

Poking around in the gearbox, Reagan thought she might be able to gauge what the problem might be. *God, how a year has changed me*, she thought, pulling a pen and poking at one of the serpentine belts. She wasn't the same woman who found herself charging for the CEO's job. Now, she was a big sister to a nine-year-old brother and just off probation for a misdeed that could have landed her in prison if it hadn't been for the testimony and faith of her father. Marcy, on the other hand, didn't fare so well. She was in for twenty years and Reagan couldn't think of a better deserving person.

"So, how's that little brother of yours doing?"

Reagan laughed, wondering if Jimbo could read minds. "He's good, adjusting well. I think finding out he had a dad was good for him. His mom…well, let's just say we're glad she's out of the picture."

"You know, I'm sorry all that crap happened to you. I mean, you've really turned things around and I know the guys and I are real proud to have you down here. I mean…" Jimbo blushed at his proclamation.

She knew what was coming next and she needed to defuse the situation before he said something he would regret.

"Thanks, Jimbo. I appreciate hearing I'm fitting

in, just one of the guys, so to speak–"

"Well, not exactly one of the guys, if you know what I mean. I was wondering if you'd like to go out for a drink sometime."

There, he'd said it before she could defuse the situation. Damn!

"I appreciate the offer, Jimbo, but I don't date anyone I work with. I tried that before and it exploded. Remember? Besides…"

"Oh, right. That whole Marcy thing, I just figured it was a phase, you know…I mean…"

Reagan slapped Jimbo on the shoulder in a good ol' boy way. "It's fine, no worries. We're good, right?"

"Yeah, we're good. I didn't mean to step over any boundaries. Sorry, you won't tell the boss, will ya?" He smiled at the implication.

"Naw, I hear she's pretty understanding, just don't let it happen again," Reagan said, hoping that he took what she implied seriously. She didn't want to have to fire the poor guy for inappropriate behavior.

Her father had revamped the employee manual to discourage dating between employees. While he couldn't stop it outside the doors of Reynolds Holdings, he could curtail any future possibilities. It was his contribution to the whole Marcy/Reagan snafu.

"Do you see what I'm seeing?" She said, pointing inside the gearbox.

"Yep, the gear is stripped down. Geez, guess all those parts stripped the teeth. I'll call and get another gear. Good eyes, boss."

"No problem. Thanks for letting me take a look at it, first." She slipped off her latex gloves and looked down at her manicure. Still looks good, she thought, walking away.

"Ms. Reynolds, please report to the main office. Ms. Reynolds, please report to the main office." The loud speaker shouted to the whole floor.

"Oh, I hope that doesn't mean bad news," Jimbo said.

"Yeah me, too.'"

Wonder what dad wants? This can't be good, she thought. She hadn't been called to the principal's office ever and it worried her now that she was.

Chapter Three

Chad relaxed, her hands behind her head, the sun warming her pale skin. She needed this vacation. Her thoughts finally sorted themselves out when she didn't need to worry about schedules, clients, and paperwork. She'd finally be able to leave the stress of the last year behind, with the help of a few girlie drinks with umbrellas. Now, if she could just get one woman off her mind, and out of her heart, she'd seal the deal she'd made with the devil to be free of her. Reagan Reynolds was like heroin; one prick under the skin and you forever chased the dragon's tail, wishing for more. The year before had been hell for Chad. She'd tried everything she could to rid herself of the memory of Reagan's lips on hers, Reagan's body pressed tightly against her own, and the sounds she made when she had an orgasm. Just walking down memory lane right now assured her she would snag a briar or two on her clothes, ripping her thinly skinned attempt at avoidance.

However, fear didn't reach her here. It didn't call her name, or need her attention. Even the sounds of fun in the pool couldn't prevent her from shutting her eyes and drifting off into a light nap. Waking slightly when the sudden lack of sun stopped warming her, she looked up into the shadow of a woman standing over her. Chad pulled her shades down partway and stared up into a tightly wrapped bikini. The sun behind the woman kept her features obscure, but Chad wasn't really looking at her face; the body was a knockout. She was curvy in all the right places. Chad couldn't help but smile.

"Could you move a little to the left please?" Chad shielded her eyes; she anticipated her demand would be followed.

"Hello."

"Hello, can I help you?" Still motioning with her hand to the left, Chad sat up on her elbows.

"Can I ask you a question?" The woman said.

"Depends."

"On what?"

"Can you move to the left? You're blocking my sun."

"Oh, sorry."

Peering at the woman, Chad realized she was more likely a college aged girl, well, woman. Girls didn't come packaged like that in Chad's world.

"What's your question?"

Chad took a sip of her melting margarita.

"Are you a lesbian?"

Margarita went spewing all over Chad just as she tried to swallow. It didn't sound like a question, but more like a declaration. Pushing her shades back into place, she peered around the pool, wondering if Marco was punking her. Across from Chad sat two other bathing beauties huddled together, giggling. She was definitely being punked. Well, she was always up for some lighthearted fun, so she'd play along. Why not? She was on vacation and what happened on vacation stayed on vacation, right?

"So, let me get this *straight*, you want to know if I'm a lesbian."

"Uh huh." The girl sat down on the lounger next to Chad, listening intently for Chad's answer. She cupped her chin in her hands, looking sweet.

"What makes you ask a complete stranger a question like that?"

Blushing, the young woman at least had the decency for her question to embarrass her. She twisted her body towards Chad and hitched her thumb towards the two giggling girls across the pool. "Ever hear of the game truth or dare?"

"Oh, I think so."

"Well, this is my dare."

"Ah, I see." Chad looked over to the girls, who waved and lifted glasses with umbrellas in them. Clearly, alcohol was involved in this dare. The girls erupted into fits of laughter.

"So tell me why you think I'm a lesbian."

She just shrugged and toyed with the fabric of the sarong that wrapped tightly around her hips. While Chad didn't deny her sexuality, she thought she *passed* for straight. Androgynous, maybe. That was how she always thought of herself. Something fellow lesbians could sniff out, but the average hetero wouldn't even suspect.

"What's your name?"

"Tiffany." She smiled and offered her hand.

Didn't that name go out in the eighties? Chad thought, shaking the limp noodle of a grip. Well, it was her turn to have a little fun.

"Chad."

"Nice to meet you, *Chad*."

Tiffany flashed Chad a toothy grin and held on to her hand. Chad played along, cupping Tiffany's hand, pulling her close enough to whisper.

"Why don't you pick one of your friends over there and meet me in room 210 tonight at 10:00 p.m.?" Making a show of checking out Tiffany's body, Chad continued, "In fact, what you're wearing is fine. It'll speed things along."

"But–"

"Oh, don't worry. Remember, what happens on vacation, stays between you, me, and your friend." Chad smiled a wicked leer, lifted her sunglasses, and winked. Tiffany eked out a half-smile, clearly embarrassed by Chad's proposition. Pulling her hand back, she said goodbye, rushing off.

Chad couldn't help but watch the girl and realize Tiffany was just a young woman messing with something she didn't have a clue about. Instead of running over to her friends, Tiffany waved them over as she walked past them. Both girls looked at Chad, frowned, and quickly ran after their friend. Chad wiggled her fingers at them and chuckled.

"That'll teach ya to play in the big kid's pool."

Settling back down on the chaise, she pulled her baseball cap off the side table and covered her face. She'd seen the last of the *queer* girls, as the younger generation referred to themselves. She'd read the stories of girls who didn't want to be labeled bi, lesbian, or straight. Their sexuality was fluid.

"Well, I'll give you fluid," Chad whispered, relaxing back into her chaise. The sun was warming her again.

⁂

Chad flipped through the channels on the satellite. Dinner had been a bust. She loved trying new things, but Creole-Ethiopian fusion wouldn't make a repeat performance on her list of menu choices. It was the last night of her vacation and she wished it would last forever. She'd told Marco she was staying longer, but the reality was she'd been gone long enough and work piled up anytime she was away from the office. The peace and solitude was wonderful and yet it was still another lonely night. One more to add to the many she'd had in the past year of self-exile. She'd distanced herself well enough from her latest heartache, Reagan Reynolds, but there were days when she would catch herself thinking of Reagan. Tonight was one of those *days*. A smile, the way a woman walked or dressed would throw her right back into a moment best forgotten and yet she couldn't forget.

Tap, tap, tap.

Chad looked down at her watch and wondered who'd be knocking on her door at ten o'clock at night.

"Shit." Chad looked through the peephole. "You've got to be kidding!"

Chapter Four

Hello Frank, you wanted to see me?" Reagan tried to keep her tone even when she addressed her father.

He'd done his best to keep her out of prison, but even a high-priced lawyer couldn't undo what she had started and Marcy had *exploited*. The gut punch for Reagan wasn't doing ninety days in jail and a year on parole for her part in the faked kidnapping attempts she had staged. Frank's lawyers with the help of Chad Morgan had proven the attempts on Frank's life had been all Marcy's doing. The fact that poisoned food had been found in Reagan's own frig only cemented that Reagan was next in line to die. It would have left Frank's son with Marcy, the sole beneficiary. That was the gut punch. Trying to prove she was ready to lead Reynolds Holdings, even in the most dire of circumstances, had opened the door to Marcy's even more diabolical plan. So being called to her father's office now wasn't just a surprise, it was a shock.

A year later and Reagan still found herself on the outside, summarily shoved off to one of the sub-contractor sections of Reynolds Holdings. She suspected it was her father's way of keeping her in the company and giving her a chance to come back in a leadership role, eventually. Reagan knew Reynolds Holdings better than anyone else and her father knew it. Frank had over fifty-one percent of the company and could dictate her return, but the board had wanted concessions and the FTC investigation didn't help.

"Good morning, Reagan. How are you this morning?"

She missed the way he called her pumpkin, or sweetheart, but she had no one to blame but herself.

"I'm good, Mr. Reynolds, thank you for asking."

"Good," he said, thumbing through some paperwork in his hand. "I hear you've gone all in on a new project." Frank signed some documents and shuffled paperwork around on his desk like a blackjack dealer in Vegas.

"We did, the laser drone project looks promising."

Frank looked up at Reagan deadpan and pursed his lips together. Reagan used to see this when she was a kid and being less-than-honest when her father asked her a question. She suspected he gave the same look to her new half-brother.

"What?" Reagan said defensively.

"Sit down please." Frank pointed to an armchair in front of his desk. "I understand we're investing in some radical 3D technology that could potentially change the way we go to war?"

"Oh that." Relief flooded her voice. His question assured her she wasn't being called to the principal's office for wrongdoing. "We've designed a new portable 3D printer." She shrugged her shoulders. "At least what we think is portable enough."

"I've heard about them, but have yet to see them in action. I'll have to come over to the division and take a look."

"I think it's pretty revolutionary, actually. The military needs replacement parts and this printer can stop them from having to wait for weeks to get small parts. It won't work for larger parts over eighteen inches, but there is potential for larger component printers in the field. They just aren't as portable."

"Well, I'm proud of the way you're keeping your finger on the pulse and knowing when and what to look at."

"Thanks." She was almost embarrassed that she was eating up the compliment. To say it had been a while since her father spoke glowing of something she did was like saying hell had a heating problem.

"The reason I wanted to see you, Reagan, wasn't about new R&D. There is a conference, The International Women in Business conference in Abu Dhabi, that I would like you to attend."

"Me."

Reagan was stunned that her father would have her attend one of the biggest women's conferences in the world. "You want *me* to represent Reynolds at the conference?" She had to ask the obvious. "You know people will talk about what happened, they might even ask me. I don't know if I should be the one to represent the company. I mean…well it's just that… well the focus will be on–"

"I know, the question will be how I could trust my own daughter to represent Reynolds. I'm sure you'll have a ready answer by the time you get there." He smiled reassuringly.

The whispers barely died down when she entered the room at her own company. It had taken a whole year of proving herself to get those to a low murmur. A conference of this scale would be daunting. Anxiety started to creep up; her chest constricted and her throat felt like it would close. Reaching into her pocket, she pulled a Lorazepam, broke it in half, and stuck half under her tongue. She palmed the other half in case she needed more.

"I trust you, Reagan, to represent Reynolds Holdings and the way to show the rest of the world I trust you is to send you out there as Reynolds Holdings." His smile, his eyes - all a portrait of a loving father who was trying to forgive his daughter.

On the other hand, Reagan wasn't the same woman as before. Her egotistical arrogance was replaced with a downsized personality, which was more retro and introspective than before. She guarded her feelings and didn't let anyone close. Now, she felt more like an abstract painting that people couldn't figure out, an unfinished sand sculpture that just needed a little more to make it work. A small price to pay for lessons she should have learned earlier in her life. How her father could be so forgiving, maybe not right away, was beyond her. She would have thrown the book at herself and then question her decision making skills, let alone her leadership. No, her father still had a lot to teach her and she realized, almost too late, that she had a lot left to learn about leadership.

"I don't know, Mr. Reynolds, I mean this is a big conference. Lots of really important women from around the world are going to be there."

"Precisely." Frank poured some coffee and motioned to her with the pot. She shook her head. She didn't want to counteract the safety pill with caffeine. "Mrs. Allegany is going to be there and if there is any way we can put on a good face with her, I think it could be beneficial to us if her husband is elected president."

"Okay, who else will be in attendance that you would like me to get cozy with?" Reagan fidgeted in her seat. Her palms were sweating as she thought about the prospect of putting herself out in such a public place. While men were the hawks of business, women were the falcons and she was about to be thrust into the nest of the biggest bird of prey in the world.

"Wait, not cozy," Frank quickly corrected.

"Sorry, I didn't mean it like that."

"I know you didn't, pumpkin."

Reagan's head popped up and glanced at her father. He was still looking into his coffee cup, but a slight grin creased his weathered face.

"Several heads-of-state will be there. Women from banking, technology, human rights, you name it, chances are they'll be in attendance."

"I see. Most of these women will know what happened and they'll–"

"I want you there. I need you there. If for nothing else than to be on a fact finding mission for us. Listen, see what's going on. Who is talking to whom and who are the major players in this little chess game?"

"I can do that," she said, unclenching her hands and trying to relax into the idea. White powder was all that was left of her safety pill. "Thank you for trusting me with this, Frank. I'll try not to let you down."

"I know you won't."

"Anything I need to be aware of before I go? Oh, and when do I leave?"

"Conference starts Monday, so I would think you should leave this Thursday, giving yourself enough time to compensate for jet lag. Just be aware of who's there. Get a feel for what these women are talking about. We need to know what's in the pipeline, politically." Frank leaned on his desk and smiled at Reagan. "You know it's often what's being said behind the conference that's important. A lot of negotiating and deal making is going on, so go with your gut."

"I will. I won't let you down."

"I know you won't. Talk to Tim. He has your travel itinerary all booked."

Tim was Marcy's replacement and unsurprisingly to Reagan, her father had selected a man and a total divergent from any of his previous assistants in the past two years.

"Thanks."

"Oh and honey?" Frank walked around the desk and grabbed Reagan's shoulders.

"Yes?"

"Be safe. Abu Dhabi is a foreign country and a long ways away from home. You know how they feel about women, so be careful when you venture out."

"I'll be careful, I promise."

"That's my girl." Frank pulled Reagan into a bone-crushing hug. She couldn't be happier than she was right now. It had been a long time since Reagan and her father had a talk like this, so it wasn't lost on her what he was really saying. At some level she'd finally found herself back in her dad's good graces, at least partially. She wouldn't blow it this time.

Chapter Five

Chad's office drag was confining. She adjusted her shoulder holster for the umpteenth time that morning. Its stiff leather constricted her movement. What she wouldn't give to be back poolside in her board shorts and tank. Smiling, she thought about the cute college girl she'd moved on at the pool.

What's that they say, pillow princess, she thought as she remembered the little swath of hair above her pubic bone.

"Hey boss, glad to see you back," Marco said, slapping her on the back.

She almost lost the folder tucked under her arm as she grabbed the paper cup of hot tea with both hands.

"I wish I could say the same, Marco."

"Awe, you missed me, admit it," he said, reaching up to pinch her cheeks.

"Stand down." Marco froze at the stern tone in her voice. "Don't even think about it."

"Why, boss, I just wanted to show you…" He reached up and squeezed her cheeks anyway. "How much I missed you," he said, gently rocking her face back and forth. "Besides, I can take you any day," he said, sprinting for the office door.

"Fuck," Chad said, cupping the top of the cup. "Asshole!"

It's going to be one of those days, she thought,

following him inside. Looking around, she expected to see a change. She always expected to see change when she took an extended vacation. However, it was just the same as when she left it, in need of a good office assistant who would turn her piles of folders into a more organized mess.

"So what did the kids do while mommy was away?" Tossing the folders on the ever-growing stack on her desk, she shucked her blazer and leaned against her desk sipping her tea. As was customary, Marco was sitting in her office on her couch thumbing through the sports section of The Chronicle.

"Same old, same old," he said, absorbed in the big story of major league baseball's implosion. Marco lived, ate, and breathed baseball. His hopes of being a baseball player on a scholarship were dashed when 9-11 struck. He graduated from college and went into the Army, Special Forces, Delta to be exact. They'd met by accident when she was recovering in the Army hospital from an attempted attempt on her life, him from a training accident that cost him his career. She stroked the scar leftover from the stabbing. The pain of it was just under the surface, never far from her mind.

"So hey, got any juicy gossip from vacation?" Marco folded the paper and slapped the table with it, wiggling his eyebrows.

"Seriously? No, I don't kiss and tell."

"Oh, someone got lucky. Was she tall, and all sexified in one of those little string bikinis?"

Chad quirked an eyebrow and tried to stop the smile before it had grown too big.

"I knew it." Marco stood. "She got legs up to here?" Marco said, hitting his hipbone.

"They usually do, don't they?" Chad chuckled at the reference she'd heard so often from men. "Where else would they be?"

"Funny, ha ha. So…"

"So, nothing. What's on the worksheet this week?"

"Not much, we still have those four active cases and one that just came in. Requires a woman's touch." Thumbing through the file, Marco glanced at her with a smile. "So you really aren't going to tell me?"

"I'm really not going tell you."

Chad smiled. Tiffany had been a nice diversion that wouldn't take no for an answer. A chill spilled over Chad; it felt similar to Tiffany's fingers as they glided down her arms. Whoever Tiffany was at the pool, wasn't the same Tiffany that showed up at her door that night. Vixen! That wasn't a word Chad ever used, but it was the one that popped into her head after her wild night with Tiffany. Chad didn't have the heart to tell Marco she'd spent the last twenty-four hours fucking like a rabid bunny. What Tiffany lacked in experience, she made up in enthusiasm. Chad licked her puffy lips. Swollen nipples, tender to the touch, made her flinch when she put her bra on that morning and she knew a hot bath would expose the rest of the over the top escapades with Tiffany. She was just what the doctor ordered, balm for her soul. God, she wished her vacation had lasted longer, 'cause even though Tiffany had left her number behind in lipstick on her bathroom mirror, Chad knew she would never make that call. Tiffany had so much life before her and Chad wasn't the teaching type, looking to school a young woman in the ways of lesbian love. It never ended well. Especially with women who claimed their sexuality was fluid. It was damn close to dating a straight girl as far as Chad was concerned. Chad wasn't against taking a few laps around the track, but she wasn't used to being the one taken for a test drive.

"Damn. You know I live vicariously through you."

Chad felt bad for Marco. He and Julie had been married for years and had beautiful daughters. So he considered himself the "old married" guy of the crew, which for Chad had been sort of a blessing. Marco handled life better married. He was more stable, dependable, and rock solid than the single, carousing Marco who had the tequila flu weekly.

"Yeah, well just imagine the body of a triathlete with the face of Marilyn Monroe. Big red pouty lips and smoldering brown eyes," she said, knowing he'd beg for more details eventually.

"Oh, no fuck?"

All she could do was nod. She didn't want to burst his bubble.

"So back to work. Pass the girlie case to Sofia. She's due."

"You might want to reconsider; besides, he asked for you."

"Who asked for me?"

"Mr. Allegany."

"Mr. Allegany, as in possible presidential candidate, Allegany?"

"Yep."

"Do you have the pre-interview paperwork?"

"Right here," Marco said, tapping the folder under the newspaper.

"What's the job?"

"Protection detail."

"Oh, no. I'm not doing another protection detail. Call him and tell him we're passing on the job."

"It's a lot of dough, Chad. Besides, that was over a year ago. You've got to let it go." She knew Marco was referring to the Reynolds case and he knew enough about what had happened, that he should have passed on this one.

"Marco." Her voice almost sounded pleading to the point of whining. "How much money are we talking?"

It always came down to green. Pushing the folder to the end of the table, he opened it to show her the check.

"You've taken a check already?"

Checking out the security green paper, she rolled her eyes. "Shit, that's a lot of zeros, buddy."

"He said you'll need it to put up with his wife for two weeks."

"Two weeks. Where the hell am I going?"

Chapter Six

Abu Dhabi," Reagan said again into the phone to her still unbelieving cousin.

"Are you kidding me? Uncle Frank is sending you to a place where women rate just below farm animals?"

Ashley Henderson had been the only family member to speak to Reagan after her "incident". Her cousin had been her closest confidant after her mother's death. They'd been pinkie tight all through college and when she went out on a date, Ashley was Reagan's "one phone call" when she found herself in a spot she couldn't get out of.

"It's the International Women in Business conference. I think they picked the Middle East for a reason."

"Yeah, as in it's hot as hell and you can get arrested for doing practically nothing. It's perfect actually. Send all the power women over there and blow up the hotel. walla, you've got your *uppity women* problem solved."

"Ash, don't be so peevish, it's just a conference." Reagan could feel her cousin's cynical attitude, but then again, surviving an abusive relationship did that sometimes. Reagan was so glad Ashley had found Tyler. She was the balm on Ashley's old lingering scar.

"Subject change, how's that hot firefighter of yours? Is she still leaving you smoldering or has the glow faded from the ember?"

"Oh, who's being pessimistic now? She's good. She wants you to come over for a barbecue. We're having a few friends over that we want you to meet."

Reagan's chest clenched. She knew that was code for *hey, we have a "friend" we want you to meet.*

"Hmm, I can't. Remember, I have a conference." Reagan didn't want to come right out and say *no setups;* that would be rude. Besides, her cousin was only looking out for her. The pain of public scrutiny was still too much to bear. It was why she'd become a homebody lately.

"Oh, no worries, we'll just wait until you get home. Besides, Tyler won't take no for an answer."

"Then put her on the phone and let me tell her directly."

"Oh come on Rae, don't be a stick in the mud. You haven't been out in months."

"Over a year to be exact, but who's counting."

"Obviously you are, so let's do something casual. Just a few friends to get your feet wet. You can't continue to hide away in your bedroom upstairs. It's been over a year since that trial. People forgive and forget, Reagan."

Maybe Ashley was right. Maybe enough time had passed since the Marcy *incident* that people wouldn't remember, wouldn't judge. Could she risk it though?

"Tell you what, I'll think about it."

"That's my girl. Well, I should let you go. Hey, if you get into any trouble over there in Abu Dhabi, you remember the signal, right?"

Reagan chuckled at the plan she and her cousin had come up with in college. When they went out on a date, they always let the other know details like person, time, and place. If they found they needed out of the date, they would dial the other. One ring meant *call me*, two rings meant *come and get me*, and if they were in dire circumstances three rings and a hang up meant *it's an emergency*. They'd used this system so much during college that it practically became rote.

"Yeah, yeah, I remember," Reagan said through a chuckle.

"Okay, what is it?" Ashley's tone was dead serious.

"Seriously?"

"Yep."

"One ring, hang up – call me, two rings and a hang up means come get me, three rings and a hang up means call my dad."

They rarely used three rings. There wasn't a situation Reagan couldn't get herself out of. For God's sake, she dated lesbians. But that notion was thrown out the door when Ashley dated…the abusive lover. It was the one and only time Ashley, now a cop, had used the three rings signal.

Ring, ring, ring. Reagan grabbed her phone to answer it, but it had stopped ringing. The signal.

Panicked, Reagan rushed to Ashley's place only to come face-to-face with Ashley's abusive lover, Leslie, ready to pound the shit out of Reagan when she arrived.

"Reagan, it was three rings," Ashley said, shocked.

"Oh, is this who you dialed? Is this your get out of jail free card, bitch?"

Reagan had a brief glimpse of a scared Ashley, swollen and bloody, holding a rag to her chin, before the door was slammed in Reagan's face

"Fuck, fuck, fuck." Trembling, she dialed 911 and reported what she'd seen. Within minutes, she saw

three police cars arrive at Ashley's. All the officers had guns drawn.

"Where's Officer Henderson?"

All Reagan could do was point to the door, tears streaming down her face. She was suddenly afraid. She didn't know what they'd find on the other side of the door, but if what she'd seen of Ashley's face was any indication of the damage this psycho could do, Ashley's life was at risk.

Reagan remembered as the whole scene played out in what took only minutes, but felt like hours before the abusive bitch came out first. Leslie smirked at Reagan. Without thinking, she ran up to Leslie and slapped her face, trying to knock the smirk sideways and yelled, "You fucking monster. If you hurt Ash, I'll kill you, you fucking bitch."

Another officer threw up his arms to deflect any more blows that might land and pushed Reagan back.

"Ma'am, if you do that again I'll have to arrest you for assault."

"I want that bitch arrested for assault."

"I think you have bigger problems to worry about, like assaulting a police officer," the cop said, yanking Leslie to the patrol car.

Reagan could hear him reading Miranda rights to the bitch as he pushed her into the back seat.

"Hey, did you hear what I said?"

"What? Sorry. I guess I was somewhere else. What did you say?"

"I said, no, three rings means it's an emergency and get help."

"Right. Look, I'm going to be in a foreign country. It's a little far to send in the Calvary. Don't you think?"

"Yeah, maybe you're right. But you never know."

"Yeah, yeah, tell you what, I'll call you every night and you can tell me a bedtime story." Reagan smiled

"Fine."

"Have a good night and don't worry, I'll be fine." These were Reagan's parting words as she hung up and settled in for the next chapter in her journey towards redeeming herself with her father.

Chapter Seven

The conference room table was covered with building plans, dossiers on all the women scheduled to attend the conference, and background material on the companies, countries, or organizations they represented, as well as travel itineraries.

"Geez Chad, this looks more like a crash and retrieval than your basic run-of-the-mill protection detail," Marco said, scanning the table.

"Nothing is run-of-the-mill and once you start thinking like that mistakes get made, things get overlooked, and people get hurt." Chad pulled building plans towards her. The conference was in the tallest hotel in Abu Dhabi. A security nightmare for her, but one of the newest and best security systems in a hotel.

The hotel management hadn't exactly been forthcoming when she'd requested more info on their building, their security in place for guests, or the conference room's layout. For a price, though, anything could be had and it was laid out in front of her for that price.

"Yeah but-"

"But do you remember who we are protecting and where?"

"Of course."

A possible first lady, who had a habit of pissing people off with her stand on women's rights, was going to a section of the world that had a polar opposite view of women's rights. Chad waited as the rest of the team came into the room. No use wasting time when she could say it once and brief everyone altogether.

"We only get two people in her protection detail." Marco reminded Chad

"That's what they say. I say we get as many as I think we need. Now…"

Chad laid out the details of the trip, who would be where, and the equipment they would be taking.

"Concealment is the word of the day," she said, making eye contact with all five people. "It's a foreign country with strict laws. We won't be able to get much in the way of weapons so we will be taking something that will level the playing field."

"Edgar?" Someone whispered.

Edgar was the nickname the crew gave a three dimensional printer that Chad had learned about when she attended a mandatory conference on Homeland Security. The licensing in the state had changed and anyone in the executive protection industry was required to take a course on homeland security. She'd thought it a waste of time, until they started a break out session that included ways terrorists were getting weapons through security checkpoints. *Edgar* had the ability to make plastic guns, sturdy enough to fire a single round. Getting rid of the evidence was as simple as setting it ablaze and watching it melt into a lump of unrecognizable plastic.

"Of course," Chad said. "That piece of equipment will allow us to pass through any security screening, keep us off the radar, but it only gives us one shot in some instances."

"Nice pun, chief," Rita said, smiling.

Rita would be the other female on her visible team. The rules of the conference clearly stated that men could be behind the scenes, but not visible. Some would have none, but the bigger personalities of the conference could have only two security personnel. Chad would massage the rules to fit her own needs. She wouldn't get hired again if she put her charge at risk because of some silly limit. If these organizers knew anything, they would cut the guest list down, keeping their attendees safe. Hotel security was often men who wore ill-fitting blazers, carried a walkie-talkie, and wore comfortable shoes. Not acceptable.

"So, I assume we're taking the goose?" Marco ticked off something on the clipboard he was studying.

The goose was a modified 747 recently purchased for their bigger operations that required cars, and big equipment. It also allowed a base of operation to be set up almost anywhere a 747 could land. Lately bigger jobs were landing in their laps, especially after the Reynolds case. She avoided thinking about that case at all costs; the cost was her heart. She lost a bit more of her humanity on that case.

"We'll need the goose. Mr. Allegany is willing to pay extra for the ability to keep his wife safe. So we need to be prepared for anything. We'll take our own vehicle, so get clearance through the government, schedule refueling, and make sure the goose is ready if we need to extract Mrs. Allegany at a moment's notice."

"Okay. I've requested a complete list of attendees, staff, and security personnel," Marco said, still scratching on the clipboard.

"Good. People, we need to be alert. The Taliban chatter is up, chatter in Iran is off the chart, and we're getting some Intel from Saudi Arabia."

"I'll make sure we get those lists before you leave in the morning."

"Morning." The team groaned.

"Sorry, we need to be in place and waiting for Mrs. Allegany the minute she gets off that jet."

She felt bad about the late notice; she'd only found out the details herself when she walked into the office.

Mrs. Allegany better be on her best behavior, Chad thought. She had enough of mouthy women for her lifetime.

"Okay team, let's get packed up, and get the gear checked, double checked, and loaded up. Zero dark thirty comes way too early. By the way, no drinking for the next two weeks." Chad looked down at her watch. "Starting now."

Another long groan hummed in the room. No alcohol meant it was going to be a long two weeks.

Chapter Eight

Reagan tossed her bags into the trunk of her sedan and suddenly wished she hadn't packed so much. Gone were the days when she'd had a car pick her up and someone to help her with her luggage. She lugged her own stuff to the car now. It was part of her father's plan to teach her a lesson.

"Hey, need help with that, Legs?" Tyler said, running over to Reagan.

"Oh god, you're a savior." Reagan released her death grip on the heavy roller.

"Geez, what've you got in here?" Tyler grunted, heaving the bag in and tossing it with a thud into the trunk.

"Two weeks of clothes, computer stuff, and alcohol."

"Alcohol?"

"Yeah, I'm not risking not being able to have a much needed drink in a country that doesn't like alcohol."

"Oh come on Reagan, surely the hotel is cosmopolitan enough to know how to cater to their international travelers."

Reagan hugged her cousin Ashley as she continued to talk. "Well, Tyler. I don't take anything for granted anymore. Besides, I plan on holing up in my room and working the whole time. It'll keep me out of trouble."

"Oh Reagan, you're not trouble."

"No, but somehow trouble seems to be able to find me pretty easily," Reagan said, tossing in her briefcase. "I'm starting to think they're selling roadmaps to my house." She chuckled softly

"Awe, I think someone needs a big old butch hug," Ashley said, pointing towards Tyler.

Tyler furled her eyebrows and shook her head. Ashley motioned her head towards Reagan and Tyler huffed toward Reagan and opened her arms.

Seeing the whole thing play out, Reagan laughed at the exchange. Putting her hands up, she said, "Thanks Tyler, I'm good."

"You sure? It isn't often your cousin pimps me out."

"I'm good. Thanks." Reagan opened the driver's door. "Well, I guess I'll see you chickies when I get back. Tyler, I hear there is a kick ass barbecue happening when I get back."

"So I hear." Tyler cast a dubious glance at Ashley. "What?"

"Group hug," Reagan said, throwing her arms open wide. "I'll see you when I get back."

"You got it," Tyler said, squeezing Reagan tight.

"Okay so… Don't forget the signal."

"Signal?" Tyler quizzed.

"She's being silly, don't pay her any mind." Reagan squeezed her cousin tight and whispered in her ear. "If I send that signal, you better come running, cousin."

A wink and a smile was all Reagan had left in her as her anxiety choked back the tears. Driving off, she waved at the pair in her rearview mirror.

"Signal? What's that all about?" Tyler said.

Reagan smiled watching as Tyler wrapped her arm around Ashley. She wished, she hoped, she would find a committed relationship like that.

"Oh, it's just an inside joke we had in college," Ashley said, tapping Tyler's stomach. "Hungry?"

Chapter Nine

The room buzzed like a swarm of bees in a mating frenzy for the queen bee. The queen bee in this case was Sylvia Allegany. She was Chad's new client and the wife of the rumored presidential candidate, Sam Allegany. Normally, Chad would be happy to be in a room full of estrogen, but this was estrogen bordering on testosterone. To her recollection, women in power were often as ruthless as men, just with nicer clothes and smelling better. Turning, she indicated it was safe and her charge walked in behind her, stopped, and surveyed the room, the same way Chad had, but with a smile.

Chad could see the wheels turning in Sylvia's mind. The world beckoned her in a way that it did people who *might* be running for president. Piranhas in a fishbowl and raw meat had just been thrown into the water. Reporters swarmed them the minute one had spotted her. Chad could read the reporters lips as she whispered Sylvia's name and then it all started to move in slow motion. The reporters circled them, crowding around Sylvia, herself, and Sylvia's assistant Jason, one of the few men allowed at the conference. Chad knew Sylvia had pulled strings to get him into the conference and she already had taken a dislike to the man who smiled in a wicked way that bothered her.

"Mrs. Allegany, is your husband going to run for president?"

"Mrs. Allegany, what does your husband think about the high unemployment rate in his state?"

"Mrs. Allegany, why isn't your husband running for governor of California, instead of leap frogging to the presidential race?"

Chad was feeling uneasy with the crush of the crowd and waited for Jason to take a queue with the surge, but he just stood there smiling. "Okay everyone, Mrs. Allegany is here as a guest speaker for the conference. Save the questions for her husband," Chad said, spreading her arms wide as if it would protect her charge from the throbbing masses.

"I'll be happy to take a few questions," Sylvia said, trying to shove Chad out of the way.

"Mrs. Allegany, I don't recommend that, you'll have time later for questions."

"Nonsense, I always have time for reporters. Ask away," she said, oozing southern charm all over the place.

Chad suspected Sylvia's trip to the international conference was more of a fishing expedition for her husband's possible presidential campaign than to bestow any pearls of wisdom to the high-powered elite. The acquiescing in Sylvia's tone was enough incentive for the throngs to push closer. Chad searched each face, and looked at all the microphones pushed in Sylvia's face for any signs of trouble. Every news agency was there covering an event that would barely make page two in the business section any other time. Business was still an old boys' club that allowed very few women past the glass ceiling. Oh, they could press their noses against the glass and look up to see what shoes the men were wearing, but that would be as close as most educated, qualified women would get. It was a shame, really, that Reagan Reynolds had screwed up as bad as she had, thought Chad. For all her faults, Reagan could have claimed her right to be amongst the power elite of the old boys' club. She tried not to keep track of Reagan after all that had happened. It wasn't her fault Reagan had trusted a woman like Marcy. Marcy had other ideas when it came to Reynolds Holdings and Reagan being the CEO wasn't one of them. Luckily for Reagan, her father had survived the attempted poisoning, but then he'd gained a son neither of the two knew anything about.

"Ms. Morgan is currently handling my appointments—"

"I'm sorry, Mrs. Allegany, that would be your assistant, Jason."

"Well yes, but you ultimately veto the sweet boy's itinerary. I just thought we could skip to the chase and you could set something up now. Won't you be a dear and do that?" Sylvia wrapped her hands around Chad's biceps and squeezed them gently, flashing her pearly veneers and then looking at the crowd around her waiting for their murmured agreements. "Please? I would hate to make all of these wonderful people who've come so far have to wait just to talk to lil ol' me, when there are so many other fantastic women who deserve their attention more."

Chad could see how she and the reporters were being played and standing right behind her was that smirking, snot-nosed ladder climber, Jason. Oh, how she wished she could smack that smile right off his face.

"I'm sorry, Mrs. Allegany. We have a vetting

process and since most of the media didn't send us their credentials, I can't just arbitrarily decide to break from the security routine." She pulled her arm from Sylvia's grasp and turned to the mass that seemed to have doubled in two minutes. "If you'll submit your credentials to my assistant at MorganExecutiveRelations.com, we'll try to expedite the process. You'll get an answer and a time to interview Mrs. Allegany one-on-one, or you'll have to wait for the press conference at the end of the conference."

She wasn't thrilled that the coordinators had put several press conferences together for the bigwig attendees, allowing them to take questions en mass. She understood why they did it, but it was a security nightmare in the making. It would be an even bigger risk for her crew, though. The organizers made it clear – security details were restricted to two security attendees at the conference and one must be female. She could've had an all-female team, but Marco was one of her most trusted friends and he was SIC, second in command, so he came, leaving Thomas and Sofia in charge back at the suite.

"Sorry everyone, I tried," Sylvia oozed. "I look forward to seeing those that get through my security detail. Don't be intimidated, her bark is worse that her bite." Sylvia smiled and scrunched her shoulders and squealed when she grabbed Chad's bicep, again.

"Mrs. Allegany, is it true you're here to land support for your husband's possible run for the White House?"

Chad stepped between the reporter's line of sight and Mrs. Allegany. Clearing her throat, she drilled the reporter with her gaze. "Look, no questions at this time, means no questions. Got it? Now, I'm sure Mrs.

Allegany needs to get to her room and freshen-up. It was a long flight, so if you'll excuse us…" Chad pulled her sleeve back, pressed a button on her watch, and said, "Are we ready for retreat?"

"We're a go. Camp is clean, trails are clear, and we're in position."

"Roger."

"Campers leaving now."

Chad pulled Sylvia's elbow and stuck her hand out, clearing a path to the elevator. Why Sylvia demanded to come in through the lobby was clear. The media wouldn't have known she was here if they had come through the more secure underground entrance. The hotel had assured Chad their security team was up to par when Sylvia made a stink about how she would arrive. For the amount of money she was being paid, Chad didn't care if she arrived on the backs of six big men holding a sedan chair, as long as, of course, it had room for her security team.

The elevator doors swished open and Chad let Sylvia and Jason in first, but just as she was about to get on, a well-dressed woman slipped past her and settled herself in the middle of the elevator. Chad looked at her then Sylvia and Jason who both shrugged their shoulders in unison.

"Excuse me, ma'am, I'm afraid I'm going to have to ask you to wait for the next elevator."

"Excuse me, I don't think so. Do you know who I am?"

"No, I'm afraid you have me at a loss." Chad lied; the woman had popped up on her radar when she ran the speakers list through her database. "Nevertheless, if you would be so kind as to step off the elevator," Chad said, her foot kept the doors from closing. "I would appreciate it." Pulling on the woman's sleeve, she waited. When she didn't move, Chad tapped on her watch. "Marco, we have a situation in the lobby elevators."

"Roger that, I'll send in the ranger."

"Is this really necessary, Chad?" Sylvia cooed, trying to be polite. "I don't mind—"

"I'm sorry, Mrs. Allegany—"

"Oh, Mrs. Allegany. I was hoping we would have the opportunity to meet. My name is Señora Colleen Velazquez. Perhaps you know my husband, Juan Diego Velazquez?" she said in a smooth as silk Latin accent.

"Well, it's a pleasure to meet you, Señora Colleen Velazquez. I'm sure my security detail will have no problem allowing you to ride up with us. Will you, Ms. Morgan?"

Chad could see Rita rounding the corner as she tapped her watch and said, "Call Ranger off."

"Roger that, Ranger off."

Making eye contact with Rita, she rolled her eyes and shook her head as she let out a flustered breath. She would have exposed the fact that she had more than two on her security detail if Rita showed up, but she didn't care. Her responsibility was to her client and not to some artificial agreement that could put her client in danger.

"Oh relax, Ms. Morgan. It'll be fine."

The southern accent was starting to get on Chad's nerves and she'd only been with the woman for two days. Chad wanted to turn her back on the bantering women, but Señora Colleen Velazquez was someone who had a reputation and it wasn't exactly a stellar one. Her husband was an arms dealer who was less than ethical, but well connected.

Pushing herself against the sidewall of the elevator, she checked out the new addition to the ride, five-four, fair complexion, blonde hair up in a conservative bun, generous curves accentuated by a flowing gown that seemed to drift with each air current as the doors opened up. A giant handbag that could hide a multitude of weapons seemed to be the one item out of place.

Pulling out a pad of paper she kept in her blazer pocket, Chad nonchalantly started to write something. What her non-observant passengers didn't know was they were being captured on video surveillance. Tapping her lip with her pen allowed her to snap photos of the woman she would use later to confirm her identity. For shits and giggles, she snapped one of Captain Oblivious, Jason, just so she had him on camera, too. Looking up, Chad noticed the mirrors on the elevator and could almost see whom Jason was texting. Snapping a few photos of the reflection, she'd have them blown up and see what information she suspected the little prick was sending. *You can't be too careful or too nosy*, Chad thought, nestling the pen into her front pocket so she could record without being obvious.

Ding.

"Aw, we are here on my floor. It was wonderful chatting with you, Mrs. Allegany. I see we have much to discuss during the conference."

"Yes, please, let's chat more. I'm sure we can be of service to each other in the future. You know men, they just look at data driven numbers and not the faces beyond the numbers."

"So true, Mrs. Allegany, so true. Well, thank you again and thank you, Ms. Morgan, for allowing me to avoid the crush of reporters." A flick of her hand and she was gone, seeming to float down the hall, her gossamer dress flitting about as she shuffled down to her room.

"Of course," Chad said to closing doors. "Of course."

"Now see, Chad. She wasn't a kidnapper or an assassin."

"Yes ma'am. May I remind you that your husband was very clear on his instructions to keep you safe–"

"Oh poo, George is a worry wart, I think he's more worried I might say the wrong thing and end up getting caned or something."

There was some validity in what Sylvia said. She was an image of opposites – a well coifed southern lady on one side and on the other side, an outspoken feminist who'd take any opportunity to chide a government for their lack of human rights when it came to women and children. The fact that the conference was in Abu Dhabi would only exacerbate the situation. The Middle East's record on human rights was fodder for a woman like Sylvia Allegany and quite frankly, Chad was surprised her husband had let her attend when it was announced she would be special speaker at the conference. She was a lightning rod and the organizers had known that when they extended the invitation. It would get them the much needed publicity for the conference and it would push George Allegany into the spotlight via his wife, Sylvia Allegany. Everybody was using everybody in this potential international crisis.

"Well, let's try and not let that happen, shall we, Mrs. Allegany?"

"Of course, Chad. What would my husband say

if some brutal dictator ordered the wife of the possible future president caned?" Sylvia laughed at what she thought was a joke.

He'd probably think you deserved it, thought Chad.

"I'd hate to think what he might say, Mrs. Allegany," Chad said, opening the door to her penthouse suite. "I'd hate to think."

Chapter Ten

Reagan's dress stuck to her like second skin. It only clung tighter each time she tried to pull it off her sweaty body. The conference in Abu Dhabi was starting to feel like a bad idea, but she needed to prove herself to her father, so she'd taken the lead to represent Reynolds Holdings at the International Women in Business conference. A cold, tall gin and tonic sounded nice right about now. Looking down at her watch still on California time, she realized that wouldn't be happening for another three hours.

Reagan spotted the camera crew as they entered the large conference room. The reporter scanned the room and briefly made eye contact with Reagan just as Reagan dipped her head, hoping the reporter would overlook her as just one of the many attendees.

"Kill me now. Please," she muttered, her head lolling back against the edge of the chair.

"Well, that's a tad dramatic isn't it?" A soft voice said to her right.

Stiffening, Reagan sat up straight and tried to glance casually towards her right. A fair-skinned woman with striking features was smiling and checking her out.

"Excuse me?"

"Oh, I'm sure you're just tired, but a request to be killed could be misinterpreted, especially in the Middle East." The woman stuck her hand out. "Hi, I'm

Señora Velasquez." The accent washed over Reagan, its soothing sound tickling her ears.

Reagan stared at the hand, and then caught sight of the reporter moving around the room getting closer to her table. Gathering her things, she shoved them in her bag, just as she saw a group of reporters swarm a woman and her staff.

"Poor woman," Reagan said to herself.

"Oh, her? That is Mrs. Allegany, the future first lady."

"Yes, I know." Reagan tried to catch a glimpse of Sylvia Allegany, but the crowd around her grew as attendees jumped to their feet to try to see the political powerhouse. It was like watching feeding time at the zoo. The animals were off leash and pouncing on a smiling future first lady, who was perfecting her swarming techniques.

Reagan turned her attention back to packing up her briefcase, hoping she wouldn't be noticed just as she heard someone mention her name. A few in the swarm who'd been entrenched in getting a story from Sylvia now turned their attention to her and suddenly she found herself waylaid by several of the reporters.

"Ms. Reynolds, how does it feel to be off parole?"

"Ms. Reynolds, can you tell us what you were thinking when you faked the death threats?"

"Ms. Reynolds, how do you feel about having a little brother?"

"Ms. Reynolds, are you still in love with Marcy?"

Reagan shook her head and gave them a disgusted look. "No comment."

"Please, Ms. Reynolds isn't here to discuss her past. She's a conference participant. Leave her alone." Shocked, Reagan looked at Señora Velasquez, who'd put herself between Reagan and the reporters. "Now go, or you'll miss your chance to spin Mrs. Allegany's words into untruths." Señora Velasquez motioned the reporters back just as Reagan worked her way past them.

Good manners and protocol dictated that she thank Señora Velasquez for her kindness, but Reagan wasn't in the mood for small talk. Usually she could've handled reporters, like a skilled surgeon handled a scalpel. She'd cut them with her razor sharp wit, laughing at their petty questions. Lately though, she didn't want to find her words, or her image, splashed across the papers. Reagan had grown tired of finding herself on the society page with the tag line, "Former future CEO of Reynolds Holdings finds herself..." doing whatever made it news worthy to report.

Chapter Eleven

Chad wiped the sweat from her eyes. The stifling heat outside the hotel kept her to once around the block and then quickly back indoors, so she passed on the quick run for a dash on the treadmill. Chad punched the buttons. She pushed herself faster until her six miles were done. Pressing them again, she slowed to a fast walk. The equipment left a lot to be desired and she found the hotel had separate gyms for the women with the better equipment for the men. Clearly, women didn't work out in Abu Dhabi. The hotel spent their budget on plants and water features that seem to be the very center of attention on every floor in the hotel. Thinking about the work schedule, she made sure Rita was with Mrs. Allegany and Marco was in the room, behind the cameras, watching as they caught the guests arriving for the conference. They were using face recognition software and with their tap into the US database, they should be able to find out who was staying in the hotel.

The short time she'd been with Mrs. Allegany had already split her last nerve. Chad doubted the woman had ever been told no before and wasn't use to the restrictions Chad had placed on her. *No little dogs.* Mrs. Allegany had thrown a fit when she was informed that Bush and Cheney had to stay home. *They wouldn't pass quarantine,* Chad lied. Pets were like little kids; they were great as long as they were

                    Isabella

someone else's. Her lifestyle didn't promote acquiring pets, or spouses.

Chad practically tripped off the treadmill when a voice squawked in her ear. "Hey boss."

"Jesus, Marco. You scared the shit out of me," she chided. She knew she should've taken her com system off if she wanted privacy and yet she was on duty twenty-four/seven, so that wasn't an option.

"Sorry, but I thought you might want to see this."

"I'll be right up. This better be good since I haven't had a minute of peace and quiet since I've been here."

"Not sure it's good, but it's important."

"See you in ten."

"Okay."

Chad tried to rack her brain, thinking of what was so important Marco had to interrupt the only half of an hour she had to herself.

Chad pushed the door to the suite open, the hum of computer equipment filled the room. A printer spit out paper that was spilling onto the dining room table. As Chad caught sight of her crew, they suddenly went silent when she walked into the room. Suspicious, she tossed her workout bag on the only clear spot on the table.

"What's up?"

Marco looked to Sofia, who'd joined the group after checking out the rest of the hotel. Sofia turned her attention to her computer screen and sidestepped the question by asking one of her own.

"Coffee, boss?"

"No, thanks." She staked Marco with a stare, her hands on her hips. "What's going on?"

Grabbing stacks of paper from the printer, he

handed photos to Chad. "Thought you might want to see this." Moving over to Sofia, he nodded at the photos and then continued, "Can you rerack the video?"

"Sure, but do you think I should?"

"Just do it. Keep an eye on the cameras and let me know who else pops up on screen."

"You got it."

Chad thumbed through the black-and-white photos then stopped on one. The face had changed in a year. It was still beautiful, but in a different way. Chad couldn't put her finger on it, but the woman in the photo almost seemed lost.

"Is this who I think it is?" Chad quizzed the room, asking no one in particular.

"We checked the hotel computer system and Reagan Reynolds is registered for the conference and just checked in."

Chad noted the timestamp on the photos and then looked at her watch. "Who's on her?"

"No one. She showed up alone. At least we don't see a shadow."

The intel surprised Chad. Reagan was in a foreign country with no one. Surely, Frank would have sent someone with Reagan. She was still with Reynolds Holdings. Chad had deliberately kept her distance from the Reynolds, especially Reagan.

"She's here all by herself?"

"We didn't see anyone with her… but we did see this woman talking to her." Marco pointed to the computer screen with a frozen photo pasted across it. Chad stared at the screen and then told Rita to play the video.

Reagan sat at one end of the table in the conference room, leaning back against the chair and said something. Chad couldn't read her lips, but she'd seen Reagan do this very thing before and knew she was tired and had probably said something like "kill me," or "fuck me." It was her usual line when she was tired or nervous. Chad was betting Reagan was tired; she never got nervous in huge groups. In fact, the exact opposite happened. Reagan fed off crowds. When she was on, she was good, engaging, and on fire. She had a chemistry that made people sit up and take notice.

"That's the woman from the elevator, Mrs.… Mrs…" Chad patted her chest, looking for her notepad. "When did she arrive?"

"A couple of hours ago."

"Why didn't you call me when she checked in?"

"We had to be sure it was her, and you were in the elevator escorting Mrs. Allegany to her room."

Marco scrubbed his chin, a sign he was uncomfortable being grilled. "We saw who she was talking to, I figured it was time to let you know." Marco slapped her on the shoulder. "Besides, it was only a matter of time before you ran into her. Forewarned is forearmed."

Chad couldn't believe her luck. Of all the place she could run into Reagan, working in Abu Dhabi wasn't one of the places she wanted it to be. They not only would run into each other, but more than likely they would find themselves face-to-face at the conference. Well, not if she had anything to say about it.

"Do we know if she is who she claims to be?" Chad said, remembering Colleen Velasquez from the elevator. "Did we do a background check on her?" Marco handed Chad the folder. The look on his face told her everything she needed to know without looking in the folder. "That bad?"

"She's married to an arms dealer turned dictator, small island syndrome. He thinks he's big enough to play with the big boys, but they won't pass him the ball." Marco looked over Chad's shoulder explaining.

"I've heard of him. Who the hell hasn't?" Chad pointed to the screen. "Great, but what's she doing here?"

"She, on the other hand, was a beauty queen that met a bad boy who just happened to be the dictator."

"Why do women always fall for these guys?" Chad thumbed through the pile, looking for answers. "Why is she here though?"

"Connections? You've got me." Marco shrugged.

"Conveniently, she bumps into Mrs. Allegany in the elevator."

"She was waiting for her?"

"Maybe. Anyone with her? Bodyguard sitting in the corner or lurking around?"

"Not sure. With the number of people milling around it's hard to say," Rita said over her shoulder.

"I think it's safe to say her husband wouldn't let her travel without protection. Word is he's running drugs and laundering money through island banks."

"So she's shopping for…"

"An American to help her and her husband get some legitimacy."

Chad tossed the file on the desk and wiped the beads of sweat that dotted her upper lip. She needed a shower and time to analyze the curveball that she'd been tossed.

Reagan.

She'd have been happy never to lay eyes on her ever again, but their paths seemed to be destined to cross; now all Chad needed to do was make sure those paths didn't intertwine.

"I'm hitting the showers. Keep an eye on her," Chad said, pointing to the screen. "That woman is up to something and I want to know who she's talking to and who she's hanging out with. Keep an eye open for any "meat" hanging around." Chad shuddered at what she just said. It was how Reagan had referred to her and funny now that she used the word. Just seeing Reagan again was already having an effect on her. "Sofia, get down to relieve Rita. Stay on Mrs. Allegany like a postage stamp."

Rita tossed her earphone on the table and picked up her com system. "You got it."

"Marco, check the cameras and make sure they're still hidden. Keep the chatter to a minimum; we don't want anyone picking up on our conversations, especially anyone connected to this woman's husband."

They had strategically placed a few cameras in the lobby, and throughout the conference areas. But their best coup had been tapping into the hotel security system. They had limited their time on the tap, not wanting to be found out, but the time it had saved was worth the effort. The only problem was that the hotel was tapped into a lot of places they shouldn't be, such as workers' locker rooms, areas guests might be in compromising positions, like the saunas, changing rooms, and the gym. The biggest surprise had been the rooms that had shown up in the rotation. They were empty right now, but eventually they would have guests. Chad figured they would put someone from the mid-echelon of the social or business structure, hoping to get lucky on a tip or some morsel of blackmail.

Chad shook her head. She saw conspiracy

everywhere now.

"Have we checked to see who's in those rooms yet?"

"You mean the ones with cameras? No, not lately. I thought you didn't want to peep in those rooms?" Marco squinted his eyes and cocked his head

"Well… I don't, but I want to keep an eye out and know who's where. You know, I don't like surprises."

"You want me to check now?"

"Naw, I'll check them myself. That way if anything happens, the team is clean and can say so." She'd rather take the blame for something than make her team lie to cover for doing their jobs. "Besides, I'm sure anyone connected to the con wouldn't be put in those rooms. All right," she said. "I'm off to get a shower. Keep your ears and eyes open out there people."

A chorus of, "You, got it," sounded through the room.

Now, if only she felt as confident as they sounded, but one thing assaulted her mind. Reagan Reynolds.

Chapter Twelve

Hey, I got this shift, why don't you take a break and go get some sleep?" Chad tapped Thomas on the back.

"You sure? You've been dealing with Mrs. 'It's all about me' Allegany all day. I'm sure you're wiped," Thomas said, still shifting in his seat in front of the monitors, grabbing video throughout the hotel.

"Yeah, I'm good. Besides, how busy could it be?" Chad assured the youngest guy on her team. Thomas had pretty boy looks, but bad boy attitude written all over. The full sleeve tattoo only added to his *trouble* mystique with the women. The only thing missing was the leather motorcycle jacket and prison *jacket*. She was sure Thomas was voted most likely to go to prison in high school, but looks could be and were deceiving. A college grad, Thomas finished well at the top of his class in computer programming. He turned down a good paying job with a top IT firm to go freelance and she'd picked him up on a job that could have sent his cute ass to prison for a long time. Instead, she'd convinced him that working with her was a better alternative than her turning him over to the government for prosecution.

Chad settled down into the seat, a cup of tea in one hand and the mouse in the other.

"Hey boss, I've set up the tablet with the security video system on it. That way you can have a peek when you're out." His finger slid across the screen and popped up the same view she was looking at on the monitors, only smaller. "You want to see one of the cameras, you just tap that box and bam, it pops up full-screen." Squeezing his fingers together on the screen, he closed the window and was back to the original six boxes.

"Yeah, but we have twenty cameras and the hotel system," Chad reminded him.

"No problem," he said. Swiping the screen again, he positioned the new set of six cameras and continued until he'd shown Chad all the cameras. "It's not as nice as sitting here, but it is more mobile. Since the screens are numbered, you can call out a number and you can pull it up and see what we're seeing. Cool huh?" He smiled.

"Very." Chad swiped her finger across the screen, checking out the cameras and then tapping a box, a woman's image popped up. Reagan. Squeezing her fingers together, she quickly closed the screen and moved on to another.

"Wouldn't want to spy on guests," she said as she quickly moved her attention to the monitors where she could see more. "Okay, thanks, Thomas. Now get some sleep."

"Thanks boss, holler if you need me." Thomas yawned and shuffled towards one of the back bedrooms.

Finally alone, Chad clicked on the hotel camera that was in Reagan's room. Her mind said no, but something else in her just couldn't resist now that she knew Reagan was at the conference. Then something dawned on her, why would the hotel put Reagan in a room with the camera? Something just didn't sit right.

Reagan wasn't some high-powered exec anymore. Chad wanted to chuckle at the irony but couldn't. Reagan had done it to herself. She was the one who lost the respect that came with being the head of Reynolds Holdings. Her integrity was questionable at best and at worst, she was being set up. She knew Frank Reynolds didn't work that way though. He had integrity; it was the reason Reagan hadn't gone to the big house. Frank had vouched for his daughter, before God, the court, and the news media, those barracudas that circled waiting to see what chum might be thrown into the water at the trial. They'd been disappointed though; Frank, and Reagan by default, had turned the tragic situation into a mythic family reunion with a little treachery thrown in for flavoring. Just what the media liked, a son that appeared out of nowhere, an ex-mistress who wanted the Reynolds dead, and an unsuspecting daughter trying to prove herself to her father. *You couldn't make that shit up,* Chad thought, remembering the look on Reagan's face when she had outed Marcy as the one who had poisoned Frank. Reagan couldn't fake surprise like that; no, she lived her life out in the open for all to see and experience.

Without thinking, Chad ran her finger over Reagan's image on the tablet cradled in her lap. Gone was the reckless fun-loving woman, her vibrant face replaced with a sober, almost stoic appeal. However, as Chad knew, looks could be deceiving when it came to Reagan. *Take her at face value at your own peril and she would make you rue the day you met her*, Chad said to herself.

Clicking the box closed, she eyed the other camera shots, one catching her attention. Standing outside smoking a cigarette was Colleen without her requisite hijab. At least Chad thought it was her; the face seemed right, at least what she'd seen of it. The blond hair flowing freely blew in the breeze away from her face. Chad wanted to zoom in, but remembered she was on the hotel security system now and it would bring attention to whoever was sitting at the desk monitoring the cameras.

She could see Colleen's lips moving but there wasn't anyone in the camera range. Pushing the record button, she hoped she could catch enough of the conversation that she could send it off and have it analyzed by a lip reader. Call her paranoid, but the wife of an arms dealer, the possible first lady, and Reagan all at the same conference spelled trouble to Chad.

Colleen spoke for a few more minutes, stubbed out her cigarette then looked up at the camera and smiled. If Chad didn't know better, she would've sworn Colleen knew she was being watched.

Creepy.

Hitting the stop button, she saved the file, compressed it, and composed an e-mail to her contact in the government. She had him to thank for the Reagan Reynolds experience and he owed her big time. He would have someone who could look at the footage and let her know what Colleen was saying and if she was lucky, who she was talking to as well.

Hitting send, she would wait a day at the most to find out what Colleen said, but it would be a wait nonetheless.

Chapter Thirteen

The darkness of the corner booth suited Reagan's mood. Thank god the hotel was a major chain and she was grateful it had a bar. Her luggage had been gone through and someone had seen fit to abscond with her alcohol. She was sure it would fetch a high price in a country where drinking was frowned upon. She hoped that was the only snafu she would encounter. Her call to Ashley had been short, both in length and in tone.

"Hey cuz, how was your flight?" Ashley's bubbly voice was an irritant and she didn't know why.

"Funny you should ask, Ash. Seems some bastard broke into my carry-on and stole my wine."

"Oh God, did they take anything else?"

"Isn't that enough?" She snapped back

"I'm sorry Reagan–"

"It's not your fault."

"Well, how's your room?" Another bubbly question.

"I'm so high I could get a nosebleed. God forbid there's a fire, I might as well just jump out a window. I'd die before I got down all those stairs anyway."

"Okay, so I hear you have jet lag, a bad room, and nothing to help you cope with the trip so far. Is this your phone a friend signal? Because if it is it's not going well," Ashley said tersely.

"I'm sorry, Ash. I guess I wasn't as ready for this

trip as I thought I was. I'll call you later." Hanging up quickly, she leaned back and found herself sinking into the soft comfort. "Great, a marshmallow booth."

She needed a drink.

❧ ❧ ❧ ❧

Reagan stirred her drink and suddenly noticed no sound, no ice. She hoped the soda was cold at least or it was definitely going to be a long night. Hell, with her crappy attitude it was going to be a long conference.

"There's no ice in your drink." The fair stranger from earlier looked down at Reagan.

"No, there isn't and I won't have to worry about catching something in the water." Reagan was too tired to care what the woman thought about her acerbic response.

"Oh smart. Hi, I'm Colleen Velazquez. Remember from earlier, and remind me, you are?"

Reagan wasn't sure if Colleen was being a smart ass or if she really didn't remember her name. Considering the reporters where shouting it with every question, it would be hard to forget.

"Alone for a reason," Reagan said, her short temper still hanging on.

"Ah, well, nice to meet you, 'Alone for a reason?'"

"You are smarter than you look."

"A joke. Good, well at least we know you have a sense of humor."

Undaunted, the woman slid into the booth and motioned for a waiter. "Another for her and I'll have a Cosmo, please."

"Of course, Mrs. Velazquez." The waiter smiled

at Colleen and then let his eyes roam over her.

Great, a lady's man. Reagan rolled her eyes.

"You must come here often, they know you by name," Reagan said suspiciously.

"I tip well," Colleen said, reaching for the newly deposited drink.

"Obviously."

Reagan had hoped that her unapproachable demeanor earlier would have stopped Colleen from further contact but she was wrong. Sliding away from Colleen, Reagan began to reach for her warm drink just as it was replaced with a fresh one.

"Ms. Reynolds." He smiled and turned his attention to Colleen, winking. "Mrs. Velazquez."

Relief surged through Reagan when Colleen returned the wink. Obviously, the woman didn't bat for her team. *Thank God, one less problem*, Reagan thought, watching the exchange between the two.

"So you never said why you're in Abu Dhabi." Colleen tried again.

Ah, it was stupid question day at the con.

Reagan barely looked at Colleen. She really wasn't in the mood to be engaging tonight. It had been a long flight, her luggage tampered with, and the fact that she was out of her normal environment didn't make for a happy Reagan.

"So Ms. Reynolds, that wouldn't be Reagan Reynolds of Reynolds Holdings, now would it?"

"The questions earlier didn't give you a clue?"

"Well, I must confess that I looked you up on the internet."

"Then I'm even more surprised you still came over and decided to chat me up."

"I don't judge, Ms. Reynolds. We all have our

skeletons, no?"

"Hmm, so it seems."

Reagan wasn't trying to be deliberately obstinate, but she wasn't ready to play nice with the corporate children yet. The conference didn't start for another day and she would need that day to prepare herself for the stuffed blouses, the ass-kissers looking for their next contract, and the media darlings, like future first lady Mrs. Allegany.

"I know you're ready for this, pumpkin."

Her father's words hung in her head. He put his trust in her and sent her to the conference and she wasn't about to let him down.

"It doesn't cost anything to be nice and smile, Reagan," Ashley told her before she boarded her flight to the conference.

"I know Cousin, I just don't know if I'm ready for something this big," Reagan admitted her fear, even if vaguely.

"Yes, I am that Reagan Reynolds," she said, offering a small smile and raising her glass in salute. "Cheers."

Now that wasn't hard, was it, she told herself. She'd need another drink if she was going to be engaging and social. Calling the waiter over, she ordered another round. Might as well be social with another American, at least the conversation was less painful.

Chapter Fourteen

The bar was too dark for Chad to see what was going on, but she could see Reagan drinking with someone.

"Damn." Why did she care what Reagan did? She had cost Chad plenty in emotional equity. Getting up, she flipped the controls to the multi-screen shot of the hotel. She didn't need to waste time on Reagan Reynolds. Stretching, she felt her scar pull as she arched backwards. It was proof that she carried enough baggage. She didn't need a new carry-on. Shivering, she flipped the AC off. Marco kept the room so cold someone could hang beef in it and the beef would not spoil. Old habits die hard, she guessed at the holdover from their military days.

"Keep 'em cold, keep 'em awake." They used to say.

She needed a new mug of tea and a distraction. Cradling the steaming cup, she walked around the small confines of the suite, doing mindless laps, glancing at the monitors as she passed each time. Nothing moved, so she stopped and switched back to the bar shot. Reagan still sat in the booth chatting with someone. She hadn't changed. One would have thought after all she'd gone through she would have made a conscious effort to be careful, but obviously she was still up to her old ways. Chad began pacing the suite again. Her replacement would be in soon and she hadn't finished her paperwork or the assignments for the next day. Tension bunched in her shoulders, and her muscles ached. Luckily, she wasn't wearing her holster; that would only add more discomfort. Chad rotated her head and wiggled her shoulders, trying to loosen them up, but the knot only tightened the more she tried to relax. Swinging her arms, she started to punch at the air while she paced the suite. A little shadow boxing would keep her loose and keep her focused on mapping out the assignments for the day.

"Geeze, who you beatin' the shit out of, boss?"

Startled, Chad pivoted and punched at the voice. Clipping Marco's jaw, she pulled her punch just enough to keep from knocking him down. Before she could land the left cross that instinctively followed, Marco pivoted, blocked her hand, and tried to smack her on the back of the head. Ducking, she sliced the air with a spear hand and tapped him center mass, causing him to gasp for air as she knocked the wind out of him.

"Uncle," he yelled, putting his hands up, sucking in air. "This is a bad version of that movie where the house boy is constantly trying to get the drop on his inspector boss." Marco rubbed his chest.

"You shouldn't sneak up on someone. You're just lucky I wasn't cleaning my weapon."

"No shit. What's go you so jumpy?"

"Nothing," she lied. "I'm just trying to work through the man power for today."

"Oh, I can do that. No biggie." He sat behind the computer and studied the monitor and then looked at Chad, frowning. "How long you been on this channel?"

"Too long," Chad said, rubbing her fingertips. "She's like a fucking drug. I get sucked in just looking at her. Pretty bad, huh?"

Her candor was surprising even to her and she wasn't sure why she was unloading her burden on Marco, but it seemed lately they had that kind of relationship. He was her longest relationship, other than her parents, and that scared her. She hadn't planned on being alone at this age, but looking at forty wasn't as bad as it sounded. Being alone at forty was worse.

"No boss, it just means you're human and love is something that never leaves us."

"Love?"

"Come on, boss. We both know you fell hard for Reagan. Hell, I fell hard for her and I didn't sleep with her."

"Funny..." Chad looked back at the monitor again and waited for any movement from the booth.

Chapter Fifteen

Chad picked up the phone and looked down at the number, Washington D.C area code. It was her contact she'd sent the video of Velazquez's wife taking a smoke in the lobby and chatting on the phone. He'd probably have the lip reader's notes and yet she didn't want to answer it. She had a slight churning in her gut, a warning she was usually right.

"Yeah?" she said, sounding rather disinterested.

"Chad?"

"Agent Dave?"

"Are *you* on a secure line? Cause that isn't funny. You know the NSA is crawling up everyone's ass and you're calling me out on the phone. Nice move Morgan."

He didn't just sound pissed, Chad knew she'd accidently stepped over the line trying to be funny. Lucky for him she was on a disposable, but probably still traceable on his end.

"Are you on a *secure* line?" She tried reversing the tables on him, hoping to squirm her way out.

"Of course. Christ, if I didn't know better I'd think you were a rookie when it came to covert communication."

"I'm on a throw-away with a signal scrambler, so relax, Dave." Chad rolled her eyes. She hated it when he was short with her; he wasn't her boss anymore. Yet, he acted like it when he had sensitive information to impart to her, so this wasn't going to be a courtesy call to let her know he didn't have anything. Her gut was never wrong, never. "You have the results of that video I sent you, Dave?"

"I do, but I have a question first. Where are you?"

"Why?"

"Because the woman in that video is married to one of those despot drug dealers, Juan Diego Velazquez, we've been keeping an eye on."

"I figured he'd be on someone's radar."

"Yeah, well he's on ours. Where are you?"

"Tell me what the video said first." Chad was starting to worry now that her D.C. connection was quizzing her. He usually passed off the information she needed, hung-up, and only called her when he needed a favor in return. Which luckily was rare lately.

"We could only get a few lines, but let me read it verbatim so we both understand the implications."

"Okay," she said, hesitating, opting not to say what she'd really wanted.

"First line reads–when will the courier arrive? Second line we got–I'll let you know when I've finished…then we go blank when she turns her head away. It looks like a guy walks by and she freaks out a little, turns her head back towards the camera. Obviously, she's trying to conceal her conversation from him as he stands a little close. The next thing we see is–three days, four max. I'll send you a message when it's done. And finally she says–antidote or antibiotics, we're not sure which. And that's all we got."

"Well, that's not much."

Chad's mind was trying to fit the puzzle pieces of the vocabulary into a digestible puzzle she could swallow, but it wasn't fitting together very well. She could speculate, maybe Colleen Velazquez had a stomach ailment or medical condition and her husband was sending medicine. Maybe he was sending a drug fix and she was talking in code. Filling in the blanks wouldn't be easy, but she knew that this woman was married to a ruthless piece of shit who had money and connections at his fingertips.

"Can you get me all the info you can on her husband? Friends, associates, anyone he's done business with in the past five to ten years."

"I'm not sure–"

"If you've been watching him, if he's been on your radar then you know what he's into and I want to know, too."

"That's a lot of information. I'll email–"

"No, did you just bitch me out about secure communications? Send it by courier. I don't trust the government. They've got eyes and ears everywhere."

"Chad, I am the government."

"Yeah, don't remind me. Can you give me some time to find out what she's up to?"

"I can give you a week at the most. Then I need to pass this video off to someone higher up the food chain than me."

"Five days *after* the courier arrives. By the way, I'm in Dubai."

Silence. Never good, but normal for a government agent who knew he was now officially over his head.

"Shit."

"I know. It changes things a wee bit, now doesn't it?"

"Christ, I can't help you there."

"Nope, I was afraid of that," Chad said, knowing

the U.S. government wouldn't meddle in the affairs of a foreign government and while she wasn't involved with a government issue in Dubai, it was still Dubai. A Muslim country that didn't take well to the U.S. tossing their weight around inside their borders, but if she told them who she was protecting they might jump feet first into the puddle of shit she suddenly found herself in, so she'd wait. Mrs. Allegany was her trump card out of the country if things went south, but she doubted she'd get the chance to play it. They'd find out soon enough and she figured she only had about a week. Velazquez's wife was up to something and she'd not only have to secure Mrs. Allegany safety, but Reagan's, too.

Shit, Reagan, too?

"Chad…be careful. This suddenly stinks."

"Ya think? Yep, thanks for the info. I'll let you know what I find out."

"Be careful." He stressed again.

"You said that already."

"Yeah, well it bears repeating. You're not exactly known for staying out of the line of fire."

"Understood."

"Besides, you owe me lunch when you get back."

"Since when?" Chad didn't make any deal for lunch. She didn't eat lunch. Her schedule rarely allowed the luxury of sitting down to a mid-day meal, let alone take someone else out.

"Since right now. It's the least I can get for five free days."

"I'll call you when I'm stateside." She knew he'd been angling for a date for years. She was surprised he hadn't picked up the fact that she was a lesbian, but then *Captain Obvious* was more like *Captain Oblivious* when it came to personal stuff.

"Great. I'll see you stateside."

Before she could respond, the line was dead. Just like him to get the last word. Chad wondered how long Dave would really give her. Five days was too long for the government to stay silent on a guy like Juan Diego Velazquez. He was a leech attached to the ass of the U.S. government, sucking blood and defecating dead bodies in his wake. It was highly unlikely his wife was here alone either. Chad needed to find her companions, and she used that word lightly, before she carried out whatever plan she and that leech had up their sleeves.

A bigger question was–what would she do about Reagan? God, why did she worry about Reagan at a time like this?

Chapter Sixteen

Well, what do we have here?" Sylvia said, looking at Reagan.

The day had started shitty and was getting worse by the hour. Sleep had evaded Chad the whole night, but Reagan's memories didn't and that was the problem. Every time she closed her eyes, there was Reagan standing in front of her smiling, laughing, or trying to kiss her. That was the last time she had tea before bed. Chad hoped she could avoid seeing Reagan or at least avoid Reagan seeing her. She'd been successful up until now. Chad turned away from the pair, listening as Sylvia engaged Reagan.

"Don't I know you?" Sylvia said, grabbing Reagan's forearm. "You're Frank's little girl, aren't you? Shame about that business last year."

Chad wanted to melt into the floor. Sylvia dropped right into the nest of snakes without thinking. Chad had worked hard to keep her name out of the news and disassociate her company with the entire incident and she'd been successful. Now, would Reagan out her to Sylvia? She didn't want to wait around to find out.

Whispering into her wrist mic, she called for a change-out.

"How do you know my father, Mrs. Allegany?"

"Oh Reagan, your mother and I go way back. I went to college with Frank. Good looking young man and your mother, well, she was a sweetheart. Not surprised your dad scooped her right up."

"Yes, well, I barely remember my mother. Perhaps we can have dinner some time and you can tell me all about my parents and their college days."

Reagan's voice sounded strained to Chad. If she was lucky that's the last time she would hear it on this trip. Waiting for a replacement, Chad kept her back to the couple and kept watch over the room. The women milling about looked as if they were waiting for their time with the *regal* Mrs. Allegany. They were keeping their distance, probably because Chad was in watchdog mood and her body language said, *stay the fuck away*. Chad didn't want to run interference if she didn't have too.

"Why don't we have dinner tonight? I believe my schedule is open, but let me check my schedule. Ms. Morgan, am I available for dinner tonight?"

Damn.

"Mrs. Allegany, I've told you before I'm not your assistant. I'm part of your protection detail."

"Yes, well I thought perhaps Jason ran my schedule by you and you might remember if I am free this evening."

"Yes, you're free this evening," Chad confirmed.

"Excellent, how about tonight, Ms. Reynolds?"

"Oh, I don't know…"

Thank god, Chad thought. At least she had the good sense to stay away from Chad. At least she hoped that's why she rejected Sylvia's dinner offer.

"Oh, please. I'm really tired of all the wrist bending and political talk. You'd be doing me a favor and besides at least we don't need an interpreter. Not that these women aren't remarkable, but I just feel so…tapped out right now."

"Well, perhaps you'd rather have a quiet dinner in your room?" Chad interjected.

"Nonsense." Sylvia grabbed Reagan's arm and pulled her close. "I'd love to have dinner with a fellow compatriot. How about you, sugar?" she said, looking at Reagan.

God, kill me now.

"I don't know–"

"Oh nonsense, you must have dinner with me, I insist."

"Well if you–"

"Wonderful. We can meet in my room for a cocktail and then head out for dinner after that. I'd love some girl talk and you can tell me all about that *stuff* that happened last year."

"Hmm."

Oh great, this is just wonderful.

"Great, fiveish? I'm in the penthouse suite. I'll see you then."

Rita arrived just as Sylvia was finalizing her plans with Reagan. Perfect timing. Chad looked down at her watch; dinner was in about an hour and she would be off, doing something far away from the duo.

"Mrs. Allegany, Ms. Reynolds," Rita said, nodding her head at both women.

Shit.

"Oh, do you know, Reagan?" Mrs. Allegany asked, surprised at the reference.

Rita looked from the two women and then back to Chad. She'd blown Chad's cover without knowing it. Now Chad would have to figure out an excuse before Sylvia asked any more questions. Before she could say a word, Reagan piped up.

"Rita and I have worked together before, back

in California. A long time ago," Reagan said, forcing a tight smile.

"It's good to see you again, Ms. Reynolds. I didn't expect to see you here," Rita said.

Stop, don't go any further, Rita.

"Well, since my replacement is here, I'd like to debrief her before I leave."

"Of course," Sylvia said, turning her attention to Reagan.

Pulling Rita off to the side, Chad was ready to read her the riot act just as Rita put up her hands.

"I had no way of knowing you were with Reagan, I'm so sorry. It was just a reaction. I hope I didn't just blow it back there."

"Obviously, Reagan is the one who could have blown it for us, but she didn't. Just keep it casual and try not to say anything unless you're asked. Be vague."

"Got it."

"I'll be in my room. Let me know if you need anything."

"Okay."

Chad walked with Rita back over to the two women for the hand-off.

"Mrs. Allegany, Ms. Reynolds," Chad said, not looking at Reagan. "I leave you in Rita's capable hands."

"Thank you, Chad. I think I'd like you to join me for dinner as well."

"What? I'm sorry, but Rita will be taking –"

"I understand that, Ms. Morgan, but I am requesting your presence and you *will* attend. Understood?" Sylvia gave Chad a look that clearly showed she meant business.

"Mrs. Allegany," Chad said, still trying not to

look at Reagan. "I've been up for a while and I really need to rest. You have a full itinerary the first day of the conference."

"Exactly, Ms. Morgan, and a little fun before all the shit hits the fan is on the agenda, don't you think? Go back to your room take a nap and we'll move dinner to seven o'clock." Sylvia turned to Reagan and continued, "How does that work for you, my dear?"

"Mrs. Allegany, if this is too much trouble we can do it another night," Reagan said, trying not to look at anyone.

"Nonsense. Seven it is. Rita, are you ready? I need to find Jason and send some correspondence. Come along."

With that, she was gone with Rita in tow, leaving Chad and Reagan standing together. Both watched the bombastic woman whirl through the doors, literally leaving papers on a nearby table rustling in her wake.

Neither woman wanted to be the first to speak, so they just stood looking at everything in the room but each other.

"Well, this is awkward," Reagan piped up.

"I didn't know you were going to be here," Chad said, finally looking at Reagan. Even though she'd seen Reagan on the monitors the night before, she was still surprised at the visceral reaction she had around her. She felt awkward in Reagan's presence and wanted nothing more than to dash out the door, but she wouldn't be disrespectful. "You weren't on the list of conference attendees."

"Yeah, well, I didn't know I was coming until the last minute. It was my dad's idea."

"How is Frank?"

"Good, thank you for asking."

Reagan bit the inside of her lip, a nervous tick Chad recognized immediately.

"And your little brother…how's he doing?"

"He's adjusting. Dad's learning to be a dad all over again, only this time to a son he's always wanted."

"Well, I'm sure he's–"

"I'm not implying he threw me over for my little brother, I just mean he's enjoying his newfound role of being a father to a small child."

"How are you handling your new role as big sister?"

Chad smiled briefly at the thought of Reagan being a big sister. Chad loved her brothers and sisters and yet she imagined it might be hard for Reagan to share Frank with someone else. The parent/child relationship was much different than watching your father with a woman. A parent/child bond was forged with unconditional love and hard to break.

"Oh, he's great. Kinda grown-up already and he's only nine. He looks just like dad, only in miniature." Reagan smiled and her eyes creased around the edges.

"Well, I should let you go. I'm sure it's been a long day for you."

Chad turned to leave, stopped, and looked back at Reagan. She started to say how sorry she was for how everything ended but thought better of it. "You feel okay?"

"Yes, why?" Reagan instinctively felt her face.

"You look a little flushed."

"I'm fine, I'm sure it's just jet-lag."

"Well, good night."

"Good night."

Chad hustled to the elevator. She wasn't about to have a break down in front of Reagan. If she was being honest with herself, she really wanted to reach out and touch her. Gently rest her lips on Reagan's and savor a kiss.

❧ ❧ ❧ ❧

The heat of the room was stifling and Reagan felt like she was going to pass out. Surely it was leftover jet-lag; she couldn't be reacting to Chad Morgan. Of all the places to run into her former protector, Abu Dhabi wasn't exactly the place she would have picked. Not that she would have picked anywhere to see Chad. She would have avoided her like the plague here if it wasn't for a stubborn Mrs. Allegany. She had her to thank for their less than joyful reunion. Chad was just as infuriating now as she was back then, but Reagan had to give her credit – Chad was good at her job and the future first lady was in good hands. Very good hands.

"Hey, I know you." The soft Latin accent gave away the woman standing behind her.

"Señora Velazquez, how are you?"

Reagan wanted to run; not the woman from the bar last night. She'd had too much to drink, not enough to eat, and way too much listening to the woman. Why couldn't god just help her out this once? Why?

"Reagan, I see you survived. How about you join me for dinner tonight?" Colleen threaded her arm through Reagan's and pulled her towards the doors to leave. "Why don't you let me buy you a drink?"

"I can't, I have to get ready for a dinner date with Mrs. Allegany."

"Ooo, aren't you special."

"Not exactly, but I doubt no one has told her *no*

in years. Probably decades."

"Probably."

"Well, then I shall let you go and get ready for your dinner. Me, I think I'm going to the bar and see what trouble I can find. If you change your mind you know where to find me."

Colleen waved over her shoulder and pranced down the hall. Lucky for Reagan she actually did have dinner plans, otherwise she'd have been stuck either eating in her room, or forcing herself to the bar for a drink. She waved back at Colleen, who grabbed the elevator and disappeared. For some reason she didn't like Colleen. A gold digger perhaps, but clearly she didn't have scruples if she was married to one of the most ruthless dictators in Latin America. It was rumored he was a king pin in the drug and gun smuggling trade, so that would make his political activities the perfect cover for money laundering, drug trafficking, and a host of other illicit activities. She doubted countries checked Air Force One after it landed for illegal contraband, so why would they check other countries' presidential jets?

No, staying as far away from Colleen was the best choice to survive the conference.

A hot bath and an adult beverage sounded perfect right now, but the hot bath would have to suffice. At least until dinner, where she would unfortunately see Chad, again. *Crap, couldn't she cut a break?*

Chapter Seventeen

Fuck me," Chad said, pulling off her harness and dropping it onto the couch.

"Excuse me?" Marco said, coming out of the kitchen with a sandwich half way to his mouth.

"You heard me, fuck me."

"Wow, this is awkward, but I'm gonna have to pass on that one, boss."

He laughed as he started to take a bite and then another and within four bites the sandwich was history. At this rate, they would have to make a food run, and she doubted they had white bread and peanut butter in Abu Dhabi.

"Funny man. Good, cause you're gonna love this next bit of news. Reagan knows I'm here."

"What?"

"Yep, she walked up as I was protecting Sylvia and to top it all off, I have to have dinner with the two of them."

"Oh shit."

"Yep, so laugh your ass off all you want. It's going to be a long damn night."

Chad walked to her room and slammed the door behind her before Marco could say anything else. Throwing herself on the bed, she covered her eyes with her arm and wished the trip was over and she could be done with protecting people. Hell, she'd trade places with a junkyard dog right about now, if it meant she didn't have to subject herself to a night of chattering hens.

Kicking her loafers off, she let her legs hang off the bed. Her feet where killing her, her back ached, and she hadn't worked out today. All of which made for a grumpy Chad. What she wouldn't do for a bourbon, a woman, or something to take her mind off her crappy day, she thought as she felt herself starting to doze.

Good, I need a power nap.

"Hey, aren't you going to come down for dinner?" a soft voice whispered across the room.

"What?" Chad said, sitting up on the bed. "Yeah, I'm coming down. Why?"

Reagan walked towards her, smiling. The soft blue dress looked good on her, tight in all the right places and generous in all the curvy ones. Chad smiled back at Reagan, but didn't know why and then it dawned on her. "Hey, wait a minute, who let you in?"

"Marco, silly. I told him I was here to pick you up, that we had a dinner date. If I'm going to suffer through Sylvia Allegany, I'm not doing it alone. She invited you too, remember?"

"I remember. How did you find out where my room was?"

Chad didn't know why she was playing twenty questions with Reagan, she should just boot her from the room and get showered and dressed herself, but Reagan looked so good in that blue dress. God, she was screwed.

"It wasn't hard. I just asked around about the tall, good looking butch and they pointed me in this direction."

"Really?"

"Uh huh," Reagan said, putting a knee on the bed

and trailing a finger down the buttons of Chad's shirt. "Or we could just eat in." She wiggled her eyebrows at Chad.

Chad's body spiked at the touch. Grabbing Reagan's finger, she stopped the torture and held them still, staring into Reagan's eyes.

"I don't know what game you're playing here, but I'm not up for it."

"No games. Just something I should have done a long time ago," she said as she lowered herself down on top of Chad. Her tongue flicked across Chad's lips, while Chad's hips arched forward for more contact. If Reagan was going to play games, she could be on the opposing team, only this time they would play according to Chad's rules. Chad reached up and grabbed a handful of Reagan's hair and forced Reagan's lips against hers. This time is was Chad's way or no way.

"Hey buddy, you need to get up if you're going to make that dinner appointment."

Marco's voice boomed in the dark room.

Chad jerked awake. *Fuck*. It had all been a dream, a sick twisted dream. What do they say about the subconscious mind? Whatever you're having a problem with during the day works itself out in your dreams.

"Great, does that mean I'm gonna…no way."

Chad rolled off the bed and scrambled for a shower and a set of fresh clothes. Combing her hair out, she looked in the mirror and made a pact with herself. "Stay as far away from Reagan as possible." She shook her comb at her reflection. "You hear me, no Reagan. I don't care what you dreamed. She's all bad news."

If only it were that easy. Dreaming about Reagan was just barely a few steps away from thinking about Reagan consciously and now her subconscious was doing a number on her, too. Chad rubbed her tattoo. *Never forget*, it said in Latin and she wasn't about to, ever.

Chapter Eighteen

Reagan powdered, primped, and dolled herself up without thinking. Looking in the mirror, she furrowed her eyebrows and then grabbed the washcloth. Running it under the hot water, she wrung it out and raised it to her face intent on wiping her make-up off, just as the phone rang.

"Reagan, dear, why don't you come up a few minutes early and we can have a drink before the hired gun arrives," Sylvia said without the usual courtesies someone of her position used when making a call.

"Oh, I was just getting ready–"

"Wonderful, I'll see you in five minutes then?"

"Well, I'm not sure–"

"Surely you're not canceling on me, are you?"

"No…of course not." Reagan said, reconsidering her plan to beg off the dinner.

"Good, see you in five then."

The line went dead and all Reagan could do was look down at the artifact from the land before technology. Dropping it into the cradle, she thought she might have to check her back for tire treads, because she'd just been hit by the Mac daddy of all Mac trucks, Sylvia Allegany.

Tossing the warm rag into the sink, she snatched up her clutch, grabbed a wrap, and cursed herself all the way to the elevator. It was going to be a long night between Sylvia chatting her head off and Chad sitting stoically across from her. God, how she wished she had a gun right now. If not for herself, then for the fool who had convinced her this would be a great idea. Now who was that fool again?

"Up please," she said to the porter in the private elevator. Guests of the penthouse weren't expected to take the hotel elevator, so they provided the private lift with a porter who waited just for those special guests. There was a time when Reagan wanted that kind of service, now she was happy not to be wearing prison pinstripes and calling a cell her bedroom. Oh, how the difference a year and the threat of prison time changes a person. She smiled when she thought about her little brother. He'd been the only good thing to come out of her experience with Marcy. A bad plan and a worse execution had almost cost her the freedom she was enjoying now. She'd wanted to be CEO of Reynolds Holdings and to prove she could handle anything thrown at her, so she'd laid out an elaborate plan. Faking death threats against herself. Trying to position herself as someone who could handle the stresses that came with being the CEO of one of the biggest military contractors. Blackwater had eclipsed everyone with their insider contacts, but Frank Reynolds had bitten into their apple by funding and producing some of the best armor the military could find. Within ten years and a Gulf War, Reynolds Holdings had taken a sizeable chunk of armored defense contracts and Frank was ready to retire and leave the company to Reagan to run, but she'd blown that with a stupid plan that backfired and almost cost Frank his life and hers as well.

The past, that was all in the past. She kept telling herself.

"Here we are, Miss." The porter directed her out of the elevator and into the lavish penthouse hallway and the one door to the penthouse.

"Thank you."

"My pleasure, Miss. Just ring when you are ready to leave."

"Thank you."

Was she ready for Sylvia? More importantly, was she ready for Chad?

* * *

Chad slipped her trademark blazer on and slipped into her loafers. *Office drag*, she lamented as she pulled her gun and checked the clip. Overkill perhaps, but she rarely left the job behind anymore and while she was in a foreign country, she wasn't on vacation. Sighing, she shoved the cold metal back into its home and prepared herself for what would surely be a grueling night.

"So you off to dinner with the boss?"

"Yes, I'm off to dinner with the client," she corrected her second in command. Marco was the master of overstatement and he liked it.

"Well, you look smashing. Get out there and kill 'em, tiger." He laughed at her perplexed look. "Just kidding. Lighten up, Chad. The stress is going to kill ya."

"If Mrs. Allegany doesn't first."

Marco rubbed his chin, tucking his other arm under and walking around Chad. Whirling his finger around, he tried to make like he was surveying Chad's attire and then he smiled. "I think you nailed that subtle, understated, bodyguard 'I'm gonna kick yer ass' style, boss. No one can pull that off like you can. Good thing you packed all those blazers." He roared at his own joke.

"I'm glad you like them, 'cause we're instituting a dress code when we get back to the states. Ties and blazers for the men and polos for the ladies."

"Haha, you wouldn't dare."

"Yep, I think it's time we start having a uniform look to the team. Hence the meaning of team, right?"

"God, I was only kidding, Chad."

"Yeah, well I'm not. Time to start cutting a sharper image. We are executive protection and we need to start looking like the executives and not the hired help."

"Great, me and my big mouth." He slapped his hand over his mouth and grimaced.

"No, just thinking it's time."

"Hmm."

"Okay, well I'm off. Let's do this again real soon, Marco. Hold down the fort and keep an eye on the monitors. I want to know what our little Senora Velazquez is up to tonight."

"You got it."

Chad stuck her penthouse key into the elevator and waited for the doors to shut. She could have taken the private elevator, but she was too lazy to cross over to the other side of the catwalk to get to it. This one would spit her out in the service entrance, which was fine for her. She didn't stand on formality and liked being inconspicuous when she could. Lacing her fingers together, she stretched as long as she could and then bent at the waist, trying to loosen up her back. She must have slept wrong because it was tighter than usual. Chad stood, a blush crawl up her neck and flame her cheeks as she remembered her dream. Fanning her face, she remembered she was on video. Making her fingers into the shape of a gun, she shot at the camera and got off the elevator. One last check, she tucked in her white button-down, patted her left side, double-checking for her gun, and ran her tongue over her teeth. Popping a mint, she felt like she was as ready as possible for dinner, a conversation dominated by an opinionated woman and Reagan.

Before she could knock, the door opened but not by Rita. Without thinking, Chad body slammed the man, tossing him on his back and straddling him. Jerking up, she pulled back her fist, ready to punch the man.

A scream pierced the air, stopping Chad as Jason threw his hands up to block the impending blow.

"Why are you answering the door? That's why Rita is here. She's handling all exits. Where is she?"

"I put her in the kitchen. She was just standing around, making me nervous."

"That's her job, to make you nervous, you little twerp." Standing, she pulled Jason to his feet.

"Well Ms. Morgan, I don't need someone hovering. Besides, I can take care of myself," he said rather tersely.

"Well good, I expect you to stay out of the way so we can do our job then. That way I won't waste any extra energy on your ass."

"Hmm."

Rolling her eyes at the queen, she walked past without as much as a retort. She didn't have time for his bravado and she didn't know why he wasted his time trying to out *man* her.

Bitch, please.

She didn't normally have an attitude when it came to gay men, but for some reason Jason had rubbed her the wrong way the moment they met. Maybe it was a family thing. Her a lesbian, him gay, but she doubted it. It was more because he was a ladder climber and he was the type to crawl over broken glass to get what he wanted.

"Ah, there you are Ms. Morgan, we were just wondering when you'd join us," Sylvia said, handing her a glass of something red.

Chad looked down at her watch, seven on the dot. *Women.* They were usually late and she was always on time, just as she was now. Lifting the glass to sniff it, she noticed a hint of cherries and something else.

"It's a beautiful red from your state of California. Napa, I believe."

"Thank you, but I think I'll wait for dinner. While I'm not on duty, I'd still like to keep my wits about me tonight."

"Ms. Morgan, I hope you're not inferring that I would get you drunk?"

"Not at all, Mrs. Allegany," Chad lied; that's exactly what she was inferring, but she also didn't drink unless she uncorked and poured the wine herself. Her years of training didn't allow for mistakes and it only took one time for someone to spike a drink and render her incapable of doing her job to end her career and her life.

"Well, Reagan and I were just chatting about vacations we've taken. Have you traveled much, Ms. Morgan?"

Chad dipped her head in acknowledgement when she saw Reagan. Her hair was swept up off her shoulders and the dress she wore was slightly understated for Reagan, but nevertheless beautiful. Chad pretty much figured Reagan could wear a burlap sack and make it fashionable. Oh, there she went again, head long into a Reagan love fest. *Shit.*

"Ah, well sort of, yes."

"Oh, I suppose you do a lot of traveling for your job. But have you ever taken a vacation out of the country?"

"Once or twice yes. How about you, Ms. Reynolds? Vacation much?" Chad was the master of deflection.

"I have, as I was saying to Mrs. Allegany–"

"Sylvia, please."

"As I was saying to Sylvia, one of my favorite trips is to northern France. I love the area and would love to have a little vacation get-away there someday."

"Dinner has arrived," Jason said, motioning to the dining room.

Chad looked around the penthouse and took in all of its grandeur. It was clear that in Abu Dhabi they spared no expense for the elite and overly wealthy. The gold furnishings were a bit ostentatious for Chad. She was sure somewhere there had to be a handbook on over the top interior decorating and design for the rich and famous. If she'd seen one golden ornamental greyhound, gold water fixtures, and picture frames, she'd seen dozens in upscale accommodations throughout the world. It was gaudy, pretentious, and just not her style.

Chad pulled back the chair for Sylvia before Jason could get around the table. Throwing her a nasty look, he pulled out Reagan's chair and smiled as sweetly as he could before pushing it under her. Smirking at Chad, he sashayed to his own seat across from Sylvia, putting Chad directly across from Reagan. Looking around, Chad remembered Rita was in the kitchen.

"Mrs. Allegany, can I ask why your protection detail is in the kitchen?"

"Oh, I made the decision to put her in the kitchen, remember I told you earlier. She's eating in there," Jason said, pulling the cover off his plate.

"The kitchen?" Chad's voice raised a bit as she directed her question to Jason.

"Well, I told her she could leave since you were here, but she refused and since the table only seats four," Jason pointed to the four of them sitting around the table. "I figured she could eat dinner in the kitchen."

The table was big enough for eight, but the other chairs had been conveniently dispersed throughout the dining room with one or two missing. *How convenient*, Chad thought, looking at the table setting. *Little bastard.*

"Mrs. Allegany, if you'll excuse me, I'd like to have a word with Rita."

"Oh now, Ms. Morgan–"

"I'd just like to have a quick word with her if you don't mind."

Sylvia waved her hand at Chad. "Of course, please hurry back. Your food will get cold."

"Of course. Please start without me." Chad stared Jason down before leaving the room to get answers.

Chad stormed through a breakfast area and then pushed through a set of doors to find Rita sitting at a table with her arms crossed, staring at sandwich and a glass of water.

"What the fuck is going on? Why are you in here?"

"Ask that asshole, Jason," Rita said, pointing to the door. "Prick told me that I was the hired help and the help didn't eat with the person who hired you."

"That little bastard."

"No shit." Rita pushed the plate across the table. "Look what he gave me, a fucking sandwich and a glass of water."

"Get down to the suite, get yourself something to eat, and then come back in an hour. Bring me two of those pin-hole cameras."

"You got it."

"Sorry about this," Chad said, pointing to the sandwich. "That little prick is going to get his if it takes me all trip to do it."

"It's not your fault. I'll see you in an hour."

Chad wrung her hands. She'd had enough of Jason. She didn't know what his game was, but she was going to find out. She suspected he was angling for a position in the government if Mr. Allegany became president. Probably Sylvia Allegany's personal secretary in the White House, but if she had her way, he wouldn't make it past dog poop scooper.

Once again Chad tucked her button-down in, patted her left side, and strode out the kitchen and back into the dining room. Chad slapped Jason on the back, the little twerp choked on a mouthful of wine, spitting it back into his glass.

"Thank you for taking care of Rita. I appreciate you making sure she ate. So often we have to do our job without the benefit of a meal." She smiled a wicked little smile at him and then winked. "So, Mrs. Allegany, where were we?" Chad said, pulling off the cover to her dinner.

❧❧❧❧

Reagan sat quietly as Jason regaled everyone with his story of the time he met a Tibetan monk in San Francisco and asked the old man what they wore underneath all those robes. She was starting to dislike the flamboyant man, but she'd learned to keep her mouth shut and mind her manners with people she didn't like, even if they were only the staff. Staff gossiped and she didn't want to be the subject of Jason's gossip, ever. She also suspected that he embellished his stories and that would translate into embellishing about her as well. So, she laughed politely, smiled, and didn't look at Chad.

"So Ms. Morgan, I bet you have some great stories about people you've protected. Do tell," Jason said, practically salivating at the opportunity to hear some juicy gossip.

Chad looked at Reagan and then back at Jason and then at Mrs. Allegany, who was craning over the table to hear what she might say. Reagan prayed Chad would pass on the opportunity to dish on her clients.

"Well, I don't protect and tell, Jason. That wouldn't keep me employed, now would it?" she said, moving some overcooked peas around her plate.

Reagan noticed she'd barely eaten her dinner, opting for conversation instead.

"More wine, Sylvia?" Jason said, standing.

"Why don't you let me get that for you, Jason," Chad offered, picking up an unopened bottle. "You've been a great host; let me relieve you of that." She reached for the corkscrew in Jason's hand.

"Oh, very gallant of you, Ms. Morgan," he said, putting his fingertips on his chest and preening.

Reagan's head felt like it was swimming. She didn't think she'd had too much to drink, but every time she looked at her glass, it was full. She had to admit dinner was delicious and the wine was the perfect accent, almost too perfect. Whoever the Somlyay at the hotel was, he or she was to be commended. What was she thinking? Who cared really? She was stuck here with Chad, a gay guy who couldn't stop talking about himself, and the possible first lady, who made her blush with some of her comments about the rich and famous. Sylvia Allegany would have to be put on lock-down if her husband became president, because clearly she didn't have boundaries.

"So, Reagan..." Sylvia slurred a little. "Is it true...?" Reagan felt herself tighten as Sylvia moved in closer and whispered loudly in her ear. "You're a lesbian?"

Chapter Nineteen

Chad could only look at Reagan in surprise as Sylvia asked the question. A cackle erupted from the end of the table where Jason sat. Jason cupped his hand over his mouth, Chad wanted to grab it and shove it down his throat as he giggled behind it. She wished she could save Reagan from Sylvia, but it was out there now and she wondered how Reagan would handle the direct question.

"Mrs. Allegany. I don't talk about my private life. That's why they call it private, right?" Reagan said without batting an eye. "Besides, I don't kiss and tell." Then Reagan reached over and laid her hand on Sylvia's with the sweetest smile Chad had ever seen. If her intent was to make Sylvia uncomfortable, it backfired.

Sylvia grabbed Reagan's hand and cupped it in her own and said, "If I was twenty years younger and unmarried, Reagan, I would hit on you." Throwing her hands up, Sylvia said, "But those days are over."

Chad's stomach clenched. Had Sylvia Allegany just hit on Reagan? Oh, the media would have a field day with her past if she was alluding to anything just now. Without missing a step, Sylvia turned to Jason, who was still laughing, and asked, "Jason, my boy, what's for dessert?"

Without batting an eye, Sylvia lifted her glass in salute and drained it in one gulp. It was going to be one of those nights, Chad thought. She'd been to enough dinner parties where the wealthy over indulged in various vices. What was it with rich people, people in power that made them so dependent on alcohol to have a good time? She remembered a certain senator who'd had so much to drink at a function that it cost his district a huge defense contract. Stumbling over the CEO's wife in the closet was not just in bad taste, it was downright raunchy even if she was a willing participant.

Movement at the kitchen door caught her eye as Rita flagged her down.

"If you'll excuse me, Mrs. Allegany, Rita is back and I'd like to have a word with her."

"Of course," she barely slurred. "Go right ahead. So where were we, Reagan?"

"I've never been so glad to see someone in my life." Chad said.

"That bad huh?" Rita looked around the room before passing a small parcel to Chad.

"You have no idea." Chad opened the box with the two wireless cameras and transmitters inside. "Thanks. You're back on and as soon as I place these puppies, I'm out of here."

Rita nodded and grimaced as Jason popped up out of nowhere.

"Coffee, Ms. Morgan? Rita," he said, giving her a disapproving glare.

"Thank you, do you have decaf?"

"I'll check."

Waiting for him to leave, she turned her attention back to Rita. "I'm going to place one of these in his room. Keep him occupied while I do that."

"You got it. What are you going to do with the

other one?"

Chad looked around and wondered that herself. She wanted as much traffic as possible or it would be a waste. Sylvia talked about a cocktail party she was having for some of the women of the conference, so they would be mingling out in the living room and dining room, mostly.

"I'll figure something out."

Chad walked over to Sylvia, made a reference to having too much coffee, and staying in character, she asked where the bathroom was. According to the plans of the hotel, Jason's room should be by the bathroom. Walking in the direction of the bathroom, Chad couldn't help but notice the place was almost as big as her house. *Lifestyles of the rich and famous* were never words that would be associated with her. Now Reagan, she might be used to this lavish lifestyle and she'd been in Reagan's house before; she knew what kind of décor Reagan favored. Remembering her introduction to the woman brought a smile to her face.

"Do what I tell you and you won't get hurt." Chad *tried to disguise her voice.*

Sudden realization hit Chad that the woman in front of her was Reagan Reynolds, the owner of the home.

Shit, she's supposed to be in Cabo right now. What the fuck?

Chad had seen Reagan leave with her dog earlier in the day. Trying to put the pieces together quickly before Reagan turned around, Chad grabbed a wrist and held Reagan still. Sniffles, it was the only thing Chad could think of now. Clearly, Reagan was sick and had decided to stay home. Chad's mind was firing in different directions at the unsettling development, but she had a job to do and if Reagan blew her cover, it wouldn't look good for her. The police would not be called, period.

"Stop." Chad had her hand on Reagan's shoulders, trying to hold her in place. "Look, don't make me do something we're both going to regret."

Reagan squirmed and fell forward over the back of the overstuffed chair with Chad right on top of her. A firm ass wiggled against Chad's crotch as she tried to steady herself.

"Oh God, please don't rape me. I'll do whatever you want, please." Reagan's desperation was evident in her voice.

"Please, don't flatter yourself, lady."

Trying to disengage herself from the struggling Reagan, Chad gently pulled her arm behind her. The contact with Reagan's ass was starting to have an effect on Chad; she needed to remove herself and fast. She attempted to stand up, and accidentally pushed on Reagan's back, sliding the silk robe up, exposing her taut nakedness.

"Shit," Chad said, as she finally stood, getting a full view. She grabbed Reagan's other arm and yanked her up off the chair. "Stop struggling, you're only making things worse."

Reagan grew perfectly still. Chad turned her around only to see tears start to fall. Geez, now she's gonna cry, great. Chad wiped the tears and looked Reagan in the eyes.

"I'm almost done here, but I can't have you calling the police, so I am going to have to tie you up. Okay?"

She yanked the belt from Reagan's robe and smiled as it fell open, exposing a set of perfectly shaped breasts. Chad tried to divert her attention, but couldn't help herself. She openly admired Reagan's heaving breasts, but before she could do anything else, she felt a sharp pain on the left side of her temple.

"Fuck." Chad grabbed the hand that had struck her and wrenched it behind Reagan's back. The action forced Reagan against Chad, opening the robe further and exposing all of Reagan to Chad's gaze. Dropping the belt, Chad grasped her head, forcing Reagan to look at her.

"I told you to knock it off, now you're pissing me off," she said as menacingly as she could sound. "Now, you're screwed."

Turning Reagan around and bending her over the back of the chair, she held Reagan's hand between her legs and wrapped the belt around Reagan's head. Wedging the belt between her lips, she tied it off. Holding Reagan's hands, Chad wrapped the duct tape twice around Reagan's wrists.

"Now, sit down." Pulling the chair around to face the door, she pushed Reagan into it. She winced and rubbed the side of her head. "Nice right hook you got there."

Finding the bathroom, she noticed one more door a few feet away. Jason's room, it had to be. The suite had opposing bedrooms and she doubted that the designers would put the guest bathroom on the master suite side of the house. Privacy was paid for and expected, along with the trashy Vegas deco. The silver and gold wallpaper was putting the place so over the top, she felt like a lounge singer would pop out at any minute. Opening the bathroom door, she looked in to see if there was an adjoining door to the bedroom. When there wasn't, she turned the water on at the sink, and shut the door. Moving down the hall, she opened the door and found what she was looking for, the room of a meticulous gay man.

A quick survey of Jason's room revealed it was embarrassingly well detailed. The desk had everything laid out perfectly in order. Beside his computer was a pad with the pen laid diagonal across it. Assorted stationary items in neat little boxes across the top of the desk were equally spaced apart. Looking across to his room, she noticed his clothes hung in the closet by color and matched, pants with shirts, and shoes were directly under the matching items. Pulling out the top drawer, she saw his belt, hankies with monograms - *who carries hankies anymore* - and socks were also color-coordinated.

"Christ, the guy's OCD," she said, trying to find a place to hide the pinhole camera.

She didn't have much time, so she needed to work fast. Placing the transmitter behind the dresser, she looked at the desk and noticed the ornate work on the back of the small secretary. Its metalwork would be perfect to hide her camera and it would be close to the action of the desk and the bed. Chad looked back and forth across the room, hoping its wide angle would pick up everything in the room easily. Pulling the paper off the back, she stuck it into the recess of one of the circular ornamentation, wiped her finger print off the lens, and then stepped back and moved her hand back and forth. She hoped whoever was on the other end would send her a signal. Before she finished the thought, her phone beeped. Pulling it, she saw the text.

"We're set."

Perfect, she thought, looking around the room one more time before she exited. Sometimes her job was just so easy. Rushing back to the bathroom, she shut the door just in time to hear Jason walk into the hallway, his fancy shoes echoing off the grey and white marble. Turning off the water, she listened to see if she could hear anything coming from his room.

Show tunes?

"Oh god, I need to get the hell out of here," she said, wiping her hands on the plush paper hand towels with monogramed A. *The hotel thought of everything for their guest*, she thought, tossing the paper in the waste bin. Just as she was getting ready to open the door, she suddenly heard talking coming from Jason's room. Waiting, she put her ear to the door, hoping to hear something, but all she heard was low, deep, muffled talking. Odd for Jason, he had such a high-pitched voice it got on her nerves. Screw it. She opened the door at the same time Jason started to dart out of his room.

Jason acted surprised to see Chad. "Well, there you are. I've put a small pot of decaf on the table with creamer and sugar. Everything okay in there?" He motioned to the bathroom. "I put a candle in there. My mother always said, travel with a little something for the bathroom and you'll make friends everywhere." He laughed at the implication.

"I'm fine, thanks. I got a little side tracked checking my email."

"Oh, you don't want to touch your cell phone after you've–"

"I washed my hands first, thanks for worrying."

"Oh, I'm all about the personal hygiene. One can never be too careful in a foreign country, you know," he said, tossing his hands up. "Well, your coffee's getting cold."

He strutted in front of her and tried to chat about something mundane, but she ignored him. Looking back over her shoulder, she looked at his bedroom door as if it would tell her who he was talking to, no luck. It was still just a door.

"So, your mother was just–" Sylvia stopped mid-sentence and looked at Jason and Chad as they walked back into the room. "Well, there you are, everything okay?" she said, pointing to Chad's stomach.

"Oh, she's fine, just checking her email. What would we do without technology?" he said, that irritating upswing ending his sentence.

Chad looked down at her watch.

"Mrs. Allegany, you've been a wonderful hostess, but I really must call it a night." Walking over, she extended her hand. "The conference starts early and I suspect you'll want to get an early start."

"Oh bullshit, I'm not getting up early. I'm gonna have a hangover and I'm going to enjoy it. When I'm in D.C. I have to play the good wife. Here, I can be my normal self."

Chad wondered what that looked like. If Sylvia was outspoken and opinionated stateside, what was Chad in for here?

"Well, I still need to get back to my suite and do a little work. So, thank you again for dinner."

"I need to get going as well, Sylvia. I've got a presentation in the morning and it's daytime at the plant back home and I have a skype meeting before I hit the hay. So, I'll follow you out, Ms. Morgan."

Great, now she would be trapped in an elevator with Reagan. This trip was really starting to suck.

"Of course, Ms. Reynolds. I'd be happy to escort you to your room." Chad dropped her hand and made a show of sweeping the way open for Reagan. She refused to let anyone know they had a past and she would be as respectful as possible. She had a reputation she needed to protect and Mrs. Allegany's protection would open a lot of doors for her, if she didn't screw it up.

"Thank you, Ms. Morgan, I appreciate the company. I'm sure nothing would happen, but one can never be too careful."

"I agree," Chad said, wishing now she hadn't attended.

"Well, Sylvia it's been a pleasure. I hope we can talk more during the conference," Reagan said so graciously that even Chad almost believed her.

"Mrs. Allegany, what time shall I pick you up in the morning?"

"I'm going to have a dreadful hangover. So, let's make it noonish. Shall we?"

"Of course." Chad started for the door. "I'll have someone replace Rita at about…" Checking her watch, she noted the time and calculated when Rita had taken over and said, "Midnight. Her replacement will have to come into the penthouse since there are two entrances."

"Is that really necessary?" Sylvia questioned.

"Well, unless you want someone staying in the suite, yes."

Chad knew it was a delicate situation if she had her way. She would do exactly that, move someone inside. Sylvia had been completely against it, thanks to Jason. Another tick in his jerk category. She spied the little weasel standing off to the side. He might think he'd won, but Chad would get her way, eventually. She always got her way.

"Well, good evening everyone. I really need to get some sleep before the conference starts in the morning," Reagan said, trying to stifle a yawn.

"Good evening and thank you again," Chad repeated.

Sylvia waved her hand and turned away from the women, summarily dismissing them. Making a stop in the kitchen, Chad briefed Rita on her replacement. Rita gave Chad a dubious look when she caught sight of Reagan behind Chad.

"I told her I'd walk her to her room," Chad offered as an excuse. She didn't need to explain her actions to anyone especially someone who took orders from her.

"Then I think you're the one who might need protection from that one." Rita straightened as she pointed to Reagan.

Chad could feel the hostility ooze from Rita. They hadn't seen each other since the episode in the limo when Chad was hired to protect Reagan a year ago.

"Ms. Reynolds?"

"Yes, are you from the service I called earlier?" The woman raised her eyebrows at the obvious, which made Reagan chuckle. "Of course you are. Lead the way."

The long black limousine was overkill for the short drive to the hotel, but Reagan had been in such a hurry when she booked it, she didn't care what car they sent, as long as she could get to the hotel and get checked in on time. She wanted to get settled and go over her notes about Alex Hamilton, the first board member she would see. Then she would eat and get some much-needed sleep.

"Ma'am?" The chauffeur held the door wide.

"Oh, sorry, I was just thinking about all the things I have to get done."

"No problem. We'll be at the hotel in about fifteen minutes. I hear they have a nice lounge at the top for VIP guests."

"Good to know. Thank you."

"My pleasure, believe me it's my pleasure," she said, smiling before shutting the door behind Reagan.

A low voice startled Reagan. "Hello."

"Hello?" Reagan said pensively.

The speed of the car pressed her firmly against the back seat as Reagan tried to focus on the person sitting in the darkness. Her chest tightened in fear and she grabbed for the door handle.

"I wouldn't do that if I were you. The car is going pretty fast."

"Who are you and what do you want?" Suddenly a woman leaned forward, pointing a gun at her. "Is it loaded?"

"Aw, it's stupid question day. Okay, I'll play along. Yes, it's loaded."

Looking around the limousine, Reagan tried to assess the situation. Something had gone drastically wrong. If karma was a bitch, she was paying for what she had done to Chad earlier at the airport. Why she would remember Chad at this point was ironic, since Chad had preached to her about travel safety on the way to the airport. She had blindly followed the woman with the sign, gotten into a car without thinking, and was now possibly being kidnapped or worse, killed.

"Please, my father will pay you. Whatever you want. Just don't kill me, please."

"Okay, take your clothes off."

"What?"

"You heard me. Take your clothes off."

"No."

"I don't think you understand how this works. I have the gun. I get to make the rules. My gun, my rules. Get it?" The woman leaned in closer and ran the gun up Reagan's leg. "Nice."

Closing her eyes, Reagan tried to block out the feel of the cold gun grazing her leg. She couldn't move even if she wanted to; fear had her paralyzed. Her heart pounded in her chest and her hands shook as she raised them in resignation. Finally finding her voice, she squeaked out, "I'm not taking my clothes off."

"I don't think you—"

"I understand just fine. I'm not taking my clothes off, so you'll have to shoot me." The quaking in her voice betrayed Reagan's bravado. "Do what you have to do."

The seat next to Reagan sagged when the woman slid closer. Her hot breath against Reagan's neck was revolting as she whispered in her ear. "Trust me, you don't want to see me pissed off. It isn't a pretty picture."

The woman's hand slid up past Reagan's knee before stopping just under the hem of her dress. "Am I making myself clear here?"

Reagan nodded briefly and closed her eyes, suddenly wishing Chad was there. If she hadn't set Chad up, she wouldn't be in this situation. She would only be dealing with an arrogant woman instead of one who wanted to kill her. If she could just reason with this woman, she was sure she could turn the situation around. Taking a deep breath, Reagan turned towards the woman and placed her hands on her chest. She gently grabbed the lapels of the woman's jacket and ran them between her finger and thumb as she slid the back *of her hands up down the woman's chest.*

"Look, I'm sure we can come to some kind of agreement. Can't we?" Reagan crooned softly.

A smile ticked up the corner of the woman's mouth, revealing a dimple. Reagan returned the smile and locked eyes with the woman. If she could play men, she was sure she could play this out in her favor. A mix of fear and success bolstered her to continue. Watching as the woman slid her tongue out and lick her bottom lip, Reagan mimicked the same behavior. Focusing on her opponent's lips, she bit her bottom lip and kept her hands moving up and down the hard chest beneath.

"You're good, but you're not that good." The woman trapped Reagan's hands and pushed her back against the seat. She pressed her firm lips against Reagan's, practically bruising them. The kiss lasted longer than Reagan wanted, but just long enough to show her who was in control. "Now, stop your shit and get your dress off, since you're so hot to see what happens next."

"But, I'm not," Reagan blurted out. "I mean, I'm not hot. I mean. I don't want to see what happens next. Oh please don't."

The car stopped quickly, lurching forward and sending both women to the floor. Pulling herself up, Reagan tried reaching for the gun and found herself wrestling with the woman as the door opened.

"Are you done?" Chad said, reaching in and grabbing Reagan off the floor.

"Lay off, Rita. We're all a little stressed."

Chad grabbed Rita's shoulder and squeezed it. That was about as much affection as Chad showed her team.

"Ay dos mios," Rita said. She had a Latin temper

that got the best of her sometimes and it was the reason she had pulled Rita from the job last time. Sending her back to home base was the only option Chad had. She hoped she wouldn't have to do it again, for the sake of the team. She couldn't afford to lose one member considering how stretched thin they already were.

"Your replacement will be here at midnight. Keep an eye out." Leaning in she whispered, "I want you to keep an eagle eye on that little queen, Jason. I don't like him."

"Me either. His dinner choices suck and I don't think I've been treated so shitty by the hired help in a long time, if ever."

"All right, stay awake, keep your ears and eyes open, and I'll see you at roll call."

"Goodnight and be careful," Rita said, the hint of warning laced her words.

"Goodnight Rita," Reagan said.

"Ms. Reynolds."

Making their way to the service elevator, Reagan said, "I don't think she likes me still."

Chad didn't respond. She didn't look at Reagan; she didn't say a word to her former lover. The less said the better. Anything more and Reagan might just think Chad and she had buried the hatchet. Except the hatchet was safely sticking out of Chad's back, sure to remain there for safekeeping. It was a reminder of what a fool she had been in a former life.

"Chad." Reagan turned towards Chad once they were in the elevator. "I'm sure this won't mean much, but I wanted to apologize for what happened last-"

"Stop." Chad held up her hand. "There isn't anything you can say that would excuse the way you used me and my team." She turned, bent over, and looked Reagan in the eye. "Trust me when I tell you that you don't need to say another word."

"But–"

"Not. Another. Word. Ms. Reynolds." Chad turned and stood ramrod straight, staring ahead.

Out of the corner of her eye, she clicked off the floors. Why the conference had to be held in the tallest hotel in Abu Dhabi was only proof that God was fucking with her. It took almost eight minutes to get from her floor to the penthouse with just minimal stops. Add more traffic and it took a good twelve minutes or more.

"I'm sorry you feel that way, Chad. I'd hoped we could talk after the trial, but you didn't return my calls, emails, nothing. I even had Dad try to set something up, but he said you refused his request to meet." Chad pursed her lips together and forced the air out of her lungs, frustrated, but Reagan continued undaunted. "I'm not that same woman you knew."

I sure hope not for your father's sake.

"I like to think I've changed."

Highly unlikely.

"I have a different perspective on work and life now."

I hear the threat of going to jail can do that to a person.

"I have a brother who looks up to me and my dad's given me a second chance."

You can pick your friends but you can't pick your family, so might as well make the best out of a bad situation.

"So, I guess all I'm trying to say in my ramblings is well...I mean...I really care about–"

The elevator doors pinged and opened, taking

Chad by surprise. She'd been listening to Reagan and having her own conversation, and she wasn't focused on the fact that the elevator was slowing down. They'd stopped halfway down on their way to Reagan's floor.

The smell of alcohol got on before the passenger.

"Reagan, oh my Reagan. How are you?" Colleen Velasquez stumbled a little and then threw her arms around Reagan's neck, hugging her tight. "This is Reagan Reynolds," she said to Chad, patting Reagan on the chest. "She's my friend. You are my fiend right?" Colleen questioned Reagan.

"Of course, Colleen. It smells like you've been partying."

"Oh, you know how uptight this fucking place is. I went to dinner, had a few drinks, went back to my room after they told me to leave and I found out all my liquor was gone. Fucking maids must have stolen it, so I'm on my way down to give the manager a piece of my mind and…" She pulled out a pack of cigarettes. "To have a smoke. Do you smoke?" She pushed the pack at Reagan.

"No thanks."

Colleen leaned closer to Reagan as Chad tried not to notice. She smelled like she had taken a bath in the booze instead of drinking it.

"Sure you don't want to join me for a smoke and some fresh air?"

The statement was more of an oxymoron and all Chad could do was wonder what a dictator like Velasquez saw in a drunk like Colleen. There had to be something underneath all that Tammy Fay make-up.

"Hey, you're that woman with Mrs. Allegany."

"Colleen, this is Chad Morgan–"

"I'm an advisor to Mrs. Allegany, nice to meet you Colleen…"

Chad waited as if she wanted Colleen to confirm her last name.

"Oh me…haha. My name is Colleen Velasquez. My husband is Juan Diego Velasquez. Perhaps you've heard of him?" Colleen leaned on Reagan more as she started to sway back and forth. Her legs were like rubber now and she had a strangle hold on Reagan, who kept turning her head away just so she could breath.

"Well, Mrs. Velasquez, why don't we take you back to your room and get you into bed? The conference starts early."

"But I need to talk to the manager."

"You know what; it's probably not a good idea until you cool down. I mean, as mad as you are right now he would probably lose his job. You don't want that to happen, do you? He probably has a family to support and ten kids at home," Chad said, hoping her story would defuse the situation.

Maybe it was working. Colleen's eyes were fading fast as she took more and more time to blink. She looked from one side, staring at nothing, and then shifting her stare to the other side, staring at nothing again before her gaze rested on Chad and then seemed to dose off completely.

Still leaning on Reagan, she popped her eyes open and smiled. "You know Reagan my country, not the U.S., cause I am a United States citizen you know, but in my other country, my husband would kill whoever stole my liquor."

Chad figured Colleen was probably right and if she made enough noise here, she wasn't certain they wouldn't do the same thing. So in Chad's mind it was important to try and distance herself from this woman and fast. If Reagan wanted to call her a friend, that was on her.

"I think Ms. Morgan is right, Colleen. Maybe we should get you to bed. Tomorrow's a new day and you can look at the situation with fresh eyes," Reagan said, surprising Chad.

"You know what?"

"What?"

"That's what I like about you, you're so positive and just so nice. Isn't she nice, Ms. Morgan?"

"Lovely," Chad said, rolling her eyes. "Just lovely."

"She is beautiful." Colleen grabbed Reagan's face and smooshed it, pushing Reagan's lips out. Without hesitation, Colleen landed a kiss on the pouty lips and proclaimed, "You know what? If I were a lesbian, you'd be my girl, Reagan Reynolds."

Oh brother, the second woman to pronounce her love for Reagan, if they were only lesbians.

Chad wished she was having a bad dream, hoping she would wake up any minute. Instead, she tapped the button for Colleen's floor when they landed unexpectedly at the lobby level. She quickly pressed the button again to close the doors before Colleen even recognized they made it that far. How did she always seem to find herself babysitting drunks?

Chad tossed Reagan a chaste look, hoping to send a message that she wasn't happy about the situation at hand.

"Well, this is my floor," Chad said when the elevator stopped and the doors opened.

A hand grabbed her jacket stopping her. "You

can't be serious. You're leaving me with her?"

"Hey, she's your friend. Besides, she was just two drinks away from being your date."

"Funny, but she's passed out. I can't carry her." Reagan was practically pleading for help.

Chad really just wanted to leave Reagan stranded with her friend. Peering over Reagan's shoulder at Colleen, Chad shook her head. Again, she had to wonder how she always got stuck with babysitting.

"Fine, but once she's back in her room, she's on her own. Understand?"

"Understood."

Stepping around Reagan, she reached under Colleen's shoulder and supported the bulk of her weight and pulled her off Reagan.

"Thanks."

Reagan stepped back a little and shook the arm that was wrapped around Colleen. "It was falling asleep."

"Well, at least something was getting some sleep."

"I see you haven't lost your sense of humor."

"I've never had a sense of humor," Chad dead panned. She refused to be sucked into a conversation, period. Hoisting Colleen up more, Chad put more hip under the woman. Colleen wasn't frail, that was for sure. She didn't look like she missed many meals, either.

The elevator dinged again, the doors swooshed open, and Chad motioned for Reagan to go first.

"Ever the gentle woman," she said, walking past Chad and into the foyer of the floor.

"What room is she in?"

Reagan turned right and then back to Chad.

"How am I supposed to know?'

"Christ, get her room key?"

"You want me to reach into her pocket and find her key?"

"Uh, yeah, or do you want me to do that, too?"

Reagan bent over and looked at the tight pants Colleen was wearing.

"Come on, she's heavy," Chad said, shifting the dead weight back up on her hip. "Check her back pocket. That's where most people stash their keycards."

Pulling the slipping woman up again, Chad caught sight of the camera in the corner. Great, someone is going to come up any minute 'cause they think we're robbing this woman.

"Hurry up, we're on video and the last thing either of us need is for the authorities to come along asking questions."

Reagan followed Chad's gaze to the camera neatly tucked in the corner.

"Oh right."

Patting Colleen's ass, she felt the hard plastic card.

"Hey, usually you buy a girl dinner before you get touchy feely," Colleen mumbled.

"We're looking for your room key."

"Room 1412," she slurred out and passed out again.

"Let's get her to her door and then we'll get the card."

"Right."

Reagan took up position on the other side of Colleen. Chad pulled her along, it seemed that they practically walked her around to the other side of the massive hotel. Passing another set of elevators, both women groaned at the same time, catching sight of them.

"Remember those are there when we leave," Chad ordered.

"Right."

Stopping in front of 1412, Chad started to say something just as Reagan produced the room key.

"Perfect."

Kicking the door open, Chad dragged Colleen through the door and stopped. The suite was huge. Every inch of the floor was covered in shoes, papers, and luggage. Clothes were strewn everywhere and Chad was surprised the woman slipping out of her grip could find anything in the pigsty, including her alcohol. Sliding her feet, she pushed through the mess and tossed Colleen unceremoniously on the bed. Her reward was a a grunt and a fart.

"Now that's sexy," she said, turning to leave.

"We can't just leave her like this."

"Oh yes, *I* can. You, on the other hand, can do whatever you want."

Reagan tossed the keycard on the desk and Chad felt Reagan right on her heels as she pulled the door open. Without a word between them, they rushed to the elevator. Both pushed the down button, Reagan's touch lingered a little too long on Chad's hand.

"Sorry."

"Hmm."

Chapter Twenty

Reagan stood frozen. Chad's hand stiffened under hers, but didn't move. Sliding her fingers along Chad's knuckles, she couldn't control the rush of energy that flushed her body. She felt like she did at sixteen, when she'd made her first pass at her high school crush. That intense spring of emotion tingled from her toes up to her scalp, her hair standing on end.

How could she get Chad to listen to her? Fate had brought them together in, of all places, Abu Dhabi. Without thinking, she pushed the stop button on the elevator. The carriage jerked to a stop, with Reagan being flung against Chad. Burying her face against Chad's chest, she inhaled, recognizing her scent instantly. God, if she let herself, she'd melt right at Chad's feet. Her pride, on the other hand, prevented her from lingering too long on Chad's hard body. A memory flashed behind Reagan's closed eyes, nakedness, arms and legs intertwined, breath mixing as kisses were exchanged. Tongues dueled for dominance the last time she laid with Chad, only moments before the truth of her deeds were exposed, and for once she regretted her arrogant mindset.

"What the hell did you do that for?" Chad tried to reach the elevator button, but Reagan pulled her hand back.

"If this is the only way to get you to talk to me,

then I'll do whatever it takes."

"Christ, Ms. Reynolds–"

"Reagan, damn it, call me Reagan."

Reagan cringed as Chad grabbed her arms and froze her with a stare. It was a look she had seen only once and it had been reserved for Marcy, when Chad was going in for the kill during her interrogation of the bitch.

"Ms. Reynolds–"

Reagan put her fingers over Chad's lips to stop her from saying something she knew would sting. "I'm sorry," Reagan whispered. "I never meant to fall in love with you. My father, a very wise man, told me that you can't pick who you fall in love with. He was right, it just happens and sometimes it takes you by surprise." Chad didn't say a word; she just stared down at Reagan, making her even more uncomfortable, but she pushed on. "I'm not telling you this in hopes that maybe we can work things out." She could feel her eyes well up with tears. She blinked them back; she'd be damned if she'd cry over Chad again. "You're the last piece of the broken life that I have to put back together." She stepped back, but didn't take her hand down. If she did, she'd knew it would be the last time Chad would let Reagan touch her.

Chad pulled her hand down and finally spoke. "Why now? Why are you telling me all of this now, Ms. Reynolds?"

Reagan knew Chad was being formal with her to keep her distance, but she wasn't going to let her stay away like that. "Why now? I've been trying to contact you to apologize, to tell you how sorry I was for what happened. You act as if I knew you would be here and I would have a chance to plead my case. That's so far from the truth. I couldn't know you would be here. In fact, to be honest, I never thought I would see you again. So don't blame me for taking advantage of the situation I find myself in. I didn't plan to fall for you and I take that with me when I leave. I don't expect you to forgive me, or to understand why I screwed up, but I am different. My priorities are different and the shame I've brought to my family, to myself has cost me dearly." Lowering her head, she whispered. "It's cost me everything."

Something passed between her and Chad, she didn't know what, but Chad almost relaxed under her touch. Without thinking, she stepped forward and kissed Chad. Soft and pliant at first, Reagan felt Chad shift and pull her close. Reagan's heart thumped so fast, she was scared she might have a heart attack. She closed her eyes and leaned into the kiss. If this was the last time she'd be with Chad, she'd take whatever Chad offered because as soon as Chad came to her senses, she'd push Reagan away again.

Chad's tongue pushed against her lips; was it an offer for more? Maybe. Reagan would take whatever was offered and cherish it. She knew she had no right to whatever Chad was offering, but she couldn't stop thinking about Chad. Chad haunted her dreams, her nightmares, and her memories. Welcoming her in, Reagan molded herself against Chad's chest, her fingertips tentatively skimming Chad's arms, finally threading in her soft hair, pulling her close. The elevator jerked back into action, forcing the couple against the wall. Reagan held on for her life, while Chad took the brunt of the blow square on her shoulders as she cradled Reagan tightly in her arms.

Reagan rested her forehead against Chad's chest

and sighed. Chad was like a drug to Reagan. Being around her brought back the yearning, the desire to be touched, and a flood of memories Reagan had tried to push down. She'd had a taste again; now what would she do? Before she could say anything, the doors sprung open and a security guard and a maintenance man stood just outside the doors.

"Oh my goodness, I am so sorry. The elevator seemed to malfunction. Are you two okay?" The security guard quizzed, looking down at his feet.

"We're fine. Thank you for fixing it." Chad released Reagan and walked past her. "Could you see her to her room? It seems she had a panic attack when the elevator shut down."

Rushing past Chad, the security guard grabbed Reagan and stared at her. "Are you okay, miss? I am so sorry that this has happened. Please accept my apologies. What room are you in?"

"How long were we in there?" Reagan didn't know why she asked. A thoughtless question, a reflex, anything to ease the punch to her gut.

"Oh, my goodness, you were in there about half of the hour. Let me escort you to your room. Again, I am so sorry. Check the panel." The security man assisted Reagan out into the lobby to the elevator across from them.

Reagan could only watch Chad push her way through the lobby and out the doors into the night. Her one shot just left the hotel.

❧ ❧ ❧ ❧

Chad's body felt like someone had taken a match to a fireworks factory. She wanted to run, run as far away as her feet could take her. Her mind raced with everything that was said and not said in the elevator. Wiping her lips with the back of her sleeve, she wished it was enough to stop the imprint that she was sure was left behind from Reagan's kiss. The heat of the night slapped her in the face and she grabbed her knees, gasping, stopping just outside the swishing glass doors of the hotel.

"So who are you running from?"

Chad recognized the slurred words. A ring of smoke wafted past her, but Chad didn't need to turn to confirm she knew the voice. She'd heard it in its drunken state earlier that night. Chad now wondered just how intoxicated Colleen had been when she had deposited her in her room.

"Last time I saw you, you were laying on your bed shit-faced."

"Hmm, well, I have a high tolerance for alcohol, besides I told you I needed a cigarette."

Chad felt she'd been played, again. How long had she and Reagan been locked in that damn elevator? Long enough for a drunk Colleen to rouse herself and stumble down to the lobby.

"Cigarette? You look like you could use one."

Chad didn't answer Colleen. She wasn't in the mood to be polite and engaging. Besides, Colleen was a possible hostile and Chad needed to be on her toes around her. If Chad played it right, perhaps in Colleen's drunken state, Chad might be able to shake a nut from that tree.

"Suit yourself."

"I don't smoke." Chad crossed her arms and leaned against the large wall of glass.

"I didn't figure you for a smoker. You're too fit

and healthy. So what demon are you running from?"

"I don't know what you mean. I'm just down for some fresh air."

"This air isn't fresh, it's swampy and hot. You could cut it with a knife it's so dirty. I have to take a shower every time I come down for a smoke. The dust is unbearable here."

"I see."

"Besides, I know when someone is being chased and you, my friend, are being chased. No?" Colleen stubbed out the cigarette and tossed the butt in the direction of the ash can. Missing it, Colleen waved her hand at it. "Psst."

Chad picked it up and tossed it in, moving a tad closer to Colleen. She didn't want to be overheard as she tried to softly interrogate the woman.

"I would need a break if I were around that woman for too long, as well."

"That woman?" Chad felt her defenses fall in place. She'd tried to keep Reagan at arm's length, but if anyone suspected she and Reagan knew each other it could potentially derail the plan she'd been formulating to get close to Colleen. Now here she stood; opportunity presented itself in weird ways, but she'd take it.

"Mrs. I'm-so-important Allegany. God she's a bore. Everyone just flocks around that woman like she's a celebrity or something." Colleen waved her hands around and almost slipped off the huge cement planter. Chad's reflexes jerked Colleen up, stopping her from falling on her ass.

"She can be a handful." Chad righted Colleen. She hoped that agreeing with Colleen presented a sympathetic ear. Chad knelt down and locked eyes with Colleen. "You okay?"

Patting Chad's hand on her arm, Colleen giggled. "Now that would have been a sight. Me on my fat ass."

Releasing Colleen, Chad stepped back and casually leaned against the glass. She positioned herself so Colleen would turn to talk to her, positioning Colleen perfectly for the hotel camera that was pointed outside. Chad wasn't taking any chances; she wanted all of this on camera. Opportunities weren't meant to be squandered.

Tapping another cigarette on the pack, Colleen lifted it to her lips and patted her pockets for a light. Before she could search further, Chad reached in her pocket and produced a pack of matches she'd taken from Mrs. Allegany's room. The ornate gilded matchbox didn't surprise Chad; they were the excesses of the rich. She was always snatching matches, sometimes as souvenirs, but mostly because she never knew when she might need a diversion. A trash can fire always created a focal point that allowed her to make a quick exit. She would look like a guest running for safety and pulling the fire alarm would pop the sprinklers, covering any evidence she might have accidently left behind, like fingerprints.

Touching the tip of the cigarette to the match, Colleen jerked back in surprise.

"Oh, thank you. For someone who doesn't smoke, you're prepared."

Cupping Chad's hand, she took a long drag, turning the tip bright red.

"Souvenirs. Here, keep them." Chad turned the pack over in her hand, making sure she hadn't written anything inside the flap, before closing it and handing them to Colleen.

"Thank you." Looking at the matches, Colleen wrinkled her brow. "Very expensive matches."

Chad shrugged. "I took them from the penthouse suite earlier."

"Ah, yes, your dinner with Mrs. Allegany. How was it?"

Chad tried to pass off disinterest, looking down at her nails. "Dry chicken, lots of alcohol, and too much talking for me."

"See, that's what I mean. At least you had that gorgeous Reagan Reynolds for dinner." Colleen broke out into a fit of laughter. "Oh did I just say that? Oh my, what is on my mind? Sorry."

Thinking quickly, Chad wanted to take advantage of the light-heartedness of the woman. "So, what brings a woman of culture like you to a conference like this? If you don't mind me asking?"

Colleen faced Chad and squinted her eyes, studying Chad. It was quiet for a moment, worrying Chad. Maybe she'd gone too far with her fake platitude. Chad cleared her throat and was about to speak when she was interrupted.

"Well…if you must know…my husband thought it would be a good idea to make a few business connections. I'm starting my own line of cosmetics and well, I have resources, I just need connections. If you know what I mean."

"Makes sense. I mean, there are so many women of business here, but it would seem to me that you'd probably make some great connections." Chad hoped she sounded a little like an uneducated airhead. All muscle and no brains.

"Yeah, that's what my husband said."

"Sounds like a smart guy."

"Oh yeah, he's got a brain for business. He successfully brought our country back from the brink of bankruptcy, he's always helping the poor, and the people adore him."

More like he'd kill them if they didn't follow blindly, she thought, listening to the lies slipping from Colleen's lips.

"Do you know that he's a self-made millionaire, probably a billionaire now." She waved her hands around. "He's…well…he's just such a wonderful man. Smart, you know?" She tapped the side of her head. "Really smart."

"Wow, he sounds great."

"Oh yeah, he is."

Looking down, Colleen picked at something on her slacks. Her appearance was more than a little disheveled and she must have noticed. She stood and brushed the ashes of her cigarette off herself. The end of her cigarette banged precariously from the side of her mouth and it was all Chad could do not to reach up and grab it and flick the ash ready to fall. Clenching her hands, she felt her knuckles grind.

Clearly, Colleen was infatuated with either Juan Diego's money or his power, or both. She'd seen photos of Juan Diego and frankly, she was surprised a beautiful woman like Colleen liked the thug look. He could barely hide his tatted up neck and arms with a dress-shirt. The gang affiliation couldn't be ignored, considering it popped out above his collar even when he was in a tie. It was rumored that he had a tattoo artist living in the presidential mansion ready at a moment's notice to do his president's bidding. It was a job she was sure no one wanted, since word was he'd killed the last tattoo artist when Juan Diego didn't like a tattoo designed to commemorate his new son he'd had with a mistress. Dirt bag of the highest order.

Colleen's turned her attention to her phone after it beeped. Chad assumed it meant she had a text message, since the woman started tapping with the tip of a well-manicured fingernail. If Chad could just get a peek at her phone; she stretched her arms over her head and arched towards Colleen, who automatically adjusted for the intrusion by turning away. Looking up at the camera, Chad had an idea. If she just moved Colleen enough, perhaps the crew back at the room could get a glimpse of her screen. Twisting her head, she nodded at Colleen and looked back up into the camera. Hopefully, someone was paying attention and would video tape their exchange. Moving a bit closer to Colleen, she played right along and contorted herself more, pointing the back of the phone at Chad and putting it in full site of the video surveillance. Chad had to smile at her suave techniques when it came to the set-up.

"Well, I'm afraid I must call it an evening. It has been wonderful talking to you...I'm so sorry. I completely forgot to ask you what your name was, where are my manners?"

"Chad."

"Well, Chad it was very nice of you to speak to me tonight. I appreciate that, good evening."

"Have a restful night..." Chad waited.

"Oh me, yes. My name is Colleen Velasquez."

"I remember, Mrs. Velasquez. I'm sure I'll see you around the conference."

"Good evening." Colleen waved at Chad just has her phone went off with another text message.

"Good night," Chad said, a smile across her face.

"Gotcha." Looking up at the camera, she hoped that there would be enough information to find out what Colleen was planning. Just as she turned to go back into the hotel, her phone went off.

"Hey, what's up?"

❦ ❦ ❦ ❦

"Hey." Chad tossed her jacket on the bar and walked over to the table where Marco was still sitting watching the cameras. "What's going on?"

"It's Reagan–"

"Reagan's off the table. No discussion, nothing. Do you understand?" Chad's tone left no wiggle room for discussion.

"It's not going to be that easy this time, Chad." Marco tilted one of the monitors in her direction. "Take a look." Hitting the play button, Marco sat back, crossed his arms, and watched Chad's face. "Better sit down."

Without thinking, Chad sat and leaned towards the monitor. On the screen was Reagan being escorted back into the hotel elevator by hotel security.

"He's from hotel security. So," Chad said, still wondering why he insisted she watch Reagan.

"Just watch."

Watching them in the elevator, Chad noticed Reagan and the man engaging in what seemed to be polite conversation. As he talked, the security guard inched closer to Reagan. Throwing his head back in laughter, he moved closer when he bent over laughing. The elevator stopped and they got out, the camera momentarily losing sight of the pair.

Chad opened her mouth to say something but

before she could get anything out, Marco beat her to the punch.

"Keep watching." He pointed to the screen.

Focusing, Chad wondered what the hell was going on and then it happened. Reagan was pinned against the wall by the security guard. Threading his fingers through her hair, he forced her head back and attacked her neck; his other hand groped her breast, then yanked her blouse up as his hand explored her body further. His body slammed against Reagan as she tried to slide to the side and get away. Chad's blood was boiling, her hands clenched into fists, and all she could think about was finding that bastard and killing him. Starting to stand, Marco pushed her back down.

"Just wait, it gets better."

"Are you fucking kidding me? Did you send anyone to her room to help her out? Why the fuck didn't you call me?"

"She's not our problem anymore, remember?"

"Yeah, but..." Chad couldn't take her eyes off the monitor, as the scene played out further. Reagan was pushing the man back, just enough that she was able to catch him with a knee between the legs. As he bent over, she lifted the same knee and made contact with his face.

Chad grimaced as blood started to leak out of his nose. Clearly agitated, the man grabbed Reagan again and forced her, face-first, into the wall. Dry humping her, he tried to hold her still, but that was like trying to force a bobcat into a burlap bag. Elbows flew, Reagan flung her head back again, making contact with his face, and turning just a bit, she caught the side of his face with her elbow and decked him. A swift kick to his stomach and Reagan extracted her keycard and slipped into her room.

Chad's stomach lurched and the only thing she could think of was getting to Reagan. Grabbing her jacket, she slipped it on, pulled her gun and dropped it on the table and grabbed a Taser pistol instead.

"If I take that I'll kill the bastard," Chad said, picking up a com system. "Next time call me when shit like this happens."

"So Reagan is on the schedule?"

"She is for the rest of this trip. Put Thomas into the rotation. Make sure he replaces Sofia at night and put her on Mrs. Allegany during the day. Rita can split the shift with the two of them, lighten the workload." Placing the ear bud in, she looked at Marco. "Be ready to kill a few cameras when I find this bastard."

"Chad?"

"No questions, Marco. Just be ready."

"You got it, but I can't keep them down that long."

"It won't take long, trust me."

"Don't get caught."

"I won't, see you when I get back."

"Okay, do you want to know what I got on Señora Velasquez?"

"When I get back, in the meantime keep an eye on her."

"And Jason?"

Her hand on the doorknob, she stopped. Fuck, things were escalating quicker than she thought, but it was good to know her gut still called them right. The little worm was in on this somehow and now she just needed to bait him, along with Colleen. First, she needed to check on Reagan. Her heart felt like it was being cut right out of her chest at the moment and she needed to make sure Reagan was safe.

"Will it keep?" She questioned Marco.

"Yeah, it looks like it isn't going to go down for another day, maybe two. They're waiting for a delivery. At least he's waiting for a delivery."

"It's time for your gay-boy routine. Sorry buddy, but we don't have many more options. We'll discuss logistics when I get back."

"But..." Was all Chad heard as she raced down the hallway. Punching the elevator button, she bounced on her toes ready to pounce. If Reagan's room wasn't ten floors up she would take the stairs and burn off the pent-up rage she felt building. She'd kill the bastard who'd put his hands on Reagan. He'd find out just how Western women handled their problems and when she was done with him, he'd be joining the eunuch caste of people. The elevator finally reached her floor and just as she was about to jump in, the man who'd put his hand on Reagan stood leaning against the panel. With his bruised lip protruding, blood had dripped down his shirt, and his hand still clutched his nuts. Smiling, Chad got on the elevator and hit the stop button.

"Oh shit, I'm sorry. I hit the wrong button." She turned toward the man and looked him up and down. "Wow, what happened to you?"

"Oh, ah, well I fell down the stairs and hit the landing pretty hard."

"That was some fall." Chad knew that the man wouldn't admit to being beaten up by a woman and that's all she needed to know.

"You want me to help you to the security office?" Pointing to his face, she continued, "That looks pretty bad."

"No, no, I'm off. I'm just going to go home and

put some ice on it. Thank you anyway. Now if you could just punch that button."

"Oh sure, no problem." Chad turned away and then circled around and landed a left-hook right where Reagan had elbowed him. Grabbing his head, she thrust her knee up and heard a crack as it made contact with chin. If she was right, she'd just broken his jaw. Picking him up, she looked him in the face and felt her teeth grinding as she spit out her next words.

"You ever put your hands on her again and I'm gonna bury you in the desert." Reaching down she grabbed his scrotum and squeezed. His eye bulged and his body shook as she squeezed harder, a pop and the pressure under her fingers was gone. He let out a hollow scream, his mouth barely moving. He looked up at where the camera was, but before he could say anything, she spoke.

"There isn't any evidence of our little exchange here, but if you want evidence, I have your attempted rape of Ms. Reynolds on tape and I plan on taking it to your boss, if he doesn't already have a copy." Chad picked him up off the floor, made a show of dusting off his lapels, and straightened his jacket. "If I ever see you at this hotel again, I'll make sure you're dealt with, do you understand?"

The man could only nod, his lips quivering as he still clutched between his legs.

"Good." Chad pushed the stop button in and hit Reagan's floor. "You have twenty six floors to decide how you want to handle this. My men will be in the lobby watching you and if you don't leave, they'll let me know."

It was all he could do to stand against the wall, but tears didn't fall as he stared straight ahead. If he was scared, he didn't give Chad the benefit of knowing. Landing on Reagan's floor, she got out of the elevator, turned, and stood watching him. Her hands clasped together, she stared him down until the doors finally shut. Watching the elevator panel lick off floors, she waited until it hit the lobby and waited.

"I want you to make sure this asshole leaves the hotel, unmolested." Chad pushed the ear bud in, listening.

"We're on it. He's got an escort out and he's taking a long drive in the desert."

"Thanks."

Chad moved towards Reagan's room. Her heart raced, wondering what she'd find on the other side of the door. Preparing herself, she knocked and waited. Nothing. Not surprised, she knocked softly and then spoke calmly.

"Reagan, it's me, Chad."

Chapter Twenty-one

The lights were off. The darkness hid the danger from her sight. At least, that's what Reagan wanted to happen. She sat in a foreign country, now the victim of an attempted rape, and all she wanted to do was go home. Her phone dangled from her fingertips. She'd left a message for her cousin Ashley. She was sure Ashley wouldn't be able to make heads nor tails from her message. She'd cried through half of it, babbled through the other half, and then called again and let it ring three times and hung-up. Panicked, she called again and left another message and here she sat waiting, desperate. Now she marked time, watching the bright dial of the bedside clock tick off the minutes. One, two, three...twenty-four, twenty-five....

A knock at the door scared her, her mind raced. She was in a Muslim country where women were second or third class citizens, in a place where cattle were more important than Reagan. She'd hit a man, broken his nose, and bloodied his face. He'd be out for revenge. Maybe she should make a run for the American Embassy? Her passport. She needed to find her passport.

Reagan got up and thrashed around in her suitcase, looking for her papers, her plane ticket, and her passport. She clutched them to her chest. Jerking the drapes back, she peered out the window, the ground hundreds of feet below. There was only one way out of the room and they stood on the other side of the door waiting for her. She gripped her paperwork tighter. They would take it and she would be stuck in Abu Dhabi forever. She'd be sent to a prison and spend the rest of her days being raped by men, spit on by women, and die a slow painful death.

"Reagan, it's me, Chad. Open the door." The sweetest voice Reagan had ever heard called to her through the door. Knocking again. "Reagan, I'd like to talk to you, please."

Reagan stood frozen by the need to be strong, but also because she was truly scared, frightened beyond belief. Chad would never believe what happened tonight. She would assume Reagan was lying about the attempted rape. *The girl who cried wolf*, she thought. She'd done it to herself, had no one to blame but herself. Maybe she'd led the guy on by being nice to him. *Small talk, it was only small talk*, she told herself. This culture had different rules for men and women. Women didn't talk to men, they didn't walk around exposing themselves, and they surely didn't accuse men of rape, or even attempted rape.

"Reagan, open the door, or I'll call security."

Panicked, she ran for the door and swung it wide. "What do you want?"

"I wanted to check in on you, are you all right?" Chad looked down at the paperwork in her hands, her forehead furrowing. "What's that?"

Dropping her hands behind her back, Reagan stiffened. "Nothing."

"Are you all right?" Chad reached up and tried to touch Reagan's shoulders but she flinched away.

"I'm fine."

"Can I come in?"

"I told you, I'm fine," Reagan said curtly, then looked to the left and to the right making sure no one was in the hallway. Reagan noticed the knuckles on Chad's hand were scraped and bloody. "What happened? Are you all right?"

"I'm fine." Chad quickly tucked her hand in her pants pocket.

"Well, if we're all fine, what are you doing here?" Reagan stepped back out of the lit hallway and back into the darkness of the room, pushing the door in front of her. It offered her a sort of protection from further intrusion and from Chad's gaze. She didn't know what she looked like, but she was certain it wasn't pretty. Reagan ran her hand over her head and tried to smooth down any hair that might have gotten messed-up in the scuffle. She refused to make eye contact with Chad, and asked again. "What are you doing here?"

"Reagan, can I please come in? It's awkward standing out here in the hallway. Please?"

What was left of Reagan's resolve melted. Pulling the door open a few inches, she motioned for Chad to come in. She wasn't going to offer her a seat; that would mean she could stay and Reagan just wanted to be left alone. She was waiting for her cousin's phone call and her safety line.

"Can I turn on a light?"

"No…I mean…I'll turn the bathroom light on." Reagan ran to the bathroom and turned the light on, then grabbed a washcloth and wet it. "Sorry for the mess, I was looking for something," she said, then handed Chad the washcloth. "For your hand."

Chad sat on the edge of her bed, gently dabbing

at her knuckles, while Reagan stood as far away as she could get. The cold window against her back, she felt the need to run, just go. Anywhere but sitting here in a room waiting for the police to come and take her away. She thought about calling her father, but she'd used up all her favors a long time ago and she needed to regain his trust. Calling him with an accusation of attempted rape wouldn't bring him running, she was sure of it.

"Reagan, sit down." Chad patted the bed next to her.

Reagan shook her head, still holding her passport and plane ticket to her chest. Her thoughts raced around in her head. The start of an anxiety attack crowded its way into her mind as she tried to untwist everything that had happened. Suddenly, Chad was next to her, gently covering Reagan's hands, pulling her into a tight embrace. Rocking her back and forth, she heard Chad whisper.

"It's going to be okay. He won't hurt you again, I promise."

"Oh Christ." Was all Reagan could say, her body stiffened, her heart sank. Chad knew.

Chad's strong arms held her tighter. Nothing, no one, could get to her if Chad held her, protected her. Words that were left unspoken between them suddenly didn't matter. The embrace warmed her as a gentle reminder of their past crept into Reagan's mind. The last time Chad had held her like this was just before being exposed as the traitor she really was.

"I won't let *anyone* hurt you again, Reagan."

An idle promise, made in the heat of turmoil. Reagan knew Chad better than that; she'd seen the scorn in Chad's eyes earlier. Chad's hardened heart hadn't changed, she was sure of it.

"Why are you here, Chad? I saw the look in your eyes earlier. You can't fool me. Is this just a ploy for sex?"

Chad jerked back, but all Reagan saw was sadness in her eyes. "I saw what that asshole did to you, Reagan. It's all on video."

"Oh god, I have to get out of here. They're going to send someone to find me and arrest me. He's going to his supervisor, he'll tell them that I was seducing him. This country isn't exactly known for their great treatment of women." Pushing against Chad's chest, she struggled to get out of her grasp, but was only held tighter.

"I don't think he's going to say anything."

"Why not? He's a man, a privilege I don't exactly enjoy." Reagan bounced back and forth; she was antsy, her flight response firmly entrenched.

Grabbing her passport – her lifeline - tighter, she blew out short breaths, trying to ease her anxiety. She rotated her head, trying to loosen up the muscles that were squeezing her neck. The tension was starting to give her a headache.

"Oh god, a migraine." She rubbed her temple, still rocking back and forth.

"Reagan, sit."

❦ ❦ ❦ ❦

Chad sat Reagan on the bed and knelt down in front of her. Gently, she worked crinkled papers from her grip, noticing it was her plane ticket and her passport. Reagan was in a bad way and it was going to take all Chad had to bring her down from her amped up panic attack.

Chad turned off her com system and looked at Reagan. "Reagan…Reagan…look at me." Chad gently lifted Reagan's chin and forced her to make eye contact with her. "Reagan, I'm sorry I wasn't there for you. But I'm here for you now."

"Why are you sorry? You didn't do anything wrong." Reagan was starting to lose more control as tears pinched their way out of her closed eyes.

"Slow your breathing down. Reagan, slow… your…breathing…down." Chad rubbed Reagan's arms, trying to warm her up. "That's it, good. Focus on my voice, Reagan. I've taken care of everything. He isn't going to be bothering you anymore. If the authorities come, we'll be ready." Chad pulled her into an embrace and gently rocked her back and forth. "Shh, shhh, shhh. I'm here now and I'm not leaving, so let it out. Go ahead and cry all you want."

A folded pile of clothes that looked like they were ready to be packed sat next to the open suitcase on the bed, so Chad picked them up and placed them in the suitcase. She straightened up more of the mess and placed it on the floor, ready to go at a moment's notice. Flicking the covers back, she laid Reagan down on the bed. She was rigid as a board as Chad slipped off her shoes. Reaching up, she slid her hands up to Reagan's knees and then looked at her. She was staring up at the ceiling, fear lining her face.

"Reagan, let's get you into something more comfortable. Maybe some sweat pants?"

"I…I didn't pack any…I figured I would be busy and it would be so hot that all I have are some sleeping clothes in there."

"Okay, can I look for them?"

Reagan nodded, but still didn't look at Chad. Chad flipped through the neat stack of clothes she'd put in the suitcase. Nothing. Looking around, she found some sleep wear in the bathroom. *Great*, Chad thought as she rolled her eyes at the skimpy camisole and silky shorts that most likely barely covered Reagan's ass. "God shoot me now," she whispered, grabbing the jammies, if you could call them that, and went back into the bedroom.

"These wouldn't happen to be them would they?"

A brief look and Reagan nodded, turning back to staring at the ceiling. "I'm not tired."

"Okay." Holding up the sleepwear, Chad wiggled it from the tip of her finger. "Wanna get changed?"

Reagan shook her head, still not looking at Chad. "I'm fine." She turned over on her side, presenting Chad with her back.

Now what? She all but froze Chad out, not that she blamed her. Chad had shown a professional detachment to her the little she had seen her this trip and now here she was, showing up at one of the most difficult times a woman could face. She was in a foreign country, worried she was going to be arrested for assaulting a man. God, it was similar to the reason Chad hated traveling through Texas. It was like a foreign country to her, considering how many times she'd been cuffed and placed in a police car. All warranted, but nevertheless, it left a bad taste in her mouth every time she drove through the state. It wasn't really the same, but she was trying to put herself in Reagan's shoes, sympathetic and understanding, something she often was accused of not being able to do.

Tossing the flimsy clothing in the suitcase, she

sat on the edge of the bed and reached for Reagan's hand, gently touching it, rubbing her fingertips over the veins popping up. She couldn't leave Reagan here. She wasn't safe and she wouldn't sleep, not until she was on that plane taking her home.

"Reagan, I'm not going to let you stay here. I want you to come back to the suite with me. I've got room and I can make sure you're okay." Chad had a pleading tone to her request, but she didn't care. She wouldn't forgive herself if anything happened to Reagan.

"I'm fine, really."

"You're not. I can get you on a plane tomorrow and you can go home."

Reagan jerked herself up and looked at Chad. "I'm not going home. My father wanted me to come here and represent, I'm not going to let him down. I can't. Not again."

"If you explain what happened tonight, I'm sure he'll understand."

"I'm not going home. I need to make this work. I just need to keep a low profile."

Pulling Reagan to her feet, Chad let her hands go and walked around the bed, grabbing clothes off the floor. "Come on, you're coming with me." She tossed a few more items into the suitcase. "Why don't you pack your toiletries and I'll get this stuff." Pushing Reagan towards the bathroom, she opened the cosmetic case and made a gesture at the make-up lying around the sink. Reagan looked at her and slowly shook her head, but started to pack up everything.

Relieved, Chad pulled stuff off hangers, shoes from the closet, and started stuffing them into suitcases. She didn't care whether they wrinkled or not, she had room service and could get them dry-cleaned. Her pace sped up and she systematically worked from one end of the room until she ended up at the bathroom.

Reagan sat on the toilet, sobbing silently as she dabbed at her eyes. Chad stroked Reagan's hair and pulled her head against her thigh. What was she going to do with Reagan? She didn't have extra manpower to cover another client, but she couldn't leave Reagan alone. She just couldn't. Reagan was pulling at her heartstrings again and there wasn't anything she could do to prevent it.

God!

"Come on, let's finish." Chad pulled her phone and called Marco, requesting someone come down and help them move Reagan's stuff. Chad finally realized Reagan was in a near state of nudity, her T-shirt barely covering anything, so that wasn't going to work. Pulling some jeans and a sweatshirt from her suitcase, she once again pulled Reagan to her feet and silently got her dressed. Reagan just went through the motions, saying nothing, and not looking at Chad. Guiding her back to the bedroom, Reagan sat on the bed while Chad slipped a pair of slippers on her feet. The rollercoaster ride was almost over and Reagan was coming down from her amped high. Now she was more manageable. Thankfully.

A knock on the door startled both women. Putting her finger to her lips, Chad moved to the door and looked out of the peephole before opening it and letting Marco in.

"Hey."

"Hey," Chad said, tossing her head towards Reagan. "She's in here. Give me a hand with the bags.

I'm taking her to my suite."

"Do you think that's a good idea?"

"You got a better one?"

Marco shook his head and tucked a small bag under his arm. "Nope." Grabbing another, he looked at Reagan. "Hey."

Putting the do not disturb sign on the door, she wanted to make sure the maid didn't accidentally notify the hotel of Reagan's departure from the room.

"You ready?" she said to Reagan.

Without saying a word, Reagan stood and looked around the room, then walked out into the hallway behind Marco. Pulling the rolling suitcase, Chad grabbed Reagan's hand and pulled her along. The late hour would mean there would be little to no foot traffic in the hallway. A relief to Chad, who definitely didn't want another confrontation.

Chapter Twenty-two

The warmth of the covers made Reagan bury deeper under them. If only she could pull them over her head and disappear forever, or at least until she got on U.S. soil. Pulling the pillow closer, she hugged it and took a deep breath. It was Chad. Her intoxicating, protective smell wrapped around Reagan like a memory that made her heart flutter. Chad hadn't questioned what had happened to Reagan. Instead, she had rushed in and saved her, wrapped her arms around Reagan, making her feel secure, and here she was now in Chad's bed. Any other time she would welcome being in Chad's bed, but Chad wasn't around, so she only had the pillow to comfort her.

The remnants of her migraine picked at her brain. The stress of the night's events brought it on; now she hoped that being safe would ease it. She hadn't packed any medication for it and there was no way she was going to call for the hotel doctor, no possible way. Licking her dry lips, she looked around for something to drink. A bottle of water sat on the bedside table with a note and two aspirin.

I thought you might need something. These are aspirin. If you can't take them, I have other things for your migraine. I'll be in the other room, so don't hesitate to let me know if you need anything.

C

Thoughtful still, was all Reagan could think after reading the note twice. Chad had loaned her a T-shirt and left her some aspirin. Was it too much to think Chad might still care about her? Probably. Chad had made it clear in the elevator that she was over Reagan.

Popping the aspirin, she washed it down, but swallowing too fast, she spilled water all over her shirt.

"Shit," she said, popping up, the water dripping down the front of her shirt. "Oh shit." Tossing the covers off, so they didn't get wet, she slipped off the bed and ran to the bathroom, grabbing a towel and trying to soak up the water. With only the light from the clock on, she didn't see her suitcase on the floor and rammed her foot into it, jamming her big toe.

"Fuck." Jumping around grabbing her foot, she lost her balance and slammed against the wall. Before she could do anything else, the door was flung wide, and Chad stood, hands up, ready to attack.

"What the hell is going on? Are you okay?" Chad was beside Reagan before she could say anything. "Did you faint?" Chad's hands were pushing Reagan's hair back and studying her eyes. Then she ran her hands down Reagan's neck, rubbing the muscles. Reagan froze at the touch. Her mind had disengaged the minute Chad put her hands on her face, her body on autopilot.

"Oh...uh," Reagan's gaze followed Chad's, looking at the wet T-shirt clinging to her breasts. She felt her face flush as she pulled at the edge of the white material, hoping to cover herself, but it wouldn't stretch far enough with her sitting on it. "I spilled water all over myself and I was getting up to grab a towel to dry off, when I stubbed my foot on my suitcase that I didn't see sitting there and then I guess I grabbed my foot and was hopping around and then I fell and hit the wall and then you came in and–"

Chad covered her lips with a finger, stopping her rambling. "Are you okay?"

Reagan could only nod, since Chad's finger was still stopping her from talking.

"Good. How's your headache?"

Reagan shrugged her shoulders and offered a slight smile. It was the best she could do considering Chad hadn't removed her finger yet. Staring at Chad, she waited for her to make the next move. They were so close, Reagan could smell Chad's cologne on her wrist. A feminine move to be sure, Reagan thought, closing her eyes and without thinking, she took a deep breath. The idea of scent tagged to memories was true, as so many memories of their past flooded her mind. Her body remembered too, her nipples responding, her skin prickled, and her heart raced.

"Could you please help me up?" Reagan grabbed Chad's upper arms, waiting.

"Of course."

Chad grabbed Reagan around the waist and lifted her to her feet. Trying to put weight on her foot, Reagan stumbled against Chad, grabbing her for support.

"Oh, sorry." Reagan pushed against Chad but didn't get very far as Chad held her tight.

"You smell good," Chad whispered.

Reagan turned her head towards Chad, her lips brushing against Chad's neck. Chad flinched, her body jerking at the contact. Before Reagan could do anything else, she was scooped up and carried to the bed. Gently deposited, Reagan kept her arms around Chad, pulling her down with her.

※ ※ ※ ※

Chad braced herself, an arm on each side of Reagan, almost nose to nose. They were so close she could feel Reagan's breath on her lips. Her inner struggle was battling with her head right now and all she could think about was kissing those lips that haunted her dreams.

"Kiss me, please," Reagan huffed against her lips.

Chad paused, lowered herself into the kiss, and let her body respond. God she was an idiot, but she couldn't help herself. Was she doing this out of pity or was she letting her heart lead her head? It didn't seem to matter right now, it felt...familiar. She craned her neck as Reagan sank further into the bed, pulling Chad's hips against hers. Keeping her arms straight, she hovered above Reagan. They were moving too fast. Did a shared past allow them to pass go and move forward to the next part of their lives? Studying Reagan's face, she'd committed it to memory a long time ago. Chad suddenly realized she'd been able to remove Reagan from her mind, but not her heart. It ached and the tattered edges were proof that it had borne the brunt of her anger towards Reagan. Reagan hadn't betrayed *her*, as much as Chad felt used. She'd been used as an alibi, a protector, and a lover. Now, Reagan sat under her begging for a kiss, a simple request, but one that came with strings, she was sure.

Before Chad could linger, Reagan pumped a hip, pushed Chad's elbow, and Chad was flipped over onto the bed with Reagan on top of her. Her full body weighed down on Chad's and all Chad could think to do was pull Reagan down into a kiss, a sizzling kiss that left Chad praying it wouldn't end. If it ended, she'd have to have time to think logically, to reason with herself, and remember the past. Could she put the past were it belonged? Was it in her to give Reagan the chance she had asked for in the elevator? She didn't know, but what she was sure of was that Reagan still had command over her body, its betrayal evident in the way it was responding to Reagan's exploring hands. Hands that didn't work fast, but instead savored the territory they were exploring again.

Chad felt Reagan's hand reach between their bodies and unbuckle her belt and her pants and heard the familiar sound of a zipper's teeth being released as it was edged down. Reagan's fingers faltered just at the top of her boxer briefs, a silent pause giving Chad a moment of clarity. Grabbing Reagan's hand, she stopped her progress and pressed it to her pubic bone. What was she doing? Did she want Reagan to touch her there, or was she enjoying the lingering touch of what could be the last time she allowed Reagan to investigate her body so intimately? Nipples pressed wantonly against Chad's chest as Reagan rubbed up against her breast. Pushing herself further up Chad's body, Reagan lowered her lips to Chad's ear and whispered.

"Let us have tonight."

Chad body didn't argue. She let her hand be pushed off Reagan's as Reagan slipped inside her briefs. A hot summer breeze felt cooler than the heat between them. Chad jerked at the glancing touch across her clit. Pushing past her hair, Reagan had no problem slipping between her lips, she was so wet.

Resting her palm against Chad's clit, Reagan slid her hand back and forth, her finger slipping in and out. The fire ignited her body and she thought she would burst into flames. Her skin felt like it was burning and she wished she was naked as the start of an orgasm sliced through her. Her legs were trapped between sheets as she tried spreading her legs wider, wanting deeper penetration.

"Pants," Chad huffed.

"What?"

"My pants, take them off," Chad ordered. It was the best she could do as she tried to wrangle the orgasm, holding off until she couldn't anymore.

Her slacks were half off, as she grabbed Reagan's hand and guided her back to her orgasm. Helping her slip two fingers in, Chad directed the action, burying them as deep as she could handle. Plunging them in and out, Chad rode out her orgasm silently, not making the slightest sound, fearing Marco would hear them. Why she was worried about Marco was one of those shiny object moments she had during sex. That clarity kept her safe out in the field, was a split second of pure thought in sex, and then she found herself folded back into another orgasm ripping through her body. Reagan's tongue filled her mouth, dueling for confirmation that this wasn't an accident. Chad's hand held Reagan's head tight against her, her lips bruising as she darted in and out of her mouth. In that moment when everything seemed right, Chad thought she could devour Reagan, to share her energy with Reagan. The need to satisfy Reagan, to protect her–at a baser level it was animalistic for Chad. Grinding through another orgasm, she felt sweat break out behind her knees and ankles, a signal to Chad that it had hit her at a deeper level than she'd felt in a long time.

Stopping Reagan's hand, she pulled it free and rolled Reagan on to her back. Pushing the T-shirt up, she started at Reagan's hip and trailed her tongue along the side of her rib cage, curling around to a taunt nipple. Reagan squealed as Chad sucked the tip into her mouth. Flicking it with her tongue, she pinched the other tip, and then gently pulled it as it hardened under her fingers. Switching to the other breast, Chad looked up briefly; Reagan had closed her eyes and thrown her head back into the overstuffed pillows. Arching her body up against Chad for more contact, Chad took the opportunity to travel south and stopped on her way down, nipping at Reagan's body, eliciting more squeaks. As if on command, Reagan spread her legs, begging for more contact, pushing Chad's head down when Chad delayed touching her.

"Please," Reagan pleaded.

"What is it you want, Reagan?"

"You know."

"You need to ask for it."

Reagan shifted her hips, raising them slightly as she looked down at Chad who could only smile. "Please...Chad...I've dreamed about you for so long...I think I might burst."

Chad smirked just before lowering her lips to Reagan's strip of hair. Flattening her tongue, she flicked it across Reagan's clit, causing her to body to jerk. Reagan let out a moan that only encouraged Chad to torture her again; this time she dipped her head further down and flicked her tongue in and out of Reagan's opening. Reagan threaded her finger into Chad hair and held her between her legs.

"Chad please," Reagan barely whispered.

Chapter Twenty-three

You know we need her. She's the only one who can get close enough without raising suspicion," Marco advised.

"I can't ask her to do this."

"I don't think you have a choice."

Chad slammed her fist on the table, rocking the glassware and toppling one over, spilling the contents. Marco rushed to get towel while Chad tried to scoop the liquid away from the maps and paperwork scattered all over the tabletop. She wasn't one for overt demonstrations of anger, but she knew this was a no-win situation.

"I can talk to her if you want. It might be easier coming from me."

Chad shook her head. "No, I'll do it. Fuck."

Chad hated the idea, but she had to agree with Marco. During the last two days of the conference, Reagan was the only one who'd spent any time with Colleen. In fact, they seemed to have become fast friends, much to Chad's dismay. Right now, Reagan was at the conference breakfast, sitting next to Colleen, chatting. Chad had advised Reagan against going, but Reagan had insisted, explaining she owed it to her father to represent Reynolds Holdings. The contacts made here could open more doors, but even more, it gave Reagan a chance to put a different face out to the public than the one they might remember from a year ago. Chad understood and knew Reagan was risking a lot, putting herself out there like that. The news rags would put whatever spin they wanted on Reagan's attendance and if she didn't give them a story, they would make one up. Chad made a decision to stay away from Reagan, so she wouldn't have to endure any more scrutiny if the media connected the dots between them. Court documents were public record; if someone dug deep enough, they would know Chad Morgan had a connection to Reagan Reynolds and Reynolds Holdings. They would know Chad had unraveled the case and made the connection between Marcy and the actual attempts on Frank Reynolds' life to set herself and their love child up to inherit Reynolds Holdings if Frank and Reagan died. Chad was only thankful that Reagan hadn't eaten anything when they'd arrived home to be with Frank, otherwise Reagan might have died. Fate had a way of creating circumstances that could save a life or take it.

Watching the monitor, Chad saw Rita and Mrs. Allegany enter the room. A whirlwind of excitement followed. Flipping to a different camera, Chad spied Colleen whispering something in Reagan's ear. Both women smiled, looking over at Sylvia. Chad wondered just how she was going to broach the subject of Colleen with Reagan. They'd just barely started talking again and Reagan would suspect the reason for their recent intimate encounter was to use her to get to Colleen. This was a no win situation for Chad. If she didn't get Reagan's help, she would be dead in the water. If Reagan did do it, she would do it begrudgingly and suspect Chad's motives. Damn. How would Chad convince Reagan it was the right thing to do, without divulging the dangers Reagan and the rest of the attendees were in?

"Yeah, but you and I know she'll think I set her up. That I was just being nice to her, so she would help me out."

"*Nice?*" Marco smiled at Chad.

"Don't go there, man."

"Okay, but if you think I didn't notice the big fat smile on your face last night before you left to replace Sofia…dude, you gotta know, you're a whole lot more manageable when you're happy."

"I'm not happy." Chad corrected Marco.

"If you say so. Anyway, we need to brief the team on what's going on. If this is what you think it is, a virus, then the clock is ticking and we're into our second day of the conference. Only two more to go before the conference is over." Marco studied the screen again, pointing at Colleen. "Do you think she wants to spread the virus here, or do you think she wants to pass it on and let everyone take it home with them?"

"Shit, I hadn't thought about that, I just figured she'd want to make everyone here sick. Hold 'em hostage so to speak. Now that you say that, I wouldn't put it past her to let it travel home and then let her husband blackmail the attendees. That's ballsy."

"Desperate men do desperate things."

"No, they do stupid shit." Chad rubbed her temples. This was worse than she thought–a contaminate carried back to each business leader's country could be catastrophic. Her government contact had every reason to be worried. Now she needed to come up with something to contain the situation. It would take a two-pronged approach to beat this back into submission and stifle it and just getting close to Colleen wouldn't do it.

⁂

"So, how'd you sleep last night? Last time I saw you, we were putting you to bed and you were out like a light." Reagan poked at her eggs. She wanted to be anywhere - well, not just anywhere, next to Chad, wrapped in her strong arms, being told they had a chance, that last night wasn't a mistake.

"Hey, you okay?" Colleen shook Reagan's shoulder and peered at her. "That's a cute dress, is it off the rack or designer?"

Reagan looked down at her dress and wondered again what she was doing here. Fashion talk, the snippy remarks some of the women made about the way others were dressed, assessment of their looks, well they might be powerhouses in business, but some of them were still catty women who took pleasure in picking each other apart until there wasn't anything left but bones. And don't get Reagan started on eating disorders and the women walking around with sunken faces and protruding shoulders and hip bones. They needed a cookie, make that a whole package of cookies and to keep their manicured fingers out of their throats. *Wow.* Reagan shook her head; here she was doing just what she was accusing the elite of, judgmental bullshit.

"Hello…Reagan…are you still with us?" Colleen tapped her again.

"Oh, I'm sorry. I had a bad night last night and I didn't get enough sleep. I feel like I'm dragging my butt behind me in a wagon."

"Huh?'

"It's sort of an American saying."

"You Americans have a way with the English language." Colleen finished her coffee without taking a bite of her breakfast. "Oh, there's Mrs. Allegany. What did you think of your dinner with her last night? Is she as pompous as she seems? I mean, god, it seems like she is on the campaign trail, but there isn't anyone here who can vote. Well, except for you, but you seem like you have a good head on your shoulders. How do you say, your bullshit meter seems to be working." Colleen chuckled at the joke.

Clearly, it wasn't lost on Colleen. Reagan wasn't surprised she could see right through Sylvia's attempt at furthering her husband's aspirations for political gain. If Sylvia played her cards right, the women in this room could help him fund a good portion of his campaign, but not without some future payback.

"Well, it sorta comes with the territory in America, lately. As for dinner, it was fine. She went to college with my parents and we chatted about that, the conference, and that's about it."

"Well, last night I saw that husky piece of meat that is working with her."

"When?"

"Oh, I had the urge for a cigarette, so I went downstairs. I don't like smoking in my room, my clothes start to smell like an ashtray, and well, it's a bad habit I'm trying to break."

Was she referring to Chad? If so, what was Chad doing downstairs? Had their conversation affected her as much as it had Reagan? Maybe she was referring to Jason, but she wouldn't call him a husky piece of meat. Heck, he was as effeminate a man she'd ever met. Skinny as a rail and that high-pitched voice, ugh.

"Oh, you mean Jason?" She tossed out.

"No, that tough looking woman always with Mrs. Allegany." Colleen raised her hand over her head, indicating height. "That woman who was with you in the elevator. Oh god, I hope I didn't embarrass myself. I don't usually drink that much, but oh, I was so stressed from the travel." Colleen rested her hand on Reagan's arm, letting out a small giggle.

If Reagan didn't know better, she would think Colleen was flirting with her. Colleen had flipped her hair back during their conversation, flicked her tongue out and slowly licked across her upper lip, moved her chair closer under the guise of not wanting their conversation heard and now she was softly touching her forearm, smiling at Reagan.

"No, no, you didn't embarrass yourself at all. We've all been there before. I don't know what your flight was like, but mine was brutal." Reagan pushed her plate away from her and grabbed her cup. "More coffee?"

"You're so sweet to offer. I would love some. The coffee isn't anything like we have at home, but it's better than nothing." Colleen bumped her shoulder against Reagan. "Right?"

All Reagan could do was smile back. She was starting to get suspicious of Colleen's motives. Why would she flirt with Reagan? She had a husband. She wanted something from Reagan; that's the only reason she was being so nice to her, it had to be. Just a few more days and she would be home. She looked around the room for Chad, briefly making eye contact with Rita; she didn't acknowledge Reagan in the slightest as she checked out the rest of the room.

"Do you mind if I asked you something?"

Reagan turned her attention back to Colleen. "Sure."

Colleen studied her, looking at Reagan's lips, licking her own seductively and then she let her gaze roam over Reagan's face. "No, I shouldn't. I like you Reagan. You're not like all these other women. You're more grounded, more interesting." Grabbing Reagan's hands, she continued. "You have such an old soul; your eyes aren't hollow like these women. They speak to me; they tell me that you and I are a lot alike."

"Really." Reagan tried not to sound suspicious of Colleen's statement, but she was intrigued to find out what game she was playing and Reagan definitely felt like she was being played.

"Are you close to Mrs. Allegany, I mean have you done business with her before?"

"My company has been involved with a few things her husband has contributed to, why?"

"Oh, I was just trying to get a meeting with her and I wondered if...forget it," Colleen said, as she turned slightly way from Reagan.

Reagan had played this coy game before with men whom she wanted something from, so watching Colleen play it now made her wonder if she was as transparent, or if men really fell for it. That was a stupid question; of course they had, otherwise she wouldn't have been as successful as she'd been. Women used their sexuality to get what they wanted, and this was proof positive that they even did it to each other, if it got the desired results.

"I understand...we all need help sometimes. What can I do to help?"

"Really?"

No, not really, but you've got my curiosity piqued,

she thought, smiling back at the woman. "If I can. It isn't illegal is it?" Reagan chuckled at what she hoped Colleen would take as a joke.

Reagan's phone went off, letting her know she had a text. "Do you mind?" she said, lifting it between them.

"Oh no, please." Colleen motioned to the phone.

Every women in that room was tethered to their homeland, company, or family in some capacity, including Colleen, who seemed to have hers practically glued to her ear. Except for now. Picking hers up, Reagan ran her finger across the screen and turned her attention away from Colleen.

It was a text from Chad and all it said was – *I need to talk to you. Now!*

Chapter Twenty-four

Everyone sat around the table, waiting for Chad to say something. She'd called the meeting to brief the crew on a possible volatile situation involving attendees at the conference. Rita was with Sylvia, so Chad would debrief her later, but this couldn't wait any longer. The more time that passed, the less time they had to put any kind of plan in place. She needed her group to be on their toes now, watching everyone, every interaction, and every conversation intensely. If they overlooked a possible lead, no matter how little or how insignificant they thought it might be, it could cost people their lives. *Shit, it could cost everyone their lives, including her crew.*

"All right, settle down everyone." She looked at Thomas and Marco, who were trying to wrestle the other to the ground. Is this what an overabundance of testosterone did to grown men? She thought, tossing them a disapproving glance. "Are you done?"

"We were just playin' around, boss."

"Yeah, well, save it for when we're home and our lives aren't in danger."

"What?" Marco tried to flash an innocent look, but Chad wasn't in the mood.

"What did you find out from my pen?"

"I haven't had a chance to pull the video and photos off it yet. I'll get on that after the meeting.

We've been sorta busy," Marco said defensively.

"Well, if you weren't wrestling maybe you'd have time to get to it."

"I'll get on it."

"Check." Chad turned her attention to the rest of the group sitting around the table.

"We have a situation." Chad pulled up the video she'd sent to D.C. of Colleen Velasquez on the phone. "I sent this to my contact in D.C. He says Velasquez's husband is on their radar and it's not good. According to their lip reader, seems she's up to something here at the conference. The lip reader couldn't get it all, but she said something about waiting for a courier and something about a having the antivirus. So we can only guess, but my suspicion is that she's going to release a virus, or a toxin, at the conference."

"How can we be sure?" Thomas pulled at his collar. His discomfort was evident.

"We can't, but I'm going with my gut and it says Colleen is up to something." Chad passed out photos of Colleen's husband, Juan Diego Velasquez. "This is her husband. He's not here, but I think they have someone here already. If not they'll be here soon."

"So what's the plan, boss?" Marco passed his photo to the right and took another, inspecting it closer. "Hey, this is that little weasel we tangled with about a decade ago."

"Yep, and he's a son-of-a-bitch. He killed the bastard who ran that little spit of a country and took it over. Went from small time drug dealer, to guerilla warrior, to dictator. He amassed an army just big enough to dethrone Martinez and killed everyone and anyone he thought was loyal to his predecessor."

"God, what does she see in someone like that?"

Sophia pointed to the picture of Colleen.

"Beauty queen likes a bad boy."

"I'm think he's either got lots of money or a big–"

"Hey, not while the kids are present," Chad joked.

Everyone chuckled at the *small* joke, but that would be the end of the levity, business was pressing.

"We need all eyes out there on the conference. Since we don't know what we're dealing with, we need to be on our toes. I want an exit strategy for Ms. Allegany; we need to be able to get out on a moment's notice. The jet needs to be fueled, the pre-flight already done, and I want the pilot sleeping in the jet. He has to be ready to go. No excuses."

"The conference is another two days. We can put Ms. Allegany on lock down and get her the hell out of here. It isn't worth her life." Marco pointed out what would be obvious to the average bear, but Sylvia wasn't the average bear. She was setting herself up for diplomatic duty as first lady and her agenda didn't quite jive with her protection's agenda. Chad suspected that no amount of talking would convince Sylvia to make a grand dame exit from the conference.

"I need someone on the inside." Chad looked at Marco.

"I'll do it." Thomas raised his hand.

"This isn't class, school boy," Sophia said. "Besides, this might take a chica's touch." She wiggled her eyebrows suggestively. "If you know what I mean."

"It's a women's conference. I think I know how to work the ladies. If you know what I mean." Thomas raised his eyebrows in response and shoved his legs out, crossed them at the ankles, and laced his fingers behind his head. A big grin creased his face. His boyish good looks might work on the college girls, but these were women with refined tastes. Women with money to burn and if they had a little something on the side, he was refined just like them. A gigolo, if they even called a boy toy that anymore, was well-groomed, well-read, and ready to please the moment they got the call.

"I'm afraid you might be out of your league here, pup." Chad slapped Thomas on the knee. "Besides, I was thinking something a little more brutish." She looked at Marco again. "The mark I have in mind might like burley men."

"Where you goin' with this?" Marco stiffened up.

"Can you guys give us a minute? Sophia, I want you and Thomas to keep an eye on Jason, Sylvia's assistant. Something's up with that man. Thomas, I want you and the rest of the crew to watch the cameras. I want to know who shows up, where they go, and do facial recon on any new faces that just *happen* to pop-up."

"You got it."

"I've texted Reagan. Let me know when she gets here," Chad said, grabbing her tea mug.

"Will do, boss."

The group scattered faster than cockroaches when the lights went on.

"What are you up to, Chad?"

Chad pulled her chair around to face Marco. He wasn't going to like what she had to say, but then again, if he didn't do it, she'd have to.

"What do we have from Sylvia's assistant Jason?" Chad sipped her tea, looking at Marco, who was looking at the monitors.

Shaking his head, he muttered something incoherent.

"What?"

"We got the dude jerking."

Chad chuckled at the thought that Marco had caught Jason as he pleasured himself. It wasn't really funny, but it wasn't the first time they had seen something like that; usually it was an intimate moment between two adults, accidently caught on tape. Hazards of their job.

"It's not funny. The dude's a freak. By the way, I wouldn't be touching any socks in his room if I were you," Marco tossed over his shoulder.

"I'll remember that next time I'm alone with him."

"Hmm."

"Anything else?"

"Dude does a lot of texting."

"Really? Any idea who he's texting?" Chad sat next to Marco, and swung the screen so it faced her. Punching through the cameras, she pulled up Jason's room. Empty. "Do we know where he is?"

"I can tell you where he isn't. He isn't with his employer, Ms. Allegany."

"Something's not right with this guy. I don't trust him."

"You're telling me? The dude must jack-off at least two or three times a day. I'm surprised he hasn't worn that thing down to a nub."

Chad smiled. Poor Marco had his fill of the nubile young ladder climber, Jason. She couldn't blame him; she'd had enough of the pompous ass, too.

"We need to get close to him. He's up to something and I want to know what. He's one of the few men at this conference and that isn't a coincidence. Don't you think?" It was a rhetorical question, but she really did value his opinion. He was not only her confidant on most occasions, he was also her sounding board, her devil's advocate, and her most trusted friend.

"Is that your gut, or your general dislike for this pretty boy?"

"Both."

"So, how do you propose we get close to this guy?"

Smiling, Chad looked at Marco and tilted her head towards him.

"Oh no, I'm not doing it."

"You haven't heard my idea, yet."

"I don't need to hear your idea. I know where you're going before you even give it voice."

"I know you can do this, buddy." Chad pushed her shoulders back and snapped her fingers back and forth. "Oh snap, girl. You can pull this off. You are *fierce*, bitch."

"Don't make me do this, Chad. Please."

"We don't have any other options, buddy. Hopefully, you can get in his pants–"

"Chad!"

"What? I was going to say, get his phone, and see who he's been texting. We just need a name and a quick look at those texted messages."

"To quote you, fuck me."

Chapter Twenty-five

Reagan was getting ready to knock on the door of Chad's suite/office when Sofia opened the door.

"Oh, is Chad here? She texted me and said she needed to talk to me." Peeking past Sofia, Reagan tried to see inside. "Is she here?"

"Yeah, she's here, but let me give you a little advice, Ms. Reynolds, don't mess with her. It took her a long time to get over you and I'd hate to see her hurt again. You get my drift?" Sofia stepped closer and looked past Reagan, her lips close enough to feel the force of her breath against her ear. "If you do anything to…well, I think you know where I'm going with this." Sofia walked past her, nudging Reagan with her shoulder, trying to knock Reagan back a step.

Reagan watched Sofia strut down the hall, shoulders back, head held high, never once looking back to see if she'd made an impression on Reagan. She didn't have to worry, she had and Reagan knew what she was intimating. Cross her and Sofia would make it a point to leave Reagan behind in the desert somewhere. Reagan hoped she was exaggerating, but the women who worked for Chad scared her witless.

"Hello?" Reagan stood at the open door, calling inside.

Nothing. Looking around, she took a step in and called out again, "Chad?"

"Hey, thanks for coming." Chad peered out of one of the rooms of the suite.

"Sure. What's up?" Reagan's heart sank when she saw Marco sitting at the bank of monitors lined up on the table. She'd hoped Chad was calling her to talk, but with Marco here that wasn't happening.

"Hey Marco." She waved at him and gave him a half-hearted smile.

"Reagan."

"I need to get back to the conference. So, what's up?"

"Have a seat." Chad tossed her chin towards one of the chairs at the table.

"Okay." Reagan felt her anxiety heighten as suddenly Chad was all business, pulling out a chair for her. "What's wrong?"

Chad cleared her throat, looked at Marco and then at her and then away. She felt like bad news was coming and there was nothing she could do about it.

"I want you to go home."

"What?" Reagan sat shocked. Who was Chad to tell her what to do? They didn't have that kind of relationship and just because they'd been together last night, it didn't suddenly give her the right to order her around.

Chad scrubbed her face with her hands and let out a sigh. "I'm sorry, I'm not saying this right. Let me try again." Grabbing Reagan's hands, Chad stared down at them and then started again. "You're in danger here. I want you to go home where it's safe, please."

"What do you mean I'm in danger? You mean after what I did to that security guard?"

Reagan felt her flight response gearing-up. Chad

was right, she should leave Abu Dhabi. She wasn't safe here.

"No. Something's going on at the conference and I would feel better if you weren't here."

"What? What's going on at the conference?"

"I can't tell you that."

"Chad, I can't leave. My father has placed a lot of trust in me and I can't let him down."

"I'll call Frank and explain that you aren't safe here."

"Wait, you'll tell him, but you won't tell me." Reagan looked at Chad and then Marco, who looked away and studied the monitors, again.

"I'll just tell him that you need to–"

"What, Chad? Do you think he'll believe that I didn't screw up, again? You call him and he'll wonder what you're doing here and why I'm leaving. It'll look bad, either way you slice it. I'm not going. Besides, if Sylvia Allegany can stay, so can I." Reagan crossed her arms across her chest and stared at Chad, waiting for an explanation.

Reagan could tell Chad was exacerbated and she knew she wasn't helping the situation, but damn Chad. If this was her way of getting away from Reagan, why didn't she just come out and say so? Reagan would leave her alone.

"If this is about last night–"

"It's not about last night."

"I'm gonna get some coffee, anyone want some?" Marco said, picking up his cup. "Okay, well, I'll just leave you two alone."

Reagan waited until he was out of earshot and then asked again, only softer. "Is this about last night, because if it is, it won't happen again. I'm sorry, Chad.

I didn't mean to take advantage of the situation. I…I just…" Reagan looked down at her hands resting in her lap and felt just like she did when she was a schoolgirl who'd just kissed her best friend, who was straight. She promised it wouldn't happen again, but she knew she might not keep that promise and she didn't. Now here she was again, making the same promise and knew the results might just be the same as they were back then, failure.

"Reagan, look at me," Chad ordered.

Reagan winced as she lifted her head and caught sight of Chad's pursed lips, and furrowed brow. She knew she was going to be admonished and just wanted to get it over with. Last night had been a mistake and now she knew it. Chad's look all but confirmed it for her.

"I'll stay away from you and Mrs. Allegany, Chad. I promise. I won't make trouble for you. I just need to make my father proud, I need to earn his trust back, and I need to make this work. I have to put on a professional face for Reynolds Holdings. My dad is counting on me."

Chad worried her lip, biting at the edges. Reagan had seen her do this when she was concentrating, only this time Chad seemed upset.

"I want you to stay away from Colleen."

"What? Colleen Velasquez?"

Chad nodded. Moving to the computer, she clicked the mouse a few times and popped an image of Colleen up on the screen. She was in the front of the hotel talking on her cell phone.

"We taped her talking to someone. I had the tape sent to Washington, to one of my contacts and we've pieced something together that makes us think she's going to pull something at the conference."

"What?"

"We're not exactly sure, but what I do know I can't tell you."

"I don't understand, Chad. You want me to leave because something's going on at the conference, but you aren't getting Sylvia out of here. That makes no sense to me, at all. Besides, Colleen seems very nice to me. We had breakfast this morning and–"

"I know, I saw you two."

"Oh, is that what this is about, you're jealous?" Reagan said, her tone accusatory.

Marco came back into the room and sat across from them. "Why don't you tell her? Maybe she can help?"

Chad's head jerked around at Marco and she froze him with a stare.

"Marco's right, maybe I can help." Reagan jumped at the statement. If it meant she could stay close to Chad, maybe she could earn back Chad's trust.

"You can't help."

"Look, you saw the way Colleen flirted with Reagan this morning–"

"She can't help us." Chad cut Marco off.

Throwing up his hands, Marco continued. "Look, I'm just saying if she can find out where the virus is, we can stop something tragic from happening."

"Virus?"

"Can I see you in the other room, please?" Chad's tone coarsened.

Reagan could hear them arguing in hushed tones. Chad's voice deepened with each sentence, shutting Marco down when he tried to say something, and then it was over. Both walked into the room, Chad red-faced and Marco wearing a smug look. Clearly he'd gotten his way.

"So you want to help, huh?" Chad pulled her chair further away from the table and motioned for Marco to sit.

"If I can." Reagan said, pleased she was being asked.

❧ ❧ ❧ ❧

Chad was tired. Lack of sleep from the night before and a sore body were her reward for a night well spent. However, sitting across from Reagan, she was torn between sharing what she knew and keeping her safe. If she had her way, she'd get Reagan out of the way and sort out her feelings later. Yet, Marco has trumped her and spilled the beans on the looming threat at the conference. Colleen was a for-sure on the suspect scale, but Jason was a maybe; her gut said he was in on it, but she'd need proof. That's where she would make sure Marco would pay for his indiscretion earlier, forcing her hand. He would court Jason, and step into the gay lifestyle tonight. Gay boys slept around and it wouldn't take much to convince Jason that Marco was just his type. Looking over at Marco, she smiled. *You're gonna take one for the team buddy,* she though as their gazes locked.

She hoped he knew he'd screwed up. They'd locked horns before, but this time was different. He defied her in front of a civilian. He had made it known that morning when she came out for her morning tea that he disapproved of Reagan spending the night. A few terse words between them had been more than they'd ever spoken in their whole working career. Suddenly, something had changed. Was Marco jealous? Was he worried about her ability to do her job? She didn't like being pushed, or her judgment questioned. She'd deal with Marco later.

"Reagan, the tape we had analyzed has Colleen on tape talking about waiting for a delivery, and then we have her on tape saying something is going down in three or four days and that she has an antidote. It's not much but it's enough to make DC worry. We're in a foreign country and they know there isn't much they can do, yet. As soon as they can work out the logistics, you can bet the feds will be here. So we don't have much time."

"What can I do to help?"

"Nothing, just keep your eyes open." Chad wanted to reassure Reagan by putting her hand on Reagan's arm. When Reagan covered her hand she felt herself try to jerk back, but Reagan held her tight.

"I think Colleen wanted to tell me something this morning at breakfast."

"What makes you think that?"

"Well, while she was flirting with me, she asked me if I could help her with Sylvia."

Chad had seen the two whispering during breakfast and any idiot could tell Colleen was flirting with Reagan. Hell, her own little green monster had poked its head out and growled at the sight. Chad looked over at Marco. The odds were starting to fall in their favor, but they needed to make sure that meeting never happened. Reagan wasn't going to be some pawn in Colleen's plan to spread a virus at the conference. But why come all this way to expose Sylvia to a virus? It didn't make sense. If this all happened off U.S. soil, it would look innocent enough. Too simple.

Something didn't quite add up, considering who was behind it, Juan Diego Velasquez. What was in it for him?

"What did you tell her?"

"I didn't, you texted me so I left her hanging."

"Hmm."

"I can chat her up at lunch. She wanted to go for drinks later. Maybe I can get something out of her then."

"No."

"What do you mean no?"

"No. I don't want you putting yourself in danger. Besides, Marco's got a hot date tonight and I can't watch you and him at the same time."

Both women looked over at the grunt Marco let out. He clearly wasn't happy about Chad's little plans for his evening, but he'd just need to deal with it. Those were the breaks and right now Chad was even less sympathetic after his little stunt earlier.

"I thought Marco was married," Reagan leaned in and whispered. Reagan's hand still rested on Chad's and she was gently caressing the back of it while she stared at Chad.

"He's going out to catch a fish."

"Huh?"

"I need him to get close to Jason. So, he's gonna do his best gay boy imitation."

"Jason? Sylvia's assistant. You think he's involved in this."

Chad shrugged. She'd like to think her gut was never wrong, but something about him wasn't right. "I don't know but he's up to something. I took a picture of someone he was texting and Marco is pulling that up now. Right?" She turned to Marco and shot him a questioning glance.

"I got the photos and video up if you want to go through them," Marco offered.

Moving closer to the computer screen, both women craned their neck to look at the screen. Chad couldn't see anything on the screen but the reflection of the phone and some text bubbles.

"Can you zoom in on that?"

"Yeah, let me see what I can do, the mirrors should give us a pretty good image. Well, as long as the phone is positioned at the right angle we should...." Marco zoomed in on the small window. Moving the photo around, he selected it and skewed the image so it was straighter. "That should do..." Marco went silent.

Chad leaned in closer and studied the screen. It should have made her feel good that it confirmed her suspicions. She was thousands of miles away from help and now it was her job to not only protect Mrs. Allegany from her own assistant, Jason, but she had to find out what he was doing. How involved he was in the conspiracy to release an unknown virus or chemical at the conference?

"It looks like he is sending a text message to the woman standing in front him. Weird," Marco said, trying to widen the screen more.

"He's sending a message to Mrs. Allegany? Well, that's not strange, is it? I mean, he probably doesn't want to say anything in front of everyone. Come on, people do this all the time. Hell, I see girls sitting next to each other on the train texting each other," Reagan reminded the group.

"That would be fine if it didn't say..." Chad looked closer. "Velasquez at the top of the text bubbles."

"Oh, wow."

Chad pointed to the screen and asked a question. "Can we see the first name of the person he's texting?"

Marco manipulated the photo more, but couldn't get a clearer view. "Nope, that's as good as I can get it. Sorry."

"Not your fault. So, he's either texting Colleen or Juan Diego. Looks like you're going to the bar tonight buddy. We need to get eyes on that phone and since he's gay…" Chad looked at Reagan and then down at herself, pointing back and forth between them. "We aren't going to get anything."

"Seriously?"

"Sorry, buddy. We don't have time to work up something different. I figure I'll try and bring him down to the bar and you can work your magic."

Marco rolled his eyes. He clearly wasn't a happy camper, but Chad didn't have a choice. Marco needed to get this guy's phone and see who he was texting.

"We'll wire you up, so I can hear everything and if need be, prompt you. I want it all on tape, that way if we need to confront him we have evidence. More importantly, if I need to take this to Mrs. Allegany, we have something she can believe in. I'm sure he's in deep within her organization and there are probably promises made about him coming with her as part of her White House staff."

Chad looked down at her watch; the conference was barely starting. Reagan needed to get back and participate as usual. The day would drag, but Chad would make sure Reagan was safe and it would give her plenty of time to plan out their take-down of Jason that night.

"Reagan, I need you to go back to the conference and act like nothing is going on. Talk to Colleen, sit by her, but don't get overly friendly. I don't want her to get suspicious. Just act normal."

"Okay, want me to see what I can find out?" Reagan's voice sounded hopeful.

"No, I just want you to act normal, that's all. Okay?" Chad needed Reagan safe. Pulling her from the conference was an option, but it might draw attention if she suddenly was absent. She didn't want Reagan to put herself in danger either, yet Chad knew she could already be in danger just being there. She was caught between the proverbial rock and a hard spot.

"Can I convince you to leave today?" Chad had to ask.

Her heart was pounding, waiting for Reagan to answer. She watched as Reagan pondered the request. At least she hadn't come right out and said no. It would make her life so much easier if she didn't need to stretch her crew beyond their limits. As it was, they were doing fourteen-hour shifts, now that they had to keep an eye on three people. This job not only got tougher, it had taken a dangerous twist that there was no way she could have anticipated. Kidnapping - yes, extortion - maybe, drunken clients – always, but a toxin being released at a conference by a third world dictator – she had to admit she was a pinch in over her head this time. Once Reagan left, she'd call her contact, Doug, and let him know the latest developments in the case. He'd have a response team here in twelve to eighteen hours, so she only had that much time to get this handled and get her client to safety.

"Chad," Reagan said quietly as she moved closer and touched Chad's folded hands. "You know my father is counting on me. I have to earn his trust back. I…I…can't disappoint him, I just can't."

"I've said this once, but I think it bears repeating – I'm sure I can call your father and explain the situation to him. I think he would want you safe, despite everything else that's happened in the past. I know it."

"Perhaps, but I need to prove to him that I can be trusted." Reagan dropped her head and whispered, "And maybe I need to prove to you, too."

Chad slipped her hands from Reagan's grasp and suddenly studied them. Her palms lined with lifelines that were too long, and relationships that according to a palm reader were many and short. Then she thought about what Reagan had said. Did Reagan need to prove something to her, really? Did risking her well-being prove to Chad she'd changed? Maybe? What did her palm tell her? *Huh*, nothing.

"You don't have anything to prove to me, Reagan. I can see you're sincere."

Grumph. Marco cleared his throat and shot Chad a glance.

"Look, why don't we talk about this later? Come here at lunch and you can debrief me on anything Colleen might have said. Okay?"

"Sure." Reagan smiled, looked over at Marco, and said goodbye to Chad.

Waiting until the room was empty, Chad turned towards Marco and asked. "You got a problem?"

Chapter Twenty-six

Reagan peeked in the doors, looking for Colleen. The panel discussion, "21st Century Business in a 20th Century Man's World" didn't sound very interesting. In fact, she suspected it probably really should have been called, "Women Doing Business in a Neanderthal's World," but that wasn't politically correct. God, where was her head? After last night's attack, she was surprised she wasn't more devastated. Maybe knowing someone was out to hurt the women at the conference was overriding her own fear. It was something she could throw herself into and take her mind off the awful prior evenings events. Then there was the night with Chad. Her head spun with everything that was happening.

Focusing back on the task at hand, she scanned the room. She didn't see Colleen. So she went to the next conference room, "Diversity, the Universal Language and How to Speak It." Popping her head into the room, she recognized the speaker, Sylvia Allegany. Surely Colleen would be in residence at this break-out session. Sliding in and backing around the corner, she practically sat on Colleen's lap.

"Hey! There you are," Colleen said, grabbing Reagan's ass.

"Oh, sorry, I didn't seen you there."

"Here." Colleen gave up half her seat and patted it. "Sit."

"Thanks," Reagan said, noticing the packed room. The future first lady could draw a crowd. Something her husband would be thankful for when they officially hit the campaign trail.

Turning her head and covering her mouth, Reagan quizzed Colleen, "How's she doing?'

Colleen grimaced and shrugged her shoulders. "A talk on diversity, given by a white, affluent woman from the United States, or as I would say, the big white hope here to save us all. What can you expect?"

The hint of sarcasm was definitely evident in Colleen's voice. Maybe she thought she was a better choice to discuss diversity. Reagan suspected the organizers would have passed on Colleen, due to her husband and his recent human rights violations. The United Nations had come down hard on the dictator, imposing sanctions and freezing assets. It surprised Reagan the media hadn't been climbing all over Colleen for her reaction to the stiff penalties, but then again given the choice between covering Sylvia Allegany and Colleen Velasquez, she knew that while the adage was if it bleeds it leads, unless Colleen pulled a knife and stabbed someone, Sylvia was the story. She was the only story at this conference, dwarfing anyone else, including Reagan. "Sorta like when the victors write the history," Colleen added.

"Yeah, I see what you mean," Reagan agreed.

"Anyways, where did you jet off to? You disappeared after breakfast."

"I had to take an emergency call from the plant back home." Looking down at her watch, she quickly did the math to make sure she got her times right. "It was late in the U.S., so I knew if they were calling, I better take it." Now she felt as if she was over explaining. So she clamped her mouth shut. Trying to avoid slipping off the seat she wiggled closer to Colleen, who pulled Reagan's hips closer and left her hand on Reagan's hips. Well, this is awkward, Reagan thought, now wishing she'd opted to stand.

"So, want to do lunch later? I know this great little place just down the hall." Colleen giggled in Reagan's ear.

"Oh, do you?" Reagan smiled back. If she played her cards right, maybe she could get some useful information from Colleen that she could pass on to Chad. God, she was turning into such a *pleaser*.

The crowd around them erupted into applause and rose to their feet. Without thinking, she stood and clapped as well. The speech had passed her by and she didn't even catch a snippet she could use later if she saw Sylvia, not even one little nugget. Colleen's shoulder bumped her and Colleen tossed her head towards the door as she passed Reagan.

"Let's make a break for it before this gets any more embarrassing."

The crowd surged towards the speaker and opened up enough to let them out. Reagan fell in behind Colleen. Her ears were still ringing as she made her way to the dining room.

"Oh god, I'm glad that's over." Colleen laced her arm around Reagan's and pulled her. "I'm starving. Hurry."

Passing the dining room, Colleen kept walking, still pulling Reagan's arm.

"Come on, I need a cigarette first."

"But I thought you were starving?"

Without warning, Colleen stopped dead in her tracks, shot Reagan a look, and then turned towards the dining room.

"Of course, how inconsiderate of me, you must be hungry. Where are my manners, it's not all about me, now is it?" Colleen sniped.

Reagan was shocked at the sudden turnabout from Colleen. *Angry much*, she thought, walking into the dining room. Clearly, Colleen was someone who liked to lead, never follow. Reagan had been around plenty of people who had flashes of anger; like hot flashes, they were usually short lived. Nevertheless, Reagan took note of the quick personality change and made a mental check to stay on her toes. Colleen picked a table at the back of the room and set her briefcase on the table. She didn't sit, but pushed the back of the chair over against the table. She motioned for a waiter and placed her drink order, an adult beverage and water, and then ordered lunch.

"Can you make sure no one bothers our things?"

"Of course, miss."

"Thanks." Colleen reached over and grabbed Reagan's thing and placed them on a plate and pushed a chair against the table. "What would you like?"

"Oh um, ice tea and I'll have the chicken salad. Thank you."

"Yes, miss."

"Come on," Colleen said, yanking Reagan's hand. "I figured you just wanted to get a good seat."

Reagan wanted to jerk her hand back and school the woman on whom she was dealing with, but that wouldn't help Chad. Again she was following behind Colleen, being dragged along in her wake.

A giant blob of people were moving towards them. In the center, Reagan spied Sylvia holding court with a group of reporters as she walked down the hall.

The moving mass was coming straight for her and Colleen. If she wasn't careful, she might find herself wedged right in the middle of the buzzing hive. Before she could react, Colleen slipped them into the service elevator hallway.

"Oh my god, did you see that? It was like a mob of moving flesh. I thought we were going to get mowed over." Colleen pulled a pack of cigarettes and tapped the end, dislodging one half-way out of the pack. Colleen offered one to Reagan, who refused and watched Colleen pull it free. She slip the end between her lips and lit it, dangling as she talked. "God, I never thought she was going to stop talking."

Reagan was hypnotized by the bobbing cigarette that seemed to be glued to her lips. Each time she spoke, it dipped up and down.

"Sure you don't want one?" Colleen offered up the pack again.

"Huh? No, I don't smoke, thanks."

"Good, don't take up the habit. It's nasty. I wish I didn't smoke but it's my only vice. If you don't count tequila, of course." Colleen laughed.

"Of course."

Reagan leaned against the wall of the elevator and wondered how she'd get Colleen to open up to her. She needed to be casual and yet focused.

"Your English is perfect."

"Why thank you. My parents sent me to a boarding school in England and then I went to UCLA."

"Ah, beautiful and smart, a deadly combination."

"That's very sweet of you to say. I was a beauty queen, too, you know."

"Really?"

"Hmm."

The slide of the doors opening caught their attention. Pushing past the crowd trying to get on the elevator, Reagan lost sight of Colleen briefly. A hand reached through the crowd and pulled at her sleeve. The hallway was hot, sweaty, and nauseating. Grabbing the hand, she felt herself pulled free of the group and face to face with Colleen, her cigarette still dangling.

"I almost lost you back there."

"God, what a mess." Reagan turned and looked at the packed elevator, sure it was going to fail to close or move up the shaft due to all the bodies crammed inside. *Sardines.*

Looking for relief, they stepped out the huge glass doors of the hotel and the heat of an oven slapped them in the face. Reagan's chest collapsed slightly under oppressive warmth. She forced her chest to rise. It was like breathing through a blanket, smothering.

Colleen pulled a pack of matches Reagan quickly recognized as one from the penthouse. She'd seen them lying in the ashtrays on the end tables throughout Sylvia's rooms. The sulfur smell itched her nose before the flame caught her attention.

Looking at the ornate box, Reagan asked, "They really go all out at this hotel, don't they?"

Turning the box over in her hand, Colleen tossed them to Reagan. "Ostentatious, don't you think?"

"A bit, yes."

As if she could read Reagan's mind, she continued. "I got these from her assistant."

"Oh, you know, Jason?"

"Jason?"

"Sylvia's assistant."

"Oh no, don't know him. I'm talking about that

tall, beefy woman that's with her all the time."

"Oh, right. Ms. Morgan."

"Yeah, her. She came out here last night and we chatted for a bit. Well, I chatted. She just stood there."

"Oh, she's not much for conversation?"

"Not really. Kind of the tall, silent type I guess. All business."

"I know the type well." Reagan lamented. A flash hit her. Reagan had told Chad she'd come back and talk to her at lunch. Shit, where was her mind? She'd need to make her excuses and get back to the room.

Stubbing out her cigarette, Colleen tossed the smoking butt in the sand pile with the pile of other butts left just from that morning.

"Let's go eat. Want to get a drink later?"

"Sure, I've got nothing else to do. I just need to make a few calls to the plant manager and check on things." Reagan said.

"Yeah, I think I'm going to check out of the afternoon sessions. I have a few calls to make myself. Lots going on back home."

"Oh yeah? Trouble on the home front?"

"Nothing I can't handle." Colleen suddenly looked distracted.

"Well, let me know if there is anything I can do to help out."

Reagan felt Colleen study her as her eyes narrowed, before she smiled. "Careful, I just might take you up on that."

Reagan tapped her watch. "You know what, I need to go back to my room and make a phone call. I'll meet you on the way to the bar, later."

"Fine with me, I think I'll take a nap after I call my husband."

Kissing each other on the cheek, Reagan grabbed the first elevator as Colleen whipped out her phone and lit another cigarette. She didn't have much to tell Chad, but if any of it helped, she'd be glad to oblige.

Chapter Twenty-seven

Tapping softly on the door just in case Chad had someone inside, Reagan felt like a schoolgirl meeting her date for a first date. Silly, she thought, tapping a little harder. She was a grown woman and Chad wasn't anything to her, not really. Well, maybe she wanted Chad to be more, but that was up to Chad. Reagan sighed; she wondered where that self-assured woman had disappeared to and if she would ever get her back. The door opened slightly as Chad peeked out.

"Hey," Chad said, opening it enough for Reagan to step through.

"Hey, I just saw Colleen and I'm reporting back as you asked."

"Good, come in. Hungry? I was just throwing something together. It isn't as elaborate as what you just passed up down at the conference, but it's something."

Reagan would take peanut butter and jelly if it meant she and Chad could spend time together. "Sounds good."

"Great, what can I get you to drink?"

"Water is fine."

Pots and pans rattled in the small kitchen of the suite, surprising Reagan. Chad cooked? Well, wonders never ceased. Looking at all the papers strewn across the dinner table, Reagan pulled a few and stacked them if they were close to each other, making two spots for whatever Chad was serving. She tried not to look down at the messy work, but something caught her eye.

"Hey, I thought we'd eat on the couch." Chad tossed her head towards the living room, waiting and watching Reagan as she reshuffled the papers.

"Sorry, I thought you might want to eat here, so I straightened a few things."

Chad's casual attitude threw Reagan off as she sat on the couch and set plates down. If what she had read was true, Chad was way too casual for her tastes. *Let it go*, Reagan thought. *This is Chad's job, not hers, and she knows what she's doing.*

"So, find anything out from Colleen?" Reagan sat closer to Chad than she should. "Hey, you okay? What happened? You look–"

"Scared?"

"Well, I was going to say, well I don't know what I was going to say, but you look – pained." Chad shoved a slice of cheese into her mouth and chewed.

Reagan knew this trick, shove food into your mouth and you don't have to talk, not if you were raised with the old saying – don't talk with food in your mouth.

"I am scared."

"About what happened the other night in your room? Don't worry, I won't let anything happen to you." Chad covered her hand and gave her a weak smile.

Reagan cupped Chad's hand and stared at it, then laced their fingers together. She brought it to her mouth and kissed the knuckles, then brushed her cheek against the strong grip. Such dichotomy in that touch. Reagan released Chad's hand and turned it over. Reagan kissed her palm and then traced her lifeline with her tongue from the base of Chad's palm to the web of her hand. Running her tongue up to the tip of her finger, Reagan felt the minute ridges of the fingerprint as she rolled her tongue back and forth over the tip. She noticed Chad's eyes were closed, but her brow was furrowed. Pleasure or pain, they both had the same look for Chad, but the way Chad's tongue traced her upper lip was a sign that it was pleasure that kept her still. Wrapping her lips further down Chad's finger, she seductively slid her lips back and forth over it. Her reward was a low, guttural moan. Without thinking, Reagan pushed Chad backwards on the couch, trapping her body against it.

"Uhm," Chad huffed out.

"Shh, I need…I need to feel protected right now. I mean I need you…" Reagan covered Chad's lips before she could lodge another protest and produce a logical reason why they couldn't do what they were doing. Reagan wanted emotion, to hell with logic right now. She wanted Chad. God, she felt like a slut. Well, maybe slut was too harsh a word. She didn't want to think, she wanted to feel and not just anyone, she wanted to make love to Chad. In the midst of all the chaos going on, all she could think about was Chad. Just Chad. In a few minutes, she would be forced to focus on the task at hand, but for right now, for these few minutes she wanted it to be about Chad. Because she knew deep down inside, she would never get this time alone again.

"Reagan."

"Chad please, just these few minutes before all hell breaks loose."

"Baby...Reagan...I."

Reagan felt her body melt against the strong, hard goddess under her. She'd called her baby. A mistake, Reagan was sure, but she would take it and hold on to it for a moment. Back stateside it would all revert back to the way it was, but for right now they had Abu Dhabi.

Reagan wedged her hand between them and slid into the top of Chad's pants. Warm, soft and pliant, Chad didn't stop her. She only pulled Reagan's head to her chest and caressed her hair. Reagan turned her hand and felt her palm rub against Chad's hip bone as she made her way to the button on her pants. Flipping it open with her thumb, she waited to hear a protest from Chad. Nothing. Reagan slowly pulled down the zipper. She felt every barb unfasten as it went down, opening Chad's slacks. Still nothing. She could feel Chad's heart start to race. The solid thumping against her ear was a testament that Reagan could still turn Chad on. The mind might say something different, but the heart doesn't lie.

Reagan let her hand rest on Chad's hip. Drawing slow circles around the bone was only adding to the tension between them. Was this foreplay? For Reagan it was torture, when all she really wanted to do was slip Chad's clothing off and lay naked next to her, Reagan's body begging for the skin-on-skin contact she hadn't had in over a year, not counting last night, of course. Did a repeat today mean anything for them? Or was it an action built out of necessity? *Enough with the mental gymnastics,* she told herself. What happens at the end of all of this really doesn't matter, does it? She'd made amends with Chad and that chapter in her life could be closed if need be.

Suddenly, Chad grabbed Reagan's hand and slipped it down into her panties. No words were spoken, no requests were made, acquiescence was the language of the moment. Reagan complied, her fingers searching for the sweet spot she'd visited many times before. That one place that Chad left unguarded. Her heart she protected, her sex, she exposed. To get off, to find release - whatever the reason, right now it didn't matter to Reagan. She wanted to the same thing and when two people were of the same mind it was easy to come to a mental agreement where no promises were made, no voice was given for a tomorrow and whatever happened, happened. The freedom to explore unrestrained, unguarded and to fuck unabashed.

Reagan's fingertips encountered the soft down hair of Chad's pussy. Warm, wet, and inviting, she slid down further. Using her fingers to open Chad's lips, she eagerly dipped into the wetness and fingered the opening.

"May I?"

"Uhm, it's a little late to ask for permission isn't it?"

"I just don't–"

Chad tilted Reagan's face up and pushed Reagan's fingers in more. Her hips started to circle on Reagan's fingers, Chad's body welcoming them inside. Pushing further, Reagan added another finger to the dance Chad was doing on her palm. A staccato was playing out, with short, quick thrusts, her palm across Chad's hard clit adding to the tempo. Chad's muscles clamped down on her fingers and she stilled her hips. Reagan's body responded to the taut body, rubbing herself against Chad's hip, the hard bone just rough enough to start her own orgasm. It started as a ripple and then Chad released Reagan's fingers and used her hand to pump Reagan's furiously into her. Reagan pounded out her orgasm against Chad's hip, while Chad arched into her, a silent scream barely breaching her lips. Reagan couldn't control hers; she let it release as a smoldering sigh in Chad's ear, a conquest survived.

Blood throbbed in Reagan's ears. She didn't move for fear of breaking the spell that they had been cast under. Chad lay still, griping Reagan's hand in her pants. Without thinking, Reagan ran her fingers through Chad's hair, the warm sweaty strands sticking to her fingers. Rows formed where she rubbed Chad's scalp. Chad looked like she was sleeping. Long deep breaths kept her chest rising and falling at an even pace, not even a post orgasm stutter.

Reagan wished they could lay there forever in that land of post orgasmic rapture. That time when couples talked of the future, of love, and lives together. She kept her eyes closed, hoping that Chad would just stay for a moment longer before they had to enter back into the chaos that was their lives right now.

"Can I ask you a question?" Reagan said quietly.

"Sure."

Reagan gently pulled herself free of Chad and ran her finger up the scar that divided Chad's body. She hated that Chad had known that kind of pain. The pain of rape, of someone who hated you so bad that they wanted to kill you and wanted to do it in the most intimate way possible, with a knife.

"Did you ever think about me?" Reagan asked.

Silence.

Reagan would confess her sins if it opened Chad up to confess hers.

"I thought about you in ways that…" Chad looked away.

Reagan stilled her fingers on the smooth skin of the scar. "That what?"

"That made me touch myself."

From the way Chad said it, it didn't sound as if she felt the same way. It was clinical.

"I see." Reagan resigned herself to the fact that maybe she was just a fuck for Chad while they were in Abu Dhabi, a convenience of sorts. "I'm sorry, I shouldn't have asked that."

There they lay, staring at the ceiling of the room. The fan whipped the air-conditioned breeze around them, breaking the tension for them. It reminded Reagan of one of those old black and white fifties movies where someone was going to get up, and light a cigarette – she could almost smell the sulfur from the match - toss the match in the ashtray, and give some speech about how this wasn't going to work out between them.

"I've thought about you, too." Reagan confessed. "In that way."

Chapter Twenty-eight

Chad scrutinized the bar for possible locations to sit. Her view needed to be unobstructed, but she also needed to be concealed as well. Lighting in the bar was low, attributing to the sleazy feeling she picked up when she entered. The crass, red velvet wallpaper harkened to a different time, and if Chad hadn't known that the hotel was relatively new, she would have thought it was right out of a lounge in Vegas. Maybe that was what the hotel management was going for; if so, they'd pulled it off.

Threading her fingers together, she hid her mouth behind her hands and spoke into her mic. "Marco, sound check again."

Silence.

Scanning the room, she couldn't see Marco anywhere. Chad knew he was still pissed about the assignment, but hell, he'd gone undercover before. Geez, he'd even dressed as a woman without questioning the needs of the assignment. He didn't exactly have the legs for it, but chicken legs were better than beefy, manly calves that could have given away his gender. So she couldn't understand why he was throwing a piss-fit over this assignment. Then it dawned on her, maybe he was homophobic. She'd known him a long time and the subject of being gay rarely came up. It wasn't a deep probing topic that they discussed unless it was her sex life, then it was the fodder for his constant ribbing. He said he lived vicariously through her, but did he mean her sex life represented all those girl-on-girl porn videos guys loved?

Movement into the lounge caught her attention out of the corner of her eye. Marco had finally arrived.

"Marco?" she said again into her mic.

"What?" he eked out just above a whisper.

He moved towards the bar, pulled out a chair, and slid onto it, one foot planted on the floor. He appeared uneasy and if he wasn't careful, he would blow it with Jason. Before Chad could invite the assistant to the bar for a drink, to set-up the scenario with Marco, Jason had made a declaration that afternoon he was ready to pop and if anyone needed him, they could find him in the bar. She'd played along, trying to dissuade him, knowing if she said she didn't think it was a good idea, like a child, he would do the exact opposite. So, here she was, waiting for the sucker to take the bait. She didn't have to wait long, as he walked in, perused the room, and spotted Marco instantly. He tossed a smug smile at the bartender when he sat two barstools way from Marco.

He pointed his body right at Marco and leaned against the bar, mimicking Marco's posture, with one leg on the floor, his legs wide. He was cruising Marco hard, staring right at him.

"God, this guy's putting it all out there right off the bat," Chad said, not realizing Marco could hear her.

Marco cleared his throat then casually looked over at Jason, gave him a nod and then went back to his drink. He was hunched over his drink; his whole demeanor was giving the impression of being a submissive. If she was right about Jason, he was a predator when it came to bedmates and he'd been without someone for at least three or four days and according to Marco, his libido was out of control.

"Throw your hand back," Chad instructed her unwilling student.

Marco waited a minute and then he went into to his routine. Running his fingers up into his hair, he flipped it and then rested his hand against his face.

"Excuse me. Would it be possible to refresh my drink?" Marco said, a little lift at the end of his sentence and he dragged out the word *drink* for a second too long.

A wide smile crossed Jason's face as he made a show of craning his neck to check out Marco's ass. Calling the bartender over, Jason said something and within a few minutes Marco had another drink deposited in front of him and Jason hopping into the seat next to Marco.

"Hey, you're an American?"

"Yep, how'd ya guess?" Marco's lisp was overkill and all Chad could do was shake her head.

"Well, look around. There aren't a lot of Americans here." Jason waved his hand around. "So what brings you to Abu Dhabi?"

"Work. Oh, thanks for the drink."

"My pleasure."

"So what are you doing here?" Marco quizzed.

"Same. Work."

"Hmm." Raising his drink, Marco quipped, "Here's to work."

"To work."

The two sat in silence for a few seconds before Jason spoke up. "How long are you here for?"

"I leave tomorrow night. Gotta put in a full day, or my boss will skin me."

"Oh, got one of those bosses, huh?"

Marco turned towards Jason and gave him a drunk laugh. "Don't tell me, you love your boss?"

"Oh, she's all right. She's a little mouthy, but she does what I tell her to do. She'd be lost without me. I set her schedule, pick out her clothes, so she looks fierce on TV and I keep all her secrets."

"Really? Who's your boss?"

"Have you heard of Mrs. Allegany? Her husband is running for president." Jason got cocky and started preen in his seat. "Sylvia, that's her first name, I'm her personal assistant."

"Ohhh, sounds impressive."

Chad shook her head. Marco was piling it on thick. His hands were flailing around and Chad didn't know whether Marco had too much to drink or if it was part of his act.

"Marco, you're laying it on thick, calm down and let him take the lead," Chad whispered into the mic. Before she could say anything else, she heard Jason talking.

"So, can I ask you a question?"

"Sure."

Jason leaned over into Marco's personal space and laid his hand on Marco's shoulder. "I'm not usually wrong, but my gaydar is just pinging right now."

Marco pulled back and peered over his drink at Jason. Chad wasn't surprised that Jason was playing fast. Marco had just stated he was leaving the next evening, so Jason didn't have time to be coy, not if he wanted to get laid tonight.

"Oh my god–" Marco started to talk, but Jason

cut him off.

"I'm sorry, I didn't mean to offend you, clearly I–"

Marco put his hand on Jason's leg and said, "Is it that obvious? Oh my god, I'm so embarrassed. If my boss finds out, he'll fire me. See, this happens when I've had too much to drink. I get all girly. Am I acting too girly?" Marco covered his face, looking at Jason through his fingers.

"Oh, no, not in the slightest." Jason reassured Marco. "Hey, do you smoke?"

The quick subject change was clever. Jason knew all the tactics to put someone at ease and divert their attention to get what he wanted. He smiled and kept running his hand over Marco's shoulder, massaging his shoulders every once in a while.

"Go with whatever he says. He's going to be a dog with a bone until you say yes. So play coy, but don't play too hard to get," Chad instructed Marco. Looking around the room, she wanted to make sure no one was watching her. The near empty bar wouldn't be empty for long; the draw was alcohol and the locals would pack the place soon. While drinking was taboo in the country, locals came to get away from the prying eyes of the community that condemned consumption.

Chad's focus was pulled back to the bar when Marco replied to Jason.

"I gave up cigarettes a couple months ago."

"No, I mean do you like to…smoke a little…" Jason searched around the room and finished. "Weed."

"You got weed? How'd you get weed?"

"I'm traveling with the next first lady; do you think they go through her stuff at customs? I just tucked a little something in her bag and boom; I've got a relaxing night and no worries."

Chad balked at the statement. The pieces were slipping into place. The little bastard was the courier.

"Son of a bitch," she said without thinking. "He's the fucking courier. He's the one with the toxin, fuck me. Of course that's how they're getting it into the conference."

Marco sat, pinned to the stool, waiting for further instructions.

"We're staying with the plan, buddy. We need to confirm what's going on and when it's going down, so we can get them both put away."

Chad's mind spun with all the things that needed to happen to get the goods on these two. Her DC contact had assured her they would be on site within forty-eight hours and ready to take over. She had to make sure her team had built a tight case and that whatever was going to happen didn't.

"So maybe, you'd like to come back to my room?" Jason's Cheshire cat smile gave his intention away.

"Hmm, I don't know. I've got some work to do back in my room."

Jason wrapped his arm around Marco's broad shoulders and leaned against him. "You're a very handsome." Leaning closer, Jason whispered into Marco's ear. "I bet you're hung like a horse."

That's your come on? Chad thought, watching Marco choking on his drink. "Hang in there buddy. We're almost in the home stretch," Chad reassured Marco.

Before she could say anything else, Reagan walked in with Colleen, followed by a large group of women behind them. This wasn't in the plans.

"Fuck!"

Chapter Twenty-nine

"Oh god, I could use a double of anything," Colleen said.

Reagan spotted Marco sitting at the bar firmly in Jason's grasp. If Marco was here, Chad was close by. This must be the plan to get close to Jason and if so, she needed to be as far away from the action as possible. She didn't want to be in the way.

"Me, too." Reagan looped through Colleen's arm and pulled her towards a booth in the back of the bar, away from the action. Slipping onto the slick vinyl seat, Reagan pushed herself into the center with Colleen and a few women who decided to join them. Without effort, a waiter was suddenly at their table with happy hour menus.

"Ladies, busy day?" He was the same man from the first night Reagan had come into the bar looking for solace in a highball glass. Instead, she met Colleen, who forced herself on Reagan. Karma, it all now seemed to have happened for a reason.

The table murmured as each woman checked out the handsome man. His dark skin, dark hair and mustache...Omar Sharif, that's who he looked like, a very young Omar. No wonder the women couldn't keep their eyes off him; his charming personality and deep, smooth as silk accent added to the mystic. Reagan doubted the young man went without a companion for very long, if the reactions from the women at the table were any indication.

"Very sweet of you to ask, thank you." Colleen spoke first. "My usual, please. Ladies?"

As the women gave their drink orders and eyed the happy hour menu, Reagan scoped out the room. Someone sat to the left of her, almost out of sight, if it hadn't been for the waiter who stopped by the table, said something, and then went back to the bar.

"And you, miss?" The waiter said, scribbling furiously.

"I'll have a rum and diet soda."

"Coming right up."

"I need to use the ladies room, can you tell me where it is?" She looked around and whispered to be let out of the booth. Sitting in the middle probably wasn't a good idea with a weak bladder like hers.

"All the way down, make a right and through the beads."

Reagan followed his hand gesture and thanked him. It took her in the opposite direction from Chad, so she'd have to figure out how to get her attention, but first, a bathroom break.

Tapping the table, she directed her comment to Colleen. "I'll be right back; all that ice tea at lunch is catching up with me." Tossing a hundred dollar bill on the table, she smiled and said. "I've got the first round, so don't start without me, 'kay?"

"Nice," Colleen said, fingering the money.

"Don't start without me, I'll be right back." Reagan followed the waiter's directions and found the ladies room. Washing her hands, she checked out her reflection. Tired. She not only felt tired but her appearance confirmed it. Pulling out some lipstick, she puckered her lips and dabbed the stick against them. Smacking them together, she wiped off a little that accumulated in the corners of her mouth. As she washed it off, the door opened and Chad stood looking at her, as she turned her com piece off.

Looking under all the stalls, Chad came up behind her and whispered just loud enough that Reagan could feel her breath on her neck. "What are you doing here?"

Drying her hands, Reagan turned around and was practically chest-to-chest with Chad.

"Colleen wanted to go for a drink and I figured I might be able to get something, but then she invited all those women. I couldn't exactly bail once I'd said yes."

"Well, as you can see, I have Marco in there trying to get to Jason."

"Sooo, that's the plan...catch Jason in a compromising position?"

"Not exactly, but we did just put a bow on that little package we think is coming."

"Oh, really?" Reagan hoped that Chad was wrong about Colleen. She was starting to like the woman and part of her just couldn't see Colleen as someone who'd let a virus loose.

"Yep, so I want you to get out of here. I want you safe and I don't want to have to worry about where you are."

"I can help," Reagan said, hoping she actually would be allowed to help.

"No, you can't. Colleen has invited all those women and there is no way she's going to be confiding in you. At least not right now."

"I suppose you're right." Reagan lowered her head, but before she could say anything else, Chad pulled her into a stall and shut the door.

"I need you to be safe." Chad pulled her into a tight embrace and lowered her nose into Reagan's hair. Reagan felt Chad's chest rub against hers as Chad took a deep breath. "Last night wasn't an accident, Reagan. I want to explore the possibilities with you and I can't focus on the task at hand if I'm watching you over at the table with Colleen."

"Okay, but I bought a round of drinks already. I think I should at least stay and have one or two or she might get suspicious."

"Have you eaten tonight?"

"Not yet. I was planning on grabbing something here."

"Order something to eat, have a drink, and then beg off. Please?" Chad pulled her chin up and kissed her. It was a long lingering kiss that weakened Reagan's knees and her resolve. Pulling Chad tighter, she pushed up and deepened the kiss. Soft, warm and almost delicate, Chad wasn't rushing, as she took her time and threaded her fingers into Reagan's hair. Forcing Reagan's lips against her own, Reagan wished they were anywhere but a bathroom stall.

"I better get back out there. I don't want Marco on his own for very long. He isn't very happy with the scenario."

Chad's smile was contagious and all Reagan could do was return it. Her mind was somewhere else, somewhere inappropriate.

"Okay, well, I guess I'll see you back at the suite. Unless you'd rather I go back to my room?"

"No! No I don't want you to go back there, not after what happened last night."

"Thanks, I appreciate that."

"So, have a bite to eat, have a drink, but promise me that you'll make your excuses and get out of here." Chad looked down at Reagan, their gaze locking. "Please."

Reagan nodded her head and backed away so Chad could open the door.

"I need to get out there, so let me go first, and you wait a minute and come out then. Okay?" Pushing a lock of hair behind Reagan's ear, she continued, "I don't want anyone getting suspicious."

"Okay. I'll see you later?"

"Later."

Chad dropped a kiss on her cheek and closed the bathroom door behind her. Looking around, Reagan couldn't find her purse, then spotted it in the stall on the ledge. Just as she grabbed it, she heard someone enter the bathroom. Panicking, she closed the stall door and sat down on the toilet, hugging her purse. *Shit*.

Chapter Thirty

Chad flipped her com piece on just in time to hear Jason proposition Marco again.

"Here, why don't you and I go for a walk, we can just talk. No pressure. I just haven't heard a man's voice in days. All these bitches and would you believe, there are no men around."

Chad turned the corner and slipped behind a booth, making her way to the back again.

"Sorry, buddy. I had to make a bathroom stop," she whispered into her sleeve, watching as Jason practically sat in Marco's lap.

Jason's phone went off for the umpteenth time, but he didn't let it distract him from his prey, Marco. Instead, he stuffed it in his back pocket and put his finger and thumb a space apart and tried to lure Marco with the idea of a walk again.

"Short walk. If you don't like my company, you can walk me back to my suite and go home. 'Kay?"

"Short walk." Marco parroted Jason's hand gesture.

"That's not my penis size, by the way."

"Hmm, good to know," Marco said, tossing back his drink and starting to take out his wallet.

"His phone is going to go off again, Marco. When it does, I want you to strike a bargain with him. He gives you his phone in exchange for a walk. Tell him you want his undivided attention, or no walk."

Marco rubbed his ear, the signal for he heard what she'd said. Thank god they hadn't come up with any other signals, except the one for abort. That signal was Marco lacing his fingers behind his head and flipping her the bird. Clever, she thought, since he'd come up with it in a fit of rage. It got the point across, so she let him have it. So far, no bird. He was a champ and she owed him and his wife a dinner at the nicest restaurant, with her doing the babysitting. Small price, she thought, if it saved Sylvia Allegany. Chad couldn't bear a failed assignment on her spotless record. Well, it was spotless until the incident with Reagan; she'd figured it all out, almost all of it.

Just as Marco tossed a few bills on the bar, Jason's phone went off like expected. When he pulled it out, Marco put his hand on Jason's and said, "Look, I don't have a lot of time, so if you want to date your phone I'm fine with that, but if you want to "take a walk" with me then I suggest you hand over your phone and I'll hold it until we're done. Sound like a deal?" Marco stuck his hand out.

Jason looked at his phone and then back at Marco's open hand then back to the phone. Marco didn't miss a beat.

"Fine, have a nice evening."

Marco turned to walk out of the bar, but Jason acquiesced and grabbed Marco's bicep, stopping him from leaving. Making a face, Jason handed Marco the phone and then smiled.

"I can live without it for a little while. Besides, I like a man in charge. It makes me giddy."

"I'll make you giddy," Marco flirted right back and stuffed the phone in his back pocket.

"Go to the bathroom, quick." Chad commanded

and then practically sprinted to the men's room. Jumping into a stall, she closed the door and looked like she was using the facilities while waiting for Marco.

"Hey, I gotta take a leak. So wait right here for me."

"Oh well, if you want to go to the bathroom, I'm down for that."

"Ah, no. I'm a germaphobe and I think you're a little better than a quickie in the john. So give me a minute, think about that walk."

Chad heard what she thought was the sound of a kiss, but knew there was no way Marco would kiss a guy.

"That's to give you something to look forward to when you get back," Jason whispered.

"Oh, I can't wait."

A minute later, Marco was slamming the door to the bathroom. "I'm alone, get your ass out here, Chad." His tone left no doubt he was angry.

"Calm down. You got the phone?"

"Yeah, right here." He handed the phone to Chad.

She hooked it up to a transfer line connected to a dummy phone she'd brought. The transfer equipment would copy everything to the phone and leave Jason's intact. They just needed a few minutes for it to work.

"Get in the stall," Chad ordered. "If he gets antsy, he'll come in here to check up on you and proposition you again."

"Are you kidding me? Fuck."

Chad shot him a no-nonsense look and took a stall, shutting the door. "Get your ass in the one next to me. When this is done downloading, I'll pass it to you under the stall and you can get rid of the little twerp."

"Fine."

Her timing was perfect as she heard the restroom door open and Jason shouted inside the tiled echo chamber.

"Marco? Oh Marco."

"Jason? I'm a little busy. I'll be right out." Marco's gruff voice chided Jason.

"Oh, come on big boy, I'm ready to take that waaallkkk," he said, singing the end.

Chad wanted to puke. Couldn't the guy give Marco a minute to go to the bathroom? He was more than persistent; he was an ass. Checking the status of the download, she just needed another minute, that's all.

Jason started talking again, but before she could make out what he was saying, she coughed and grumbled.

"Oh, someone's in here. Sorrrryyy," he said. "I'll wait for you outside, Marco. Hurry, handsome."

The slamming door signaled his exit, but just to be sure, Chad peered through the crack in the door and searched for him. Nothing.

"Is that thing done yet?" Marco's voice pleaded.

"A few more secs buddy."

"Christ."

The signal on the transfer flashed green, letting Chad know the transfer was done. Disconnecting it, she handed it under the stall wall to Marco.

"Here ya go. Let him down gently," Chad said, laughing.

"Yeah, I'm gonna come down on him like a load of bricks. Fuckin' prick is annoying. A man can't even go to the bathroom without being bothered."

"You're not really going to the bathroom, are you?"

Chad heard the telltale signs of a belt being buckled and the toilet flushing.

"Of course, might as well take care of business, too."

"Oh gross."

"Chill-out, I just had to pee."

"Wash your hands, you don't know where this thing's been," Chad said, suddenly holding it with her fingertips and remembering the latest data on what cell phones were covered with. *Yuk.*

Marco snatched the phone out of Chad's two-finger grasp and said, "See you back at the suite."

"Be gentle. He's a sensitive guy."

Chad couldn't help herself. She knew the minute Marco was out of here, he was going right out and dumping Jason. Knowing Marco, he'd tell Jason that coming into the bathroom had been his first mistake. Outing him to whoever was in the stall next to him was his second. He'd toss the cell phone at him and stalk out of the bar, pissed more at her that he'd had to endure the whole thing in the first place, but channeling that anger at Jason.

Poor Jason.

Chapter Thirty-one

Reagan couldn't help but notice the scene being played out at the bar, even if it was being done covertly. Marco had stormed out of the bathroom, confronted Jason, and tossed the phone at him. Putting his finger in Jason's chest, he lowered his head to within earshot of the man and said something before storming off.

"Ooo, lover's quarrel," one of the women at the table said before chuckling. All the women turned and looked at the exchange. It was almost entertaining, if it wasn't so desperate looking. Reagan caught site of Chad exiting the bathroom and slinking off in the darkness. She lost sight of her, but knew she was on her own, but she'd made a promise to Chad. She'd keep it; she owed that to Chad.

"Well ladies, I have to call it a night." Reagan dabbed at the sides of her mouth with her napkin and then dropped it on the half-eaten plate of French fries.

"What? You're calling it a night?" Colleen said, wedged between two women in the booth.

"Yeah, I'm pretty tired." Standing, she brushed her skirt. "Ladies, if you'll excuse me. I'll see everyone in the morning. Colleen?"

"Of course, but I didn't get a chance to buy you a drink," Colleen reminded Reagan. "So sit down and let me return the favor."

"No, really I'm good."

"It's bad manners not to let the hostess reciprocate," Colleen insisted.

Reagan was relieved she was across the table and not close enough that Colleen could physically stop her as she'd done earlier when they'd left the breakout session. Colleen didn't have any qualms about putting her hands on people to get what she wanted, whether it was going for a cigarette and wanting company, or anything else she had an eye on, Reagan suspected. That made her even more dangerous, now that she thought about it. Chad was right; Colleen was probably involved in whatever was going to happen at the conference. All the more reason to get away while she still was sober. God only knew what would happen if she stayed.

"Well, good night ladies. See you in the morning." Reagan patted the shoulder of the woman next to her and waved at the rest, who all wished her pleasant dreams. All but Colleen who turned to the woman next to her, ignoring Reagan, and said something that made the woman laugh.

"Well, okay then," she said, walking to the door. She heard another round of laughter at the table. If she lacked self-confidence, she would have worried Colleen was laughing at her, but she didn't and it would take someone whose opinion she valued to make her feel less than adequate. Striding quickly to the elevator, she punched the up button and hoped the elevator wouldn't make her wait too long. She wanted to remind Chad she'd kept her promise, and hopefully reignite what Chad had started in the bathroom.

The download seemed to be taking forever; time moved more and more slowly. Her anxiety was reaching a fever pitch as Chad waited, strumming her fingers on the table and watching the computer screen. Finally, it stopped and opened the operating system of the phone. The transfer program had scrambled the names of the folders so Chad had to open the folders one by one. She peered inside one and then moved on to the next folder, finally finding the one she was looking for.

Reading the text messages, her mouth moved with each truncated word and then stopped. It was exactly as she suspected, they were all in danger. They needed to move quickly or more than just the women at the conference would die. Where was Marco? Where was Reagan? They both should have been back by now. She heard a door open and jumped to her feet. Before she could get far, she almost knocked Reagan over in her haste to confront Marco.

"Oh, it's you?" Chad knew the moment it left her mouth she shouldn't have said it.

"Sorry to disappoint you. I can go back down to the bar and join Colleen."

"No, no, I'm sorry; I didn't mean it like that. I'm glad you're here." Chad took Reagan's hands and led her to the sofa. Their knees touched, but neither woman said anything. Chad wanted to look at Reagan, tell her exactly what she'd found out and how scared she was right now, but she just couldn't drop the hardcore, butch facade. She couldn't let herself be seen as weak, no matter what the situation. Instead, she just rubbed her hands against Reagan's folded hands. Her heart lurched. What was she going to do about Reagan's safety? This wasn't the United States and what she was about to do could land her in a foreign jail, dead, or at a minimum burn a few bridges she might have to cross back over somewhere down the line.

"What's wrong? What's going on, Chad? You look like you've just been told your puppy was run over."

"Okay, a little dramatic, but I was just going through Jason's text messages and–"

"How did you get his phone? Oh, that's why Marco was playing with Jason." Reagan slapped her head. "God, I didn't see that coming."

"Don't feel bad, Marco didn't see it coming either. I thought you were him, actually, but I am glad you're here."

"Well?"

"Well, what?"

Reagan pointed to the computer and raised her eyebrows in inquisition.

"Oh, yeah, I need to pull the team together. We don't have a lot of time. I want you to pack your stuff, you're leaving now."

"What? You can't be serious."

"I think it would be best, for now." Chad continued to rub Reagan's hands. She didn't have the guts to look her in the eye, when all she really wanted was to kiss Reagan. To scoop her up, take her to the bedroom, lay her on the bed, and make love to her. Looking at the possible end of your life had that effect on people, she suspected.

"No, if you're staying then so am I."

"Listen to me." Chad pulled Reagan over. "I don't need to worry about your safety. I need to focus on getting Mrs. Allegany out of here and I need to make sure Jason doesn't succeed."

Chad wrapped her arms around Reagan and squeezed her. God, all Chad wanted was to take her somewhere safe and try to put the past behind them. Start over, trust Reagan again.

Reagan's hands framed Chad's face and pulled her forward. Reagan kissed Chad's closed eyes, and then brushed her lips against Chad's. Chad couldn't look at Reagan, she felt childish, but she knew if she did, she'd give in to whatever game Reagan was playing. Covering Reagan's hands, Chad held them against her face.

"Reagan, you need to listen to me. Jason's the courier, he's got a virus that he plans on releasing at the conference."

"Okay, how can I help?"

"You can't, you don't have training for a job like this. He's dangerous, more dangerous than I thought."

"So he is working with Colleen." It was a statement waiting for confirmation.

"Actually, yes and no, I doubt she knows exactly what's going on. From what I've read so far, it's disjointed, but he's working with Juan Diego Velasquez, himself."

"What about Colleen, how does she figure in all of this?"

"I'm not exactly sure, but I think she could be a patsy. I think she's just the delivery system and doesn't know exactly what's going on. That's why I need to talk to Marco. We need to get into Sylvia's penthouse. He's hiding the toxin in there. That's how he got it into the country." Chad pulled Reagan's hands down and put them back in her lap, but didn't release them. "He knew that customs wouldn't check her luggage and if they did, it would be a cursory search, at best."

"Wait, I thought you had video of Colleen confirming delivery of something."

"We do, and Jason's been texting both Colleen and Juan Diego at the same time. It's clear Juan Diego is calling the shots."

Reagan rubbed her forehead; the furrows smoothed out a little but returned as soon as she stopped. "I can't believe I'm smack dab right in the middle of something so unbelievable."

"You're not, you're going home."

"I'm not."

"You are."

⁂

Reagan didn't like having her life dictated and she wasn't about to let Chad decide when she was leaving. She wanted to help, to prove to Chad she was worthy...worthy of another chance...god, she felt desperate. Her mind raced with options she could throw out, but would Chad listen? She stiffened, straightened her back, and squared her shoulders, searching Chad's face for any glimmer of wavering.

"Let me help, please." She would do anything if Chad just asked.

Chad stretched her neck; the muscled cords flexed for a brief moment before she cleared her throat. More signs Reagan recognize from their prior history. Chad was about to deliver her, *I'm the boss* speech and *you do what I say*. The only thing missing was Chad beating her chest and howling.

Reagan put her hand up before Chad could open her mouth, trying to circumvent the obvious. "You aren't my boss, I don't work for you, and I am not leaving, period."

"Reagan–"

"And unless you plan on physically restraining me and putting me on a plane - by the way, I'd like to see you explain that to the flight attendant - I'm staying."

"I don't take threats lightly, you if anyone should know that," Chad stood, thrusting her hands into her pockets, her back towards Reagan.

Aw, the silent, stubborn treatment. Let see if I can melt that, Reagan thought, standing behind Chad and sliding her arms around Chad. As Reagan had said before, a woman uses the tools in her toolbox and any woman who says she doesn't use her sexuality to get what she wants is a liar. Chad was stiff as a board, but that was okay, she'd shown her hand last night when they'd made love. Now all Reagan had to do was remind Chad that she needed another body in the mix to free up her own people to try and control the threat.

Leaning in, Reagan pressed herself against Chad's back. Her breasts made contact first and then she felt Chad tighten her ass as it touched Reagan's hips. Tightening her arms around the stout body, Reagan laid her cheek against shoulder.

"I could stay with Sylvia. Once you lower the boom on Jason, she's going to be all alone. She'll freak and her husband won't get here fast enough to be of any help. Besides, since he hasn't officially declared, there are no Secret Service personnel to protect her. It's just you, Chad. How much further can you stretch your resources, both human and electronic? Once Jason is in custody, unless you plan on turning him over to the government here, he's going back to the United States for prosecution, right?"

Chad just stood silent. Reagan was positive that what she had just said was a confirmation of what she already knew. This was a shit pile of epic proportion and the goal would be to find the toxin, to get Jason contained, and figure out what to do with Colleen and Juan Diego since they weren't United State citizens. She knew Chad would contain Colleen and turn her over to the government and Reagan didn't want to be anywhere near Colleen when they slipped the silver bracelets on her.

"You know I'm right, Chad." She persisted. Chad's cologne was settling for Reagan as it enveloped her. It took her back to different times and those experiences they had shared, their history. "I can sit here, doing this all day." Reagan let her fingers strum against the tension in Chad's stomach.

"I'd like to sit here and tell you that you're safe, Reagan, but I don't want to lie to you. The toxin or virus, whatever it is, could already be released." Chad patted Reagan's hands and then peeled them off her. Facing Reagan, Chad tried to smile, but it was a weak attempt at best. "We don't have time to talk about niceties, a walk down memory lane or rekindle what happened last night, as much as I'd like that. I agree, you could be helpful with Sylvia. Considering we might have to make Jason talk and that *will* get ugly if he's unwilling to cooperate."

"What do you mean by ugly?" Reagan recoiled from the look Chad gave her. "Are you kidding me, are we talking torture? You wouldn't."

"I have a job to do and that job means that I have to take care of Sylvia Allegany. It would be catastrophic if something happened to her when I could have prevented it."

"Look, I know Jason's irritating and all, but surely he'd see the error of his ways if you explain the consequences to him."

"He's a grown-ass man, Reagan. He knows exactly what he's doing. I haven't figured out the why yet, but I don't like the possibilities. At a minimum, he's an event opportunist, taking advantage of his position and the conference. At worst, he's working for someone else and Sylvia isn't the only person on the list of people to hurt. Think about it. If he wanted to kill or hurt Sylvia, he could have done it anytime, anywhere. It didn't have to be here. Now, think about all the women who will be at this conference and the lives they touch when they go back to their homelands, to their businesses, to their husbands. That circle gets wider, deeper, and has far-reaching implications."

Reagan didn't like the dots Chad was connecting for her. Jason as a terrorist, for lack of a better word, was almost unimaginable. Shaking her head, she couldn't wrap her mind around everything laid out before her. Colleen she could believe, but Jason, really?

Chapter Thirty-two

Okay, so let me get this right, Jason is connected to Colleen and her husband. Have you seen them together?" Holding up her hands, she stopped Chad before she could say anything. "I know you have Colleen on tape and you have Jason's text messages, thanks to Marco. I guess I'm just having trouble believing someone like that could get so close to Sylvia."

Chad wished she had time to sit around and debate the issue with Reagan. Time wasn't on their side. Chad pulled her sleeve back and noted the time. Marco was late, very late, and it was going to throw her schedule off. She tapped her watch.

"I need to find out where Marco is, so if you'll excuse me, Reagan."

Just as Chad reached for her phone, it vibrated across the table. Timing was everything. Without thinking, she flipped it open and answered.

"Marco?"

"Hmm, no."

"Dave, uhm–"

"You're not alone."

"No, not at all, can I call you back?"

"This won't take long, Chad. Bad news, we can't get you that special wine you ordered."

Beautiful, Dan was talking in code, which meant someone was listening on his end, so she couldn't risk divulging too much information.

"What? I don't see why we can't get a nice white."

"Sorry Chad, since you're in a country that doesn't allow drinking we don't want to risk the political fallout if we do deliver your wine."

Was he kidding? Didn't they remember whom she was protecting? Without thinking, she went off script.

"You do know who's here?"

"Oh, they know all right, but the administration isn't ready to end their term with an international incident."

"Are you kidding me, Dan? They're fucking afraid of an *incident*. We're talking about the possible first lady here, Dan. Her fucking husband is going to announce when we get back stateside and you're worried about pissing off a few government officials?"

"Don't get pissed with me, it's not my decision. This one is coming down from the top. I do have a special wine, though, in country, just found out about it yesterday. But I'm not sure about the logistic, yet. I've tried to track it down, but it got lost at the airport."

"Great, so you do have some wine here."

"Some, but we're just not sure where or how long it would take to get to you."

"Who makes it? Does it have a name? Cause we can't have just any wine for Mrs. Allegany."

"Understood, I just found out myself. If I had more information, I'd pass it along. I'll call you when we've located the bottle and let you know where to pick it up."

"Well, can you at least get me clearance at the airport so I can do the extraction and get the fuck out of here?"

"I'll see what I can arrange. What are your plans?"

"I'm not telling you shit; besides the walls have ears."

"Roger that. I wondered when you would realize that."

"I'm good on my end, Dan. I've got the scrambler on. It's your end I'm worried about."

"Look, if I can't find that special bottle of wine, can you get to the airport in the next twenty-four to thirty-six hours? We can guarantee an open window. After that, it's a crap shoot."

"I'll be there. You just make sure you have it clear."

"It'll be clear; you just make sure you don't leave any trash behind. We don't like clean-up duty."

"Neither do I." Chad finally had the last word with Agent Dan. It was little comfort, considering she'd just been told she was out on a tight wire without a net below.

"Bad news?"

Chad had forgotten Reagan was in the room. She'd heard everything Chad had said. Shit. This day was just getting worse by the minute. Chad touched the com unit as it popped in Chad's ear.

"Look, I just need to take a walk," Marco said to someone.

"I'm sorry, I don't know what I said to upset you, but let me make it up to you." Jason's whiney voice cut through.

Chad raised her cuff to her lips and spoke. "Marco, listen to me carefully. We need to get Jason back to his room. We'll have to step this up a level. We have a twenty-four to thirty-six hour window to get this taken care of and there's no back-up coming. So we're on our own."

"Why don't we go back to your room? You can figure out a way to make it up to me."

"Okay, okay, sure. I'm up in the Penthouse."

"Good job, buddy. I'm on my way. I'll meet you up there." Chad scrambled, putting a few things in a gym bag and slinging it over her shoulder. "Stay here." She directed at Reagan.

"Oh no, I'm not staying here by myself." Reagan stepped closer to Chad. "I can help."

"How, Reagan?" Chad wondered aloud.

"Well…well, Sylvia is going to be there right? Well, I can keep her calm. I can talk to her and make sure she stays out of your hair."

Chad had to admit, Sylvia was going to be a problem. She would come to Jason's defense immediately, trying to stop Chad from extracting information from her assistant. No matter how much evidence Chad had to prove Jason was the mole on her *team*, it would take a massive amount of work to turn Sylvia's mind. He'd been with her for a while and she was grooming him to be her personal assistant when she was first lady.

"Fine, but keep Sylvia away from the phones, in her room, and occupied." Chad thrummed her fingers against the gym bag resting against her hip. "In fact, get her packed up, so she's ready to get the hell out of here."

"Sure, anything else?"

"You take care of that and I'll owe you big."

Reagan smiled at Chad. Oh, this was going to be a bad idea, Chad was sure of it.

"Well, I plan on collecting that debt."

"I'm sure you will, I'm sure you will."

Chad opened the door for Reagan, flipped her cell phone out, and dialed the other members of her team. She needed the suite packed up and ready to go. Securing the room, Chad shook her head, walking down the hall. It was never easy guarding the rich and affluent, never.

Chapter Thirty-three

The room vibrated with tension. Marco pushed Jason back onto the chair and warned him not to move again, or he'd be sorry. Chad felt sorry for Reagan; the blank stare took Chad by surprise. The self-assured, self-appointed future CEO of Reynolds Holdings looked more like a scared child. Jason, his bluster firmly intact, tried to stand again, but this time Chad stood over the little worm and spoke to him as if she were speaking to a child.

"If you move one more time or open your mouth even if it's just to yawn, I'm going to duct tape it. Do you understand me?" Her teeth ground as she spoke through a clenched jaw.

"You are going to be so sorry. Just wait until Sylvia gets here. You'll never work another day in your life, bitch."

"Oh, I can't wait till your boss gets here and we tell her what you've been up to, trust me, I'm not the one who's going to be fired today." A smirk etched its way across Chad's face. "Tie this little bastard up, Marco."

Chad turned to Reagan. She didn't want Reagan here when they started tearing things apart. Jason wasn't going to be volunteering any information, so that meant they would have to resort to other means to get it. Reagan wouldn't be in the room, period.

"I need you to go find Sylvia and keep her busy.

We're going to toss this place, starting with Jason's room."

"And if it's not there?"

"Then we will have to do Sylvia's room."

"Chad, I don't think that's a good–"

Putting her finger up to stop Reagan, Chad shook her head. She ducked her head and whispered in Reagan's ear, preventing Jason from listening. "I don't have a choice. It's here somewhere and we need to find it before he passes it to Colleen."

"Oh, isn't that cute, the two love birds," Jason quipped.

Chad shot him a look and then ordered his mouth taped. Jason tried to fight with Marco, but Marco's bulk had Jason wedged like a vise as Sofia laughed and taped his mouth shut.

"Oh shit. He stuck his tongue out. Looks like I need to take it off and do it again." She giggled. "This time can you keep his jaw shut, Marco?"

Sofia yanked the tape across his face, Jason threw out a line of cuss words that would make a nun blush. "You fucking bitch, you did that on purpose."

Sofia looked down at what was left of his mustache on the sticky back. "Ouch, that's gonna leave a mark."

"You fucking dyke bitch. I'm gonna–"

Marco tapped underneath his jaw and squeezed down on his head, forcing his mouth shut. "If you can't say anything nice, then keep your mouth shut. If you'd been more cooperative we might have put some baby powder on the fancy cookie duster and saved it for your boyfriend back in the states." Marco laughed.

A bigger piece of tape was slapped against his face and then Marco and Sofia taped him to the chair.

"How is he going to be able to help you find whatever you're looking for if he's tied up?" Reagan whispered to Chad.

"Well, he could have cooperated, in which case he wouldn't be tied up, but he refused. Now, we have to toss the place and hope we can find it without his help. If that doesn't work, I'm thinking a dunk in the toilet is in order."

Chad heard Jason mumbling and trying to squirm out of his chair at the last statement.

"Of course we have the advantage of the tub and a towel, if we need to. We're very familiar with the process of waterboarding."

Reagan sucked in a sharp breath. "You wouldn't."

Chad nodded her head. "If I have to protect Mrs. Allegany, I'll do whatever it takes to keep her and the rest of us safe. I don't feel like sitting in a decontamination chamber for days, maybe weeks until they can figure out what it is this little prick is spreading, do you?"

Reagan shook her head. Chad knew this was the part of the job that sucked, but sometimes when it came to executive protection, you risked your life for the client. Unfortunately, this was one of those times.

Chad's com system buzzed in her ear.

"Chad, heads-up Mrs. Allegany is on her way up to her room."

"Roger that. Can you delay her?"

"Negative, she says she's tired and she needs a nap. Wants to know where Jason is."

"Roger. We'll clear the living room, try and get her into her room and close the door."

"Roger."

"Okay everyone, Mrs. Allegany is en route. Let's

get this guy into the kitchen. It's the furthest away from Mrs. Allegany's room. If he starts to make noise, smack him."

"Chad."

"Reagan, I think you're going to need to go. You won't be able to stomach all of this, go find Mrs. Allegany and keep her company. Act as if you just ran into her and you want to talk to her."

"But…"

"Reagan, this is part of the job. Granted it's not a big part of the job, but the government has left this in our hands, so we need to do whatever it takes to get him to tell us where the virus is." Chad grabbed her hands and rubbed the back of the knuckles. "I'm sorry, it's never something I wanted you to see, trust me."

"I know but…"

"Reagan, go. You said you wanted to help earlier, well go find Sylvia and make sure she doesn't come in here. Okay?"

Reagan could barely shake her head. She started to look over at Jason, but Chad grabbed her chin and kept Reagan's focused on her. It wouldn't work if Reagan was feeling sorry for what was about to happen to Jason, so she needed to get her out of that room and fast. Pulling her through the door and to the hallway to the elevator, she laced her fingers in Reagan's and rubbed her arm, pulling her close.

"I need you to go now okay? Find Sylvia." Chad tapped her com and talked into her mic. "Rita, where are you ladies?"

"We're just now leaving the podium and she's making her way through the throng of reporters."

"Good, keep her there for a few minutes, I'm

sending Reagan down to join you." She looked at Reagan and kept rubbing her arm. "See if you can get Sylvia to the bar for a drink, anything that will give us some time to search the suite. Okay?"

"I'll see what I can do." Reagan gave a half-hearted smile.

"That's my girl." Reagan shot Chad a look. "We'll talk about it later." Chad smiled, knowing it was a long overdue discussion for them.

"Rita, I'm sending Reagan over, behave."

"Yes, boss."

"I mean it. I'll let you know when it's safe to bring her back to the room."

"Roger."

Chad still had Reagan's hand grasped firmly in hers. The next few hours were going to turn her into someone Reagan might not like, so it was better if she wasn't around for it.

"Be careful, Colleen is out there and we don't know where in the plan they're at. Cut her a wide path, please."

"I will."

"Sylvia's down in the vestibule playing diva, so she should be easy to find. Good luck!"

"You too."

Chad placed a light kiss on Reagan's cheek, then opened the door to the hallway leading to the elevator. "Call me if you run into trouble."

"I will, but I'll be with Rita, and you know how much she likes me. So I should be fine."

"Play nice with the Latina."

"Be careful, please."

"Go," Chad said, shooing her out the door.

Before Reagan prolonged the good-bye, Chad

closed the door and watched her through the peephole. On cue, Reagan looked back and shook her head at the door. Chad didn't even have to wonder what Reagan was thinking, it was written all over her face. It didn't matter, Chad had to do what she had to do. Now, she needed to deal with that little worm, Jason.

Chapter Thirty-four

Mrs. Allegany, when is your husband going to announce for the presidency?"

"Mrs. Allegany, do you know who he's going to pick for vice-president?"

"Mrs. Allegany, over here."

A flash popped down the hall and the flesh mob, as Reagan was starting to refer to it, slowly moved towards her. Well, she'd found Sylvia, the only question was – could she get close enough to grab her and make a run for it. Reagan spotted Rita, who only gave her a passing glance as Rita pushed the crowd back so Sylvia could take two more steps before being stopped again. It was the final days of the conference and it seemed that the reporters had waited until the last minute to get their questions in. Pushing into the crowd, Reagan took up the opposite side of Sylvia and whispered. "Let's get a drink?"

"Oh my god, a familiar face. Bless your heart." Sylvia smiled and grabbed Reagan's hand.

"Well, I couldn't leave a damsel in distress, now could I?"

Before Sylvia said anything, she heard Rita cough loudly on the other side of Sylvia.

"Honey, I would kill for some good ol' Kentucky bourdon."

"Well, isn't that a coincidence? I just happen to have some in my room ladies." Colleen surprised everyone when she popped up behind them.

"Well, if your room is close then I think we should hide out there, don't you?" Sylvia winked at Colleen.

"Just a few doors down." Colleen looked at Rita and gave some directions for her. "Move the crowd down like we're making for the elevator and when we get close to my room, right-hand side, we'll move Mrs. Allegany right and I'll open my door and we'll get her inside without incident."

"I don't like it," Rita said, eyeing the crowd.

"Well, I do, so let's make it happen," Sylvia instructed.

As if on cue, the group stopped at Colleen's room. She slid her keycard and they backed into the room without so much as a word between them. Slamming the door behind them, Colleen just laughed and slid part way down the door.

"Oh my god, do you have to go through that every time, Mrs. Allegany?"

"Well…it isn't usually that bad for me, but my husband is mobbed constantly."

Rita came out from the bathroom and announced the room was clear. "All clear."

"Really, what did you expect, chica? A bomb or something?"

Rita crossed her arms in front of her and stood ramrod straight as she addressed Colleen. "You never know what you might find from some despot dictator, now do you?"

Colleen jumped to her feet so fast that Reagan barely had time to get between them.

"That was uncalled for, Rita," she said, putting her hands on Rita's chest.

"Ms. Reynolds, if you'll remove your hands, please. I need to call my superiors and let them know about the change in plans."

"Of course." Reagan turned towards Colleen and asked, "So how about that drink?"

"Good thing you stopped her, I would hate to mess up that pretty face."

Reagan caught Rita's grimace as she looked over at Colleen. God, you have no idea who you're screwing with, Colleen, she thought, patting Colleen on the back. Flashing Sylvia a smile, she continued. "So Sylvia, straight bourbon or a little something with it?"

"Honey, bourbon is meant to be savored. So straight it is."

"Colleen?"

"Oh, I'll get it. I've got a whole bar stocked just for moments like this. I have tequila from my country if anyone is interested."

Rita grumbled something under her breath, but didn't look at anyone. Reagan figured she was talking to Chad about the exchange between her and Colleen. Now that Reagan could think about everything, she wasn't too sure it was a good idea to be in Colleen's room if she was connected to Jason. If Colleen was the part B of the plan then they could all be in danger.

"I've called security and they should have the hallway cleared in a few minutes and then we can make it back to your suite, Mrs. Allegany." Rita addressed her comments to Sylvia but shot Colleen a venomous look.

"Hey, no problem here. More for me to drink." Colleen raised her glass. "Salute."

Chapter Thirty-five

Chad had Jason's chair teetering back and forth on two legs. Pushing it back, Jason flailed, as much as he could tied to the chair, jerking his head forward each time Chad pushed it backwards. "Look, before we resort to violence, let's toss his room." Pulling her foot off the chair, it started to topple forward, Jason almost landing face first before Chad grabbed the back and yanked him up. "Careful there pretty boy, I'd hate to think you'd ruin those good looks."

"Sofia, break out the sniffer and see if there are any other bugs or cameras in the room other than ours. If you find one, reroute them to a picture we've taken of the room, cut 'em, or black them out. Do that same thing with the whole suite. We don't need to alert anyone that we might be on to them." She looked down at Jason and hissed, "Now do we?"

Looking at Marco, she directed, "When she's done, bring him into his room. Maybe he'll want to give us a hint if we get warm. Right?"

"So Marco, you've been here, sorta. Where do you think we should start?"

Pointing to a drawer, Marco advised, "Don't touch that drawer. That's where he puts all those socks he uses to jack-off."

Jason's neck popped when he jerked his head around to Marco.

"What? You think we didn't bug your room? You must think we're some low rate operation that you could pull one over on. We're the best at what we do. Oh, and by the way, I'm not gay, asshole."

Jason mumbled something, jerked his hips in Marco's direction, and then laughed. Marco raised his hand as if to backhand Jason, but Chad stopped him. Unless he was going to spill his guts, Chad wasn't interested in his civil rights at this moment and should just let Marco go off. It was obvious Jason was taunting Marco, but she needed him in one piece. Maybe later she'd let Marco use his persuasive way with Jason.

"Don't, not yet."

"He's pissing me off, Chad."

"I know, but let's see what we can find before you beat his ass."

Sofia came back with her tools still in her hand. "It's surprisingly clean, with the exception of our stuff."

"Good. Toss it," Chad said. "But do it orderly. I don't want to miss anything. Sofia, go get some trash bags from the kitchen. I'm sure they have a few there and the bathroom." Chad pulled a marker out of her pocket, ready to label bags. "Pull the bedding off, fold it, and set it in that empty corner over there." Chad picked the only corner that was fairly clean, and would allow her to keep some order in the room.

"Want to tell us where the virus is?" Chad asked one last time before chaos took over. Jason sat silently and stared straight ahead. He wasn't going to be any help, at least not right now. "Okay, have it your way. Pull each item off the bed, fold it, and stack it. Then flip the mattress, but leave it against the wall." Chad held up her hand. "Wait. I want every picture off the wall, Sofia, and when you take them all down, I want the wall tapped and check for weak spots. Also, Sofia, I want you to sniff Mrs. Allegany's room and the rest of the suite. We've been doing sweeps every day, but with this little pimple..." Chad ruffled Jason's over-styled hair. "I wouldn't be surprised if he stashed something, moving it around every time we came in to do a sweep. So go slow."

"You got it."

"Don't touch anything in Mrs. Allegany's room. I want her to be here when we go through it."

It was slow going in Jason's room, as each item was touched and retouched, folded, and placed in a bag. Chad noted where the items came from and then sealed up the bag. So far, nothing was exposed except some condoms, lubricant, and porn magazines. Chad picked each item up by the edges, glad she was wearing latex gloves, otherwise she might catch something. Gross, she thought, tossing them into a plastic bag. She didn't have to wonder how he got the porn. Being Sylvia's assistant, he could use his position to get just about anything he wanted on the black market that she was sure was running just underneath the surface of the hotel. The staff were so poorly paid that it wasn't uncommon to find a few churning a profit in drugs, alcohol, and anything else the country might view as contraband.

"Want to make this easier on yourself, Jason?"

He didn't move, still just staring straight ahead.

"I can make him talk." Marco made a show of cracking his knuckles in front of Jason's face and once again raised the back of his hand as if he would strike Jason.

"Marco."

"Fine." Marco leaned in and whispered, "Trust me, it will be my pleasure to smack you around."

Jason jerked his head away and closed his eyes. He didn't seem intimidated, so Chad was a little surprised. If he was just a mule, he should be shitting his pants at the thought of what he faced when he returned stateside. Something wasn't adding up.

The room had been tossed and Chad's team was coming up empty. It had to be in Sylvia's room and if it wasn't there, it was either handed off already or somewhere in the hotel. If that were the case, Chad's only option was to get Sylvia and Reagan out of the country and fast; it then became the government's problem. Chad called Rita to bring Sylvia to the suite. Maybe Jason would listen to his boss.

❧❧❧❧

"If you ladies will excuse me, the boss has asked me to bring Mrs. Allegany back to the suite." Rita kept her hand on her earpiece, still listening to instructions from Chad. "Roger that, we're on our way."

The women moved towards the door, a round of air kisses and thank yous exchanged. As Reagan moved towards the door, Rita stopped her.

"I'm sorry, but Ms. Morgan didn't say anything about you coming. In fact, she specifically asked that you go back to the room."

"Really?" Reagan was shocked. She thought she and Chad had an agreement. Reagan would accompany Sylvia back to the suite to help keep Sylvia calm. She wondered why the sudden change. "Well you can tell her that–"

"Why don't you let me talk to Ms. Morgan? You

know how gruff she can be." Sylvia said, trying to defuse the situation.

"I'm sorry, Mrs. Allegany, but I have my orders. Now if you please." Rita swung her hand towards the open door.

"I'll call you once I get to the suite. I'll have the hotel send up some dinner and we can all have a wonderful last meal together. What do you ladies think?"

A chill went up Reagan's spine when Sylvia said last meal together; she hoped it wasn't a premonition, but she was getting the feeling that things were getting ready to go bad, and quickly. At least that's what she felt in her gut.

"That would be wonderful, Mrs. Allegany. I would love to have dinner with you," Colleen said, clearly excited. If Chad was right, Sylvia was playing right into Colleen's hands. Oh god, what now?

"Maybe you and I should have dinner together, Colleen, and let Mrs. Allegany rest. She's been so busy all day today, with speeches, and the reporters. That would make anyone desperate for a hot bath, a glass of wine, and a big fuzzy robe."

"Oh pasha, besides I left my big fuzzy robe and slippers at home. What do you say, I'll call you in about half-an-hour to come up for drinks, and then we'll have dinner. You know I just love entertaining."

"That sounds wonderful. Maybe we can discuss my women and children's center I plan to open when I get home. Maybe you'll come to the dedication?"

"Well, never say never. I'll have to check with Jason and see what my schedule looks like, but let's chat over dinner, shall we?"

Before anyone could say anything else, Rita

cleared her throat. "Mrs. Allegany, please." Rita insisted, practically pushing her out of the door.

Reagan was a little anxious now that Colleen had a dinner invitation and Jason would be in the same suite as Colleen. It was starting to look like the perfect storm brewing. If Colleen wanted to poison Sylvia, she could do it. If she was looking for a way to get the virus or toxin or whatever the hell Jason was going to give her, Sylvia had just made their jobs easier. Reagan felt her chest clench as she tried to think of a way out of the impending doom. How could she keep Colleen from attending dinner? Shit, she'd have to think fast.

"Oh, how exciting. I'm finally going to have dinner with the future first lady. I've got to text my husband and let him know. He'll be so impressed." Colleen searched the room for her phone.

"Would you like another drink while we wait?"

"Oh, help yourself. I want to call Juan Diego and give him the good news. I have a new bottle of bourbon here, since it seems we finished the last of it. Here." Colleen handed the bottle to Reagan and turned her attention back to looking for her phone.

Reagan was barely able to grab the wide base of the bottle before it dropped to the floor.

"Oh, sorry about that," Colleen said nonchalantly, still searching for her phone.

Reagan hefted the weight of it in her hand. She didn't have time to spare if she was going to try to stop an international incident from happening. Just as Colleen found her phone, Reagan grasped the bottle by the neck and raised it up and smacked the back of Colleen's head with it, knocking her out. Colleen's arms dropped to her side and she landed face first on the couch, rolling off onto the floor. Reagan stood stunned for a moment. Had she killed Colleen? God, she was creating international incidents left and right. First defending herself against a potential rapist and now trying to kill a dictator's wife. Stepping closer, she poked at Colleen with her toe. Nothing. Leaning down, she tried to see if Colleen was still breathing. If she killed her and it saved Sylvia's life and the lives of the women at the conference, she'd be a hero, well maybe not, but at least no one would die. A trickle of blood started to mat the hair on the side of Colleen's head. *Oh god, blood,* Reagan thought as anxiety started to creep through her. She could feel her need to run building in her. If she could get to the suite, grab her things, she could be at the airport and on the next flight to the U.S. before Colleen's body was discovered.

"Okay, just calm down," she said to herself. "You did the right thing."

Reagan's hands started to shake as she moved closer to see if she could feel for a pulse. Hesitating, she tried to touch Colleen's neck but she stopped. What if Colleen was dead? She'd never touched a dead body before. *Oh god.* Reagan's hands were shaking so badly she didn't think she had it in her to touch Colleen.

Brrriiinnngg

Reagan's jumped to her feet when her phone went off. Pulling it from her slacks, she recognized Chad's number. *Oh god, should I answer it? She's going to kill me, oh shit.*

Brrriiinnnggg

Pushing the screen, Reagan tried to control herself. "Yes."

"Reagan?"

"Yes."

"Are you still there with Colleen and is she close

by?"

Reagan looked down at Colleen and rolled her eyes. "Yes."

"Okay, don't say anything. Tell her that the hotel called and you need to go down to the business center and pick up a fax. I want you to come up here and help me handle Mrs. Allegany."

"Okay, is everything all right?" Reagan couldn't believe she got the sentence out half-normal.

"Well, she's wondering where Jason is and why we're all here in the suite. I need you to help me divert her attention for a little while more, so we can see if we can crack Jason."

"Sure, I'll be right there."

"Good, I'll tell her you're on your way–"

"For dinner, she invited us for dinner."

"Perfect. Just tell Colleen you'll meet her here. Jesus, this is a fucking mess."

"You have no idea," Reagan whispered.

"What?"

"I said I'll see you right there."

"Great. Hurry, our window to leave is closing quickly."

"On my way."

Reagan couldn't take her eyes off Colleen as she tapped the screen to end the call. What was she going to do now? Shit, this was getting worse by the minute. She couldn't pick her up and put her on the couch. She didn't want to touch anything. Hell, her prints were everywhere. She was fucked. Clenching her hands together, she took a deep breath and bit the inside of her mouth. The pain made her focus. Chad was expecting her. When she got to the penthouse, she would pull Chad aside and explain what happened. God, all she needed was Chad pissed at her again. Why did her life seem to twist out of control at moments like these? Because these were moments that life twisted out of control. Damn. Focus.

Grabbing the bottle of bourbon, she wiped it with her shirt and put it in the bar. Stepping over Colleen, she whispered an apology and thought about stopping to say a prayer, but she wasn't that religious; maybe she should just to be on the safe side. No, she needed to get the hell out of there before she was found out. Rubbing her hands down her slacks, she looked around for something to open the door with. Grabbing a washrag, she wrapped it around the door handle, opened the door, peeked out, and made sure no one was coming. She lobbed the rag on to the bathroom counter and almost reached down and grabbed the door handle to close it. Pulling her shirttail, she grabbed the handle and pulled it shut.

She could never be a criminal, it was too much planning and work, she thought as she tried to casually walk down the hall to the elevator. Rolling her finger, she pushed the button with her knuckle and jumped on the elevator when the doors opened and made sure no one was on it. Slinking against the wall, *now* she was ready for that breakdown.

Chapter Thirty-six

Ash?”

"Reagan? What's wrong?"

"I just killed someone, oh god, I'm not going to be able to come home, Ash. You know what they do to women in this country." Reagan felt herself hyperventilating.

"Slow down, Reagan. Take a deep breath and tell me where you are and what happened."

Reagan took a deep breath as ordered and then another and another. She put her head between her knees and welcomed the cold feel of the metal stairs biting into her ass. The stairwell was private and concealed her, concealed her evil act, kept her from harm's way.

"Reagan?"

Her head was swimming. *Did it really help to put your head between your knees,* she wondered, trying to take a deep breath doubled over. It wasn't working. She couldn't breathe and she was just about to go ass over teakettle if she stayed in her current position.

"Reagan!"

"Oh god, Ash. I have to get out of here and I don't know what I'm going to do. Oh Christ, this is bad. Oh god, oh god." Her anxiety ticked up so fast she felt like a stopwatch that was waiting to be punched. Trembling, Reagan pushed the phone against her face. "What am I going to do, Ash?"

This was way beyond their safety call. This was her life hanging in the balance. As soon as they found Colleen's body, they would start searching for the killer, for her. The whole placed was wired with video cameras everywhere. Panicking, she looked up into the alcoves of the stairway and noted a camera pointed right at her.

Fuck!

"Ash, I'm going to get my bags and get the fuck out of here."

"Reagan, I'm calling Uncle Frank. He'll know what to do."

"NO. You can't call my father, you can't. Promise me you won't call him. I can fix this. I'll get my shit and get the hell out of here. I mean, I'll go to the airport and get a flight out of here."

"Reagan, stop."

"I've got to get out of here." Something beyond panic laced Reagan's voice.

"Reagan, where is Chad?"

"Chad?"

"Yes, where is Chad?"

"Uhm…" Her thoughts were all over the place; she couldn't corral them if she were riding a horse and swinging a lasso. Closing her eyes, she pinched the bridge of her nose, wishing for pain. "She…uhm… she's with Sylvia. Yeah, she's with Sylvia because Jason is going to let a virus loose or something." Reagan slammed her hand across her mouth. She couldn't believe she just said that aloud. *God, did the camera's read lips? Of course they couldn't read lips*, what was she thinking. Reagan tried not to look up at the camera in front of her, they were everywhere; she cupped the phone and started to cry. Oh shit, now she was having a nervous breakdown. *Great!*

"Reagan, listen to me. I want you to find Chad. Tell her what's going on and stay with her. She'll get you out of there."

"Oh god."

"Reagan, did you hear me?"

Reagan rocked back and forth. She was a mess.

"Reagan, listen to me," Ash said so sternly that Reagan stopped rocking. "I want you to find Chad. Tell her what happened. I'm sure after everything that's happened to you two this week, she'll make sure you get the hell out of there. If you don't, I'm calling Uncle Frank and it's…" There was a pause. "It's 3 o'clock in the morning here."

"I woke you up, didn't I?"

"Nope, I'm on shift. Listen to me, what are you going to do? Tell me what you're going to do, Reagan."

"I'm going to find Chad and tell her what happened."

"Good, don't stop and talk to anyone. Get yourself to Chad and stay with her. Understand me? When you get there I want you to call me and let me talk to her."

"Why?"

"I want to make sure you're with Chad. I know you, Reagan, you'll try and fix this on your own, but you can't fix this, Reagan. Trust me, they aren't going to let you have a lawyer, they aren't going to let you leave, they are going to put you in the dirtiest prison and you'll wait until Uncle Frank can work something out. So find Chad and stick to her like glue. You said she's protecting Sylvia Allegany?"

"Yeah."

"So she's got her stuff together, she'll protect

you. Now hang up and get your ass to Chad right now. Okay?"

"'Kay."

"Rea, I love you. You're going to be fine. Pull yourself together, you're tough. You've been in tough situations before so don't fall apart now."

"Okay, okay. I'm hanging up and finding Chad."

"Call me when you get there."

"I love you Ash."

"I love you too, honey. Now go."

⁂

Reagan looked down the hallway and ran to the penthouse door and tapped on it quickly. Barely able to stop her shaking, she leaned on the doorframe, her head against her hands. She just wanted to go home. She wanted to be safe again and shut herself behind that door that kept her secluded away from the outside world. In two days she'd almost been raped, reignited a flame, and accidently taken the life of a person. Her life wound out of control so fast that each time she tried to grab it and take back control, she ended up with a handful of barbs leaving her bloody.

"Reagan?"

"Oh god, Chad, I killed her."

Reagan felt Chad pull her into the penthouse and guide her to the couch. "Who, who did you kill?" Chad whispered.

"Colleen."

"What? How? Are you sure? Okay, let's start from the beginning. What happened?"

Reagan clutched her chest; it felt like it was seizing. She was too young to have a heart attack, but the reality of the situation was setting in.

"Rita, get me some water. Slow down and take a deep breath." Chad rubbed her arms. "Here, take a sip of this and tell me what happened."

Reagan rocked back and forth, wishing she was home in bed, with the covers pulled over her head. She wasn't the rock everyone thought she was; she was more like a pebble the water washed over, pushed around with the ebb and flow of the tide, slowly wearing down.

"Reagan, what happened?"

Chad shook her, or was she still shaking, she couldn't tell until Chad lifted her chin and made Reagan look directly at Chad. Tears finally fell.

"I killed Colleen. I hit her over the head with a bottle of bourbon, at least I think it was bourbon. I don't know, it could have been whiskey. Shit–"

"Reagan." Chad shook her again. "Why?"

"She was going to come here, to dinner with Sylvia and I knew you were here with Jason and if she found out what was going on she might try and stop you and she might–"

Her mouth was covered, stopping her from babbling further.

"Rita, I want you to get on the phone and see if Thomas saw anything."

"You got it."

Reagan could hear Rita questioning Thomas in the background. Oh god, she was screwed. She wasn't going home; she was going to spend the rest of her life in a dirty prison, just like Ashley said. *Oh god*.

"Hey boss, Thomas says he can't see real well in the room. The lights are off, but he's got it on tape. She dropped her..." Rita's chin jutted at Reagan. "With a bottle to the back of the head."

"Shit." Chad sat on the couch next to Reagan. "How am I going to survive you Reagan?"

"I'm sorry, I panicked. She said she was going to come down here right now and I knew you were questioning Jason and she was going to blow everything."

Reagan was pulled into Chad's chest where she could weep without anyone seeing. Chad patted her back dispassionately, a clear sign she'd probably lost any chance at being with Chad.

"Don't worry, I'll work this out." Chad stroked her hair and rocked her slightly as she barked orders to her team in the penthouse. "I just need a few more hours and we'll get you out of here, Reagan. Just a few more hours."

Could she keep it together that long? God, she hoped.

Chapter Thirty-seven

Everyone in the room jumped as something crashed against the penthouse door.

"What the fuck?" Chad said, automatically reaching for her little one-shot plastic gun. Her whole crew had the one-shot wonders, so that meant there were at least four in the room. "Marco, cover the right side, I'll see who's at the door."

Chad eased her way to the door, hoping that one of the potted plants in the hallway had fallen over. Just before she could grab the handle, the soft sound of a silencer and the crash of a bullet splintered the door between the handle and the deadbolt.

"Shit," Chad said, jumping back and pointing her gun at the door as it eased open under its own weight. The door only opened so far before it was shoved completely open. Framed in the doorway was a visibly pissed off Colleen Velasquez. Blood matted down the hair on one side of her head. Her hand gripped a Glock with a silencer and she held a black leather wallet in her other.

Out of the corner of Chad's eye, she could see Reagan start to shake. Reagan was sure she had killed Colleen by accident earlier, but here she was in the flesh and pissed.

"What the fuck is going on here?" Colleen spat out. Her gaze lighted on everyone in the room.

Who did this woman think she was? Chad

wondered and where did she get that Glock, and with a silencer on it no less. Something didn't smell right and Chad had to think fast if she was going to flip the situation. She didn't have time to deconstruct what she thought she knew. Before she could say anything, Marco had given up his position and tried to rush Colleen. She leveled the gun at his head and stopped him cold in his tracks.

"I'll drop you right here, Marco."

How did she know his name? Marco turned to Chad; the look in his eyes told Chad he was thinking the same thing.

"Why don't you put your weapon down, Colleen? Clearly, we have you out gunned. Besides, I would hate to have a stray bullet hit someone." Just as Chad said that Sylvia edged out of her bedroom door and hesitated.

"Is everything all right? I thought I heard something fall out here." Her voice trembled. She was visibly shaken as she scanned the room, looking at all the guns drawn. Sylvia tried to go back into her bedroom as if it would offer some protection, but Colleen stopped her.

"Not so fast, Mrs. Allegany, please have a seat."

"Oh god," she said meekly.

"Now, why did you have to come along and fuck up my plans, huh?" Colleen walked over to Chad and pushed the silencer into her chest.

"Hey, leave her alone," Reagan piped up.

"Oh, now *you* want to be a betty-badass. Are you fucking kidding me? You're the reason I have this splitting headache." Colleen pulled her hand back as if she was going to strike Reagan, but Chad stepped between them.

"Look, I'm sure we can all sit and talk about this like adults."

"You don't even know what the fuck is going on here, do you?" Colleen shoved Chad back on to the sofa and brandished the gun in her face. "Do you Ms. Chad Morgan? Let's see…" Colleen put the tip of the silencer to her hips and said, "Your wife killed herself two years ago, you have a scar from your belly button to your sternum, and a tattoo that says *Never forget*, and this piece of shit…" She pointed the gun at Marco. "This piece of shit was your *compadre* in the Army. How'm I doing so far?" Colleen twirled around and ordered everyone else in the room to sit as well.

Chad was at a loss for words. How did the wife of a two-bit dictator know anything about her? How did she get that gun into Abu Dhabi and what happened to her accent?

"Well, you have me at a disadvantage, Ms. Velasquez. You know so much about me and yet I don't know anything about you."

"No, you're not supposed to, Ms. Morgan."

"Then why don't you share a little something about yourself with the group?" Chad was pushing her luck, but she didn't care.

"Well, everything was fine until you sent that picture to DC. Then all hell broke loose."

"I don't understand; are you trying to tell me you're with the U.S. government?"

"Don't look so surprised, Ms. Morgan. I might have been a beauty queen, but there's a brain underneath that tiara."

Colleen walked around the room, letting her gun glide over the back of the sofa. She was a hot mess. Her hair, still matted with blood, gave her a deranged look that really didn't instill much confidence in Chad, especially considering Reagan had been able to get the jump on her.

"I'm not surprised, Colleen. I've seen worse things than a beauty queen turned government agent," Chad said.

Chad had seen men buried so deep in undercover that they started to lose who they were. Guys joining biker gangs suddenly sporting tats, beards, and the requisite leather, with young chicks riding bitch; the whole time they had wives and lives outside of that operation. She worked with a guy who was so buried down into the inner working of the gangs that he passed his wife in the mall and she didn't even give him a second look. Unfortunately, to prove he was a one-hundred percenter, he started doing drugs and running them to prove his loyalty to the club. It was ugly when they finally busted the gang for RICO. He never quite adjusted to life outside the gang. His wife left him, his kids never knew him, and for what? For a case the government could hang their hat on and make some superior's career look better. Sometimes that's how it worked with black ops and undercover work and Colleen was with a son-of-a-bitch like Juan Diego, so the government could get the goods on him.

Chad shook her head; she knew what Colleen had to do the last four or five years to convince Juan Diego that she was only a beauty queen looking for a rich husband. Chad could imagine exactly what her handler has said to her.

"Make him think you're interested in him. Schmooze up to him, you know, turn on those feminine charms and he'll be putty in your hand. Besides, we don't need you inside for very long, just long enough to

get the goods on this dirt-bag."

Chad had been there, been in a situation like that, which always ended badly. She didn't know if she should congratulate Colleen for a job well done, or pity her. Her life after this would be up to her to decide what happened next, but she would never be able to forget or forgive. If she could compartmentalize the job and move on, she'd make it. There would always be another assignment, another dictator to cozy up to, but as a woman, she'd be the government's whore, if she wasn't careful. What she did next would seal her career status.

"I really should thank you though. I'd been trying to get out, but my boss wouldn't let me. I'd been with Juan Diego for four years. What started as a simple assignment to get close to a drug dealer turned out to be the assignment from hell."

"I'm sorry," Chad said, and she meant it. "I can't imagine the kinds of things you've had to do."

"No, I'm sure you can't." Colleen looked down at the Glock in her hands and grimaced. "Ms. Reynolds, why don't you take Mrs. Allegany to her room? I'd like to talk to Ms. Morgan alone." Chad looked at the rest of her crew and nodded her head in the direction of the master suite.

"But..." Reagan started to protest, but Chad's hand on her arm stopped her.

"It's all right, I've got this. Just take her to her room and get her packed and be ready to go as soon as I say. Understand?"

Reagan nodded, never taking her eyes off Colleen. Grabbing Sylvia's hand, she took the grief-stricken woman and led her to her room, but before she shut the door, Reagan looked at Chad and gave her a weak smile.

Chad's heart lurched. She needed to get all of them out of the country, screw Jason and his plot to do whatever he was planning with the virus. Colleen was the fly in the ointment, though.

"Ms. Morgan."

Chad turned defiantly, crossed her arms, and stared at Colleen. Agent or not, she wasn't Chad's superior and even if she was, Colleen had crossed the line brandishing a weapon and threatening Reagan and Sylvia.

"Ms. Morgan, as I see it you don't have many options. So let me tell you what happens next."

"Mrs. Velazquez–"

"Shepard."

"What?"

"Agent Shepard, my name is Colleen Shepard, Agent Colleen Shepard." Colleen repeated it as if breaking a curse that had been her life for the last four years.

"Agent Shepard, I don't give a shit about your mission. My job is to get Mrs. Allegany home and in one piece."

"And Reagan, what's your mission with her?"

"Excuse me?"

"Puleezzee, I've seen the way you look at her. Christ, only a blind man wouldn't be able to catch the invisible act you two are trying to play."

"She has nothing to do with any of this. I found out about you and Jason as part of my job."

"Well, then you're very good at your job, Morgan."

"I'd like to think so."

"Oh, no false modesty there, I see." Colleen

clucked instead of laughing. "This is how this is going to go down."

"What, *this*?" Chad quizzed and made a circular movement between her and Colleen. "I have a job to do and you're making it a little hard to do."

"Not anymore. You've blown my cover and I seriously doubt you'll get out of here without my help. Where's Jason?"

Chad tossed her head towards the kitchen. "In there."

Colleen took an exaggerated deep breath and let it out, sighing. Her shoulders sagged under the weight of the last four years. Just above a whisper, she looked off somewhere and said, "I was in so deep an enema couldn't get me out; my handlers wouldn't pull me because I was right where they wanted me. So you see, as I said before, I really should thank you. This kind of mission sucks the life right out of you. You know what I mean?" She looked down at a busted nail in a handful of manicured French tips. "Of course you know what I mean. That scar is courtesy of a government job. Maybe not a job like this, but still courtesy of Uncle Sam."

"We don't have the toxin. Jason didn't give it up."

Colleen studied Chad before she said anything. "It's a virus, one designed to lay dormant for a few weeks to a month. By the time these women get home, they would have infected thousands, hundreds of thousands. It starts with a short cold, gets passed through touch, sputum when someone sneezes or coughs, and then the symptoms are gone, but the virus is moving through the human chain of contact. Can you imagine all the people on the flights these women would be on to go home? Then their families, their employees, their friends, and then everyone those people come into contact with and you have an epidemic."

"Is there an antidote?"

"Sure there is and you know who has it. For a price, Juan Diego will parse it out to the highest bidders."

Chad felt sick to her stomach. To know that a piece of shit like Juan Diego could hold the world hostage made her blood sear through her body. If she were close enough to him, she would take pleasure in making him beg for his life.

"So again, this goes down my way. I'm not going back to Juan Diego after tonight. There's a team in country ready to pick him up as soon as Jason calls him and lets him know that the virus has been delivered to me. I think the job your girlfriend did on my head will probably work in my favor. What do you think?"

"I'm sure she feels awful."

"I bet, but not as bad as I do right now." Colleen pushed a bloody strand of hair out of her eyes. "Definitely not as bad as I do."

"Let's get this dog and pony show on the road. I've been told that there is a van at the hotel loading dock. It has diplomatic plates on it so you should be able to get to the airport and get the fuck out of here."

"What about Jason?" Chad wasn't leaving without finding the virus. "Has he dispersed the virus?"

"No, that was my job, at least that's what he's supposed to think."

"I have a question, first. How long has he been planning this? I mean, someone like him just doesn't think he's suddenly going to poison the future first-lady and get away clean?"

"Oh no, it's bigger than that; he's been working on this plan for a year. He's thinking he's going to be the hero and save Sylvia. He has one antidote on him," Colleen said, looking around the room. "Somewhere. So where do you have him stashed?"

"Kitchen."

Colleen looked at the closed door and grimaced. "Okay, I'm going to go in there and find out where he's put the virus. As soon as I have my hands on it, you're out of here."

Chad wasn't sure, the plan sounded too good to be true. Her duty, though, was to Sylvia. She wanted her feet on U.S. soil as soon as possible, so however that happened was more than fine with her. "What about Jason?"

"I'll take care of Jason."

"Sylvia is going to ask questions. I need to have answers for those questions." Chad stood. She wasn't about to relinquish control of the situation so easily.

"Let me go in and see what Jason has for me. Go into Sylvia's room and wait."

"I don't think that's a good idea."

"I don't care what you think. I have the gun and I get to make the rules. I've been working with Jason for over a year and you've just known him, what, two weeks? You think that's going to trump my relationship with him? I don't think so. Besides, I'm the bad guy remember?"

Chad grumbled. Colleen made a modicum of sense, but barely. "I'll be waiting."

Reagan sat on the bed, holding Sylvia's hand. They were both scared out of their wits and could only hold hands. Words couldn't seem to come to either of them. Seeing Colleen alive was a relief, but whatever relief she felt was short lived the more she looked at the bloody mess she'd created. Reagan was surprised that Colleen hadn't shot Reagan on sight. Not that she would have blamed the woman.

"What do you think is happening out there?" Sylvia finally said.

"I'm sure Ms. Morgan is handling Colleen." Reagan patted Sylvia's hand, trying to reassure her new friend. Rita cleared her throat and gruffed something out. "What was that?"

"I'm sure Ms. Morgan has everything under control, Mrs. Allegany."

"Yes, she seems quite capable." Sylvia seemed lost as she ran a finger over her slacks.

Reagan's heighten anxiety was back. All she could think about right now was getting home, back to her job, and putting all of this behind her. What she wouldn't give right now for her little office back in the R&D department of Reynolds Holdings. It would be a long time before she took another trip outside the United States. Hell, it would be a long time before she left the comfort of her own house. She was taking a vacation when she got back, if she got back.

The door of the room swung open and everyone jumped to their feet, except Sylvia. Chad stood framed in the doorway. Reagan could see Colleen behind her, walking into the kitchen. Oh this was bad, Colleen and Jason together. They were the whole reason everyone found themselves in that room, scared.

"What's happening?" Reagan said.

"She's going to go and find out where the virus is stashed." Chad tried to sound more confident than she looked.

"Is she going to kill us?" Sylvia asked, a frightened tone to her voice

"No, she's arranged to have a van with diplomatic plates waiting for us at the hotel loading dock. As soon as she finds the virus, we're out of here. I need you to take Reagan back to the suite and get all our stuff packed and ready to go. Grab a laundry cart and stuff all of our stuff into it. I want you to look like you're part of the hotel staff. Can you make that happen?" Chad looked at Rita. Reagan knew Rita could not only make it happen, but she'd have everything signed and sealed and wrapped in a bow if Chad asked her, too. "I've called the rest of the team and they're already packing, so get down there and move it to the van. If I'm not there in thirty minutes, I want you to leave without me."

"No," Reagan yelled.

She felt Chad's hands on her arms, shaking her slightly, pulling her off to a corner. "I need you to get Sylvia down to the van and out of here. I have no idea what's going to happen in a few minutes, so trust me to get to the airport. I don't want to be here any longer than possible, either." Somehow Chad didn't seem as reassuring as Reagan had hoped, but she needed to trust her. "Besides, you and I need to have a conversation. I'm not going to duck out on that." Chad smiled briefly before turning to Rita. "Get a carry-on ready for Sylvia. Nothing but her passport, some clothes and nothing else."

"But what about my stuff?" Sylvia protested.

"I'll bring it down, Mrs. Allegany. We need to go through everything. I suspect the only way Jason could get the virus in the country was to put it in your things. He knew you wouldn't be subjected to the same search as he would be, so it's safe to assume he put it somewhere he thought he could get it through customs. While you're not a diplomat, you'd have the same immunity, to a certain degree, as a diplomat."

"Oh gosh, I still can't imagine Jason would do such a thing." Sylvia shook her head in disbelief. "I just didn't know."

"It's not your fault. How could you have known?" Reagan rubbed Sylvia's arm reassuringly. "Let's get a few things packed and get to the suite. Okay?"

Sylvia nodded. Reagan glanced at Chad, who was deep in conversation with her team. *God, would this nightmare never end?* she thought. She hoped that by this time tomorrow she was home and in a hot bath, trying to forget about the conference.

"Mrs. Allegany, please let Rita check your bag before you put anything in it."

"Of course."

Poor Sylvia, Reagan thought. She looked like a lost soul, so different from the vibrant person just hours earlier.

"Reagan, can I talk to you?" Chad motioned her over. "I need you to keep Sylvia calm and composed. I can't have an outburst. She'll draw attention. I've called Thomas to see if he can find a Burqa for both of you to wear. You'll blend in that way."

"Isn't that a little extreme?"

Chad narrowed her gaze at Reagan and continued. "We aren't in the United States, Reagan. I don't have diplomatic immunity or a diplomatic passport, so we are flying blind right now."

"I'm sorry, of course you're right. I'll get Sylvia to the room, get her changed, and wait for you in the van."

"If I'm not there in thirty minutes, you're going to the airport. I've arranged everything. If I don't make it there in time, you'll leave without me and I'll catch up with you in the states. Okay?" Chad lifted Reagan's chin. "Okay?"

Reagan could feel herself losing control and averted her eyes. "Okay."

"Good." Reagan leaned in as Chad wrapped her arms around her and then whispered in her ear. "I'm not through with you, yet. I'll see you in a few minutes."

Reagan rested her head on Chad's shoulder just long enough to feel a sense of relief. Maybe she'd get another chance with Chad, just maybe.

Chapter Thirty-eight

Everyone froze when the door swung wide and Colleen strode through, her hair still matted down, her face frozen in what seemed to be a perpetual bad mood.

"Okay, he says the virus is in a perfume bottle."

"What?" Sylvia looked horrified. "You mean I've been spraying a virus on me this whole time?"

"Not likely. He said it's in a box that looks brand new, with a sealed bottle in it. He said it's in the bottom of your cosmetic bag."

"Where is your makeup bag, Mrs. Allegany?" Chad walked around the room and moved over to a lit vanity. Moving a few things around, she picked up a bag and said, "Is this it?"

Sylvia could only nod as she shakily sat down on the bed, Reagan sitting next to her, comforting her again. "It'll be okay."

"I just want to go home. God, this is a nightmare. Wait until everyone finds out, oh, this is a disaster."

"Don't worry, no one is going to know anything. Are they Agent Shepard?"

"Not from me. That would just involve more paperwork and I'm not a paperwork kinda gal."

"Why did he do this? Did he say why?" Sylvia's voice wavered as she asked. "I want to talk to him," she said, standing.

"I don't think that's a good idea. I told him that

you were all dead. That I killed you."

A chorus of *what's* made the rounds, each woman shocked at the statement.

Chad brought the cosmetic bag and dumped it on the bed. A wrapped box landed on top of everything. It looked just like a normal perfume bottle. Everyone just sat and stared, no one moved to touch it. Thankfully.

"That isn't even my brand." Sylvia said, pointing at the bottle.

"That's probably why he did it. He knew you wouldn't touch it," Colleen said. "I need a zippered sandwich bag or something we can seal this in. Everyone look around and see what you can find."

"The kitchen, there has to be something in the kitchen. Is Jason still tied up in there?" Chad questioned Colleen.

"Yep, I told him I didn't trust him and until I had the virus, I wasn't going to release him."

"Okay, so now what?" Chad didn't trust Colleen. She hadn't instilled great confidence and Chad wasn't sure what was waiting for them at the loading docks.

"We leave," Colleen said so matter-of-fact that she acted as if it were that easy.

"What about Jason?"

"What about him?"

"He's a fucking terrorist."

"Look, you and I both know that this won't see light of day. If word got out that a U.S. citizen tried to infect thousands of people across the globe, shit would hit the fan."

"So…what are you saying?" Chad looked around the room and then pulled Colleen over to a corner.

"He's not going back to the U.S. He makes it home and he'll squeal like a pig. Are you ready for that?"

"You're not saying what I think you're going to say, are you?"

Colleen just shook her head, popped her neck as she twisted it, and pursed her lips together. "I'll take care of it. I've got a clean team coming. They should be here within the hour. No one will ever know that Jason was here."

"Are you kidding me?" Chad knew they couldn't let Jason make it back to the States. Allegany wouldn't stand a chance to be president if Jason was brought back to face charges and a trial would overshadow everything else, including a run for the top office. The government was good, not great at burying things it didn't want to see the light of day. Jason's death would most likely be attributed to a car accident, or something less suspicious.

"I wish I was, but I have my orders. The agency doesn't want any blowback from this, period." Colleen looked over at Sylvia. "I don't know what you're going to tell her, but I would just say that the government is going to be questioning him for an extended period of time."

"I'll handle it. Christ, I'm so tired of cleaning up government shit."

Colleen smiled. "And we love you for it, trust me. It's one less thing I had to add to my report. Now grab your crew and get out of here. Time's wasting."

"Well..." Chad stuck her hand out. "I wish I could say this was a pleasure."

"Yeah, I just want to thank you again for flashing my picture around the agency. Otherwise, I wouldn't be out from under Juan Diego." Colleen shook Chad's hand vigorously. "I hope I never get the chance to meet you again, Chad, and if I see that little number over there–"

"You aren't going to do anything."

"No, I probably won't, but just tell her that I owe her one," she said, pointing to her matted down hair.

"I'll pass it along," Chad said, knowing she wasn't going to say a word to Reagan.

"All right. Out now."

"Take care."

❧ ❧ ❧ ❧

Looking through the mesh, Reagan wondered how Muslim women could handle being so confined. She felt claustrophobic; at the same time, she felt like she stood out like a sore thumb and yet the streets below were filled with women wearing the same thing. She'd blend in more than adequately; she'd just be another woman behind the man, Marco, leading a harem. Chad was the only one not wearing a burka.

"Where's yours?" Reagan asked, wondering why Chad was exempt from the confining style.

Chad didn't say anything, letting her face convey the fact she wasn't going to be wearing one. "Everyone ready?"

"What about Jason?" Sylvia questioned.

"We've got to get to the airport, Mrs. Allegany. I'll brief you once we're in the air and on our way home. Right now though, I need to get you home safe and sound." Chad swept her arms wide and waited for the women to lead the way out the door. "I understand he's going to stay behind and help with the investigation." Chad lied.

"Oh, well, can I at least say good-bye?"

"I'm afraid not," Chad said, making a show of looking at her watch. "We have a small window of time to get you out of the country. I'm sure you can send him a text." She knew he wouldn't answer the phone, couldn't answer the phone.

"Okay, I'll do that." Sylvia pulled her phone and stopped to start her message.

Chad gently grabbed her elbow and said, "Mrs. Allegany, can you do that on the airplane? We really do need to go, now."

"Of course."

The group moved down the hallway and to the service elevator. If luck were on their side, no one would see them or question them. Rita and Sofia had stolen some maid's uniforms and were pushing their cargo down the hall. It was risky, but Reagan knew Chad didn't have any choice; she needed to get them the hell out of the hotel, and fast. Reaching down, Reagan let her hand brush against Chad's as they pulled up the rear of the group. Chad always played sweeper and Reagan wanted to be next to her, knowing that was probably the safest place to be in this herd.

Reagan smiled at Chad, but she knew Chad couldn't see it, so she squeezed her hand in response and smiled.

"Scared?"

Reagan shrugged and quirked her head, but didn't say anything, afraid her voice would give her away.

"Don't worry, just stay close to me. Okay?"

Again Reagan could only offer a squeeze as she wrapped her hand around Chad's arm, moving a tad closer to her protective space.

Moving closer to the service elevator, it dinged,

the doors opened, and a man wearing a janitor's uniform got out and held the elevator for the crew moving towards it. Rita looked over her shoulder at Chad and Reagan felt her heart lurch. Before she could say anything, Chad stepped in front of Sylvia and whispered something in her ear, just as the janitor said something to Rita.

Rita responded to the man in a language she didn't recognize and the group split. Rita and Sofia entered the elevator while Marco, Chad, and the women walked past them down the hall.

Panic set in as Reagan wondered what they were going to do. Their protection just entered the elevator and they were alone in the hallway. Stopping in front of a door, Marco looked as if he was going to open it. Chad stood watch, making sure the janitor was far enough down the hall before she said anything.

"Let's get back to the elevator."

"But they're gone; maybe we should take the stairs?" Reagan said.

"We're twenty-three floors up," Chad stated.

Reagan was pulled along with Sylvia back towards the elevator.

Rounding the corner into the small lobby, Rita and Sofia were standing there, the elevator doors pinging, trying to close.

"Come on, they're going to know we're holding the elevator." Sofia tossed her head in the direction of the elevator. "And send someone to check it out."

"Hurry," Chad ordered.

Chapter Thirty-nine

Chad glanced around at the mish-mash of cohorts filling the elevator. Her most urgent need was to get everyone back on U.S. soil, safe and sound into their loved one's arms, and divest herself of another nightmare job. She couldn't see Sylvia's face, but she didn't need to. Chad knew she was a mess. The depth of Jason's treachery wouldn't sink in for a couple more hours and when it did, she would be in denial, then pain, and then anger. The trust that was built between those in politics was a foreign concept to Chad. Politics made for strange bedfellows and Jason was an opportunist that wanted nothing more than to capitalize on his relationship with Sylvia Allegany. Only now, Chad suspected it would cost him the thing he least treasured, his life. No one who plays with fire the way Jason did valued anyone around them, much less their own life. A generation of people grew up on daily doses of violent video games that taught kids that killing, raping, and stealing was the way to get ahead. Things like *affluenza* and *entitlement* were a way of life for younger people today and would set them up for failure later in life.

Dipping her head, she tried to look at Reagan, who was quietly sitting beside her. Reagan's hands twisted her passport to the point that if she continued, she might render it unusable at the airport. Chad placed her hand over Reagan's.

"It'll be okay."

Reagan's covered head looked up at her, but Chad still couldn't see her face. It was disconcerting knowing that she couldn't read Reagan, that the burka kept her hidden away so well that Chad could only hope Reagan was flashing her usual smile in response.

"I hope you're right." A whisper came from behind the fabric.

"I promise, I'll get you home safe and sound. Okay?"

A brief nod and Reagan looked down at Chad's hand on hers and then over at Sylvia, who was off in her own little world.

The ding of the elevator took everyone by surprised. They'd stopped on a floor and it wasn't their destination. Before Chad could respond, Sofia put her back at the opening, crowding out any potential boarder.

"Oh, sorry, looks like you are full. I'll grab the next one." The man wearing a janitor's uniform said. At least that's what Chad thought he said.

"Sorry, too full." Sofia said, not looking behind her. She reached up and punched the close door button and then pressed the basement button.

"Once we get to the basement, I want everyone to move quickly to the outer doors. Thomas has his equipment loaded already and he's just waiting with the driver to load this stuff." Chad motioned to the laundry carts. "Don't talk to anyone. Don't stop, even if they tell us to. Just keep moving and I'll handle anyone who tries to get in our way."

"What if you're stopped?" Sofia looked at Chad and then at Reagan. Chad could tell what Sofia was thinking and she needed to put everyone in check.

"Do not stop. Get in the van. If someone stops me, I'll take care of them. If I can't make it to the van, I want you to get the hell out of here, Sofia. Do you understand?" Sofia didn't answer; she didn't have to. Chad knew she would follow her orders to the T. "Once you're at the airport, ditch the burkas. I don't want you drawing any more attention to yourselves by having someone ask why you're wearing them. Understand, everyone?"

Chad waited for confirmation from Reagan and Sylvia, but Sylvia didn't move.

Chad lowered her head closer to Reagan's and whispered. "I want you to take care of Sylvia. Sofia will have her hands full watching for boogiemen and Marco will help unload the carts, so I don't have a person to spare. Besides," Chad rubbed Reagan's hands. "I need your help, Reagan. Sylvia trusts you."

"Of course." Reagan's hands stilled under the weight of Chad's.

The coolness of the basement was the first thing Chad felt as the doors opened. Light filtered through the open cargo door, as darkness edged everything else in the large expanse.

"Okay everyone. Let's go." Chad stood to the side outside of the elevator as everyone exited. Everyone bunched into a group with Marco leading the way to the van. The blacked out windows made Chad uneasy. Marco must have sensed it too; his fist shot-up, everyone stopping.

"What's wrong?"

"Where's Thomas?"

Chad peered around the corner of the open bay. "Good question."

"I don't like this." Marco pulled up on her

flank and searched the empty lot behind the hotel. "Shouldn't this place be bustling with people?"

Pulling her sleeve back, Chad checked her watch. "Break time?"

"Maybe."

"Check out the van."

Before they could move, Thomas jumped out of the cab. "Boss, what took you so long?"

"Where is everyone?" Chad searched the parking lot, motioning Marco to load the van.

"Prayer time." Thomas pushed a box into the van.

A moment of relief coursed through Chad. She couldn't believe she'd forgotten the Muslim ritual of prayer time.

"Let's hurry before they get back." Chad assisted Reagan into the van and then Sylvia, slamming the door shut. "Let's go. We've only got a short window to get to the airport and get the hell out of here."

❧ ❧ ❧ ❧

The burka cloaked Reagan's fear. Her heart pounded so hard in her chest, it felt like she was having a heart attack. Her hands worried her passport, her only lifeline back to the US. Reaching over, she clutched Sylvia's shaking hand. They were connected to each other through their fear, their need to get home. Sylvia was lost in her own thoughts and barely moved, except to touch the back of Reagan's hand briefly. Reagan's mind raced at the possibility of being stranded in Abu Dhabi, of never seeing her father again and…she looked at Chad sitting across from her. Chad, her hand stuck in her jacket. Reagan was sure she was clutching her gun, or maybe it was that big knife she'd seen Chad tuck into a sleeve in her harness. Reagan wished she was as calm as Chad appeared. She wondered if anything rattled Chad, ever. This wasn't the same as the situation with Marcy last year, it was different, dangerous, and Chad could be the poster child for dyke Gap ad. Her pressed khaki's crossed at the ankles, her spit-shined loafers, a light blue button-down, and her ever-present blue blazer all presented a well put together picture of leadership in the face of adversity.

The van buzzed with uncertainty as Sofia and Rita divested themselves of the maid uniforms and slipped on slacks, guns, and settled into their rough demeanors, like slipping on a mask. Reagan envied them at some level. They didn't seem to be afraid of anything and the look Sofia shot Rita made it clear to Reagan they might be a couple. Marco sat in front with Thomas, giving the impression that the women in the back knew their place. They'd enjoy it for a brief second, because as soon as they hit the airplane, Chad was back in charge.

The van stopped at the first checkpoint at the airport. The diplomatic license plates made a wave through possible. The second checkpoint, wasn't so easy.

"I see that you are from Columbia?" A man's voice said.

"Shit," Chad whispered.

"What's wrong?"

"I didn't think to check out the diplomatic plates. I just assumed they were US. Christ."

In the worst Spanish accent Marco could muster, he replied, "Is there problem, officer?"

Chad peered out the windshield and could see their plane only yards ahead of them. The door was open and ready to accept passengers, the cargo hatch was down, and the tail end of the SUV was being loaded into the plane just as the cargo door was being shut.

"Fuck. Take off those burkas. I don't want them thinking we are kidnapping Muslim women."

"So what do you have in the back of the van?"

"I'm sorry, but we have diplomatic immunity and we are in a hurry."

"This won't take but a moment, I assure you," the guard said, trying to poke his head in the window.

Chad pulled her phone and called the pilot. "Start those engines, we're going out hot."

"You got it. ETA?"

Chad looked back up at the front of the van. "Three minutes. Pull two Berretta Storms out and make sure they're loaded. Set 'em at the door."

"Roger that."

"Rita, I want you to get out and see if you can divert the guard's attention. Sofia, you and I will get the women to the plane. You in front and I'll bring up the rear. Be sure to keep them between us."

Reagan felt herself amping up. She'd run as fast as she could and nothing would stop her from getting in that plane, nothing.

"We're going to die, aren't we?" Sylvia whispered. "I don't want to die in a foreign country, Ms. Morgan."

"Chad's not going to let us die. Are you, Chad?"

"No, that isn't in my game plan today. Now ladies, no matter what happens, I want you to run for the plane get in and lay down on the floor. Do you understand me?"

"Oh god, we're going to die," Sylvia said, this time a little more frantic.

Reagan squeezed Sylvia's hand and shushed her. The guard was walking around the van, as she heard Rita say something in Spanish to him.

"I'm sorry, I don't speak Spanish."

"No problem. I speak English, you speak English?"

The wall blocked their view, but they could hear the whole exchange play out.

"I do, but I have a job–"

It was suddenly silent.

"Now!" Chad pushed the side door open and shoved Reagan and Sylvia out behind Sofia, who was running towards the plane. Reagan could hear panting as Sylvia loped towards the plane and then two shots rang out. One whizzed right past Reagan and buried in the asphalt in front of her.

"Shit, they're crappy shots," she huffed, moving fast towards the plane. It was amazing how fast you could run when your life was at stake.

"Stop." The command was given behind them and then two more shots. Pop, pop.

Reagan heard someone grunt as the second pop sounded. Turning just enough, she heard more shouting and saw Chad stumble to her knees. Reagan stopped dead in her tracks, Sylvia almost running her over. Sidestepping Sylvia, she started to run towards Chad, but Sofia grabbed her arm and pushed her towards the plane.

"She's all right. Get your ass on the plane."

"But she's shot."

"Get the fuck on the plane."

"She needs help."

"I have my orders. Get your ass on the plane, NOW."

Reagan scrapped her shins against the metal ladder, forcing herself up the steps. More shot rang out and spurred Reagan to step it up. One last look over her shoulder and she could see two men running towards Chad and the plane. Sofia picked up the Berretta assault rifle, chambered a round, and aimed at the guard, just a few feet from Chad. Time seemed to move in slow motion. Reagan heard Sofia take a deep breath, watched as she pulled the rifle to her shoulder, rest her cheek against the butt of the gun. Squint her eye and move her finger to the trigger. As she squeezed the trigger, she heard Sofia exhale and then there was a puff of smoke as the rifle ejected the hot shell at her feet.

She blinked and turned, thinking she could follow the bullet to its target, but by the time she looked at Chad, the man behind her was falling forward, clutching his leg.

"Oh shit, you missed him."

"No, I didn't."

Reagan looked again and there were two men down, one lying in a pool of blood and the second writhing in pain, holding his thigh.

"Two'fer."

Sofia handed Reagan the rifle and ran down the stairs towards Chad. Rita grabbed the rifle from Reagan and drew a bead on the two women making their way to the plane.

"Get this thing out of here, now, damn it," Chad yelled, barely halfway up the steps.

"Oh my god, you're hurt, Chad." Reagan panicked, seeing the bloody leg being dragged behind

Chad.

"Out of the way Princess. We need to close the door and get off the tarmac."

Reagan felt herself being pushed aside by Sofia, a bloody hand print dead center of her chest. The warm, coppery smell made her stomach lurch. It was Chad's blood on her chest and now she was frantic to help in any way she could. She wasn't about to lose Chad, not now.

"Get her in the back, bring the med kit. Where's Marco?"

"He's loading the last of the equipment."

"Fuck the equipment, tell him Chad's been shot. Let's get this flying pig off the ground now."

"It's a hot take off. Everyone strap in," came a voice over the intercom.

"Strap in, Reagan." Chad cupped Reagan's hand. "I'll be fine, it's just a nick."

The blood all over the mattress told a different story. Reagan sat frozen, holding Chad's hand. She couldn't budge if she wanted too.

"I'm staying right here."

"You need to get your ass in a seat and strap in or else." Rita glared at Reagan.

"You're gonna have to shoot me, because I'm not leaving her side. Understand?" Reagan stood and was nose-to-nose with the Rita.

"Ladies, please. Both of you get your asses out of here and find a seat." Marco commanded, his voice booming in the metal cigar tube. "I'll take care of Chad. Now, sit your asses down." Marco pulled a phone and yelled, "We're ready for take-off. Go!"

Reagan had barely sat in her seat when the plane pulled a steep ascent, the feeling similar to one of those roller coasters that climbed at sixty degrees before cresting and dropping so fast your stomach was in your throat. The force pushed Reagan back into her seat and kept her there for the time being. Reagan turned to search for Chad, the door to the back was closed and Sofia sat in a seat, her gun resting across her lap. The look on her face definitely told Reagan she wasn't getting in there anytime soon.

Chapter Forty

The sticky warmth of blood coated her hand. The smell threw her back into a distant memory before she could stop herself from going there.

The sharp stick of the blade piercing her skin made her muscles violently contract. The next stab took more force to push the blade deeper inside.

"You fucking bitch." The rough male voice reached into the deep recess of her mind. Adrenalin coursed through her veins as her only thought was to fight back. Kicking at her attacker, she tried pushing him back, but he was built like a brick shit-house and she only succeeded in dislodging the knife blade.

Another slash.

Another kick.

Chad raised her hands; the blade sliced across her palm. Her defensive wounds would tell the story of her fight to save her life, if her lips couldn't. She wasn't about to let her attacker get away that easily. Reaching up, she raked his face with her nails, leaving a blood trail behind.

"Argh, you fucking bitch." He reached up and ran his bloody hand across his face.

Another stab and she blacked out.

"Chad? Chad?" Her body shook. "Chad, wakie, wakie." Marco pulled an eyelid up.

Jerking her face away, she slapped at Marco's

hand. "What the fuck?"

"You passed out while I was probing for the bullet." He held up forceps, the bloody lead slug shimmering. "I can give you something for the pain, but it's going to put you out. I thought I would ask, since Reagan's been banging on the door wanting to see you. Do you want to see her?"

Chad looked down at her leg, her pant leg cut off so Marco could get to the bullet. The blood soaked bandage would need to be replaced, but she could see Reagan first.

"Send her in and shut the door behind you."

Marco smiled at the command, but before she could say anything else, he stuck her with a needle.

"Shit."

"Well, if I waited, you'd tell me no, and you need to rest. It isn't serious, but you still need to take it easy. I want you to sleep on the way home." Marco looked down at his watch. "And by my calculations, that should be about eighteen hours."

"I'm not sleeping eighteen hours."

"No, but you will sleep for at least four or five, so there." He tossed the syringe in the med-pack and cleaned up the last of the bloody gauze.

Reagan popped her head around the corner. "Hey."

"Hey." Chad grimaced as she shifted her hips and patted the small space next to her. "Sit."

Reagan did just that. Grabbing Chad's bloody hand, she picked at the dry blood on Chad's nails and started to cry.

"Hey, what are you crying for?"

"You could have been killed out there." Reagan threw herself across Chad's chest, sobbing.

Chad sat frozen at the contact for an instant and then wrapped her arms around her, trying to comfort Reagan.

"I'm fine. Don't worry. Marco took the bullet out and stitched me up." She wanted to run her fingers through Reagan's hair, but stopped when she saw the blood. "Look at me." She framed Reagan's face with her hands. "I'm sorry you had to see that. It isn't something you should ever have to see."

"I...I...was so scared."

"It's okay, I'm okay." Chad leaned up and kissed Reagan. It was all she could think to do. She could taste Reagan's tears on her lips. She never wanted Reagan to worry about her, the job she did, or anything. Startled by the thought, she pulled off the kiss.

"What's wrong?"

"Nothing, a...Marco...Marco gave me something for the pain and it's starting to hit me. I don't want to start something I can't finish. I mean, I don't want to..." Chad's leg started to throb as her pulse raced. It would only get worse if she didn't stop it now. It wasn't a lie as much as she needed time to think about Reagan and the last few days. Her heart knew what it wanted; now she just needed her mind to cooperate. At least that was what she wanted.

"I'm sorry, I guess I was just so worried that I didn't even think about," Reagan sat-up and pointed to Chad's leg. "Your leg or what if...you know." She shrugged at the suggestion.

"Look, I'm fading fast here. Why don't you lay with me? Keep me company."

"You sure?"

"Yeah, I would like that."

Reagan tucked herself tight against Chad's

side, careful not to touch her leg. Chad let her arm rest against Reagan's shoulder, her fingers twisting a strand of hair.

"Chad."

"Hmm." Her eyes closed and she was almost out.

"I think I…"

⚜⚜⚜⚜

A soft tap woke Chad.

"Hey Boss?"

Her leg felt like it was on fire and throbbed with every heartbeat. Reagan stirred against Chad side.

"I think you need to see this." He opened the door and Sofia and Rita popped their heads in too.

"You okay, boss?"

"Yeah, fine. Hey, great shot back there, Sofia."

"Got a twofer." Sofia smiled, holding up two fingers. Her sharpshooter training came in handy once again. Tactically, she was one of the best trained on the team. Her competition shooting was clearly an advantage.

"Nice job."

"So, what do I need to see?" She gently slid a waking Reagan over and tried to sit again. This time Marco extended a hand and helped her upright.

Sliding his finger across the screen, he tapped a news app that started to play.

"Breaking news! It's been reported that her protection detail and the CIA have thwarted a death threat against Sylvia Allegany. An insider reports that Mrs. Allegany's personal assistant, Jason Redman, and despot dictator Juan Diego Velasquez were working together to release a virus at the International Women in Business conference in Abu Dhabi. The Abu Dhabi government claims they have no knowledge of such a plot, but our sources tell us that CIA agent Colleen Shepard and Chad Morgan, head of Mrs. Allegany's protection detail, discovered the plot during the conference. Agent Shepard had been deep undercover for the CIA, acting as Velasquez's wife for the past few years. We'll have more details as we get them. Sid Tossle reporting, back to you–"

Marco closed the app and smiled at Chad. "Guess your stock just went through the roof."

"Shit, anyone call Mr. Allegany?"

"No, but Mrs. Allegany has been on the phone with him for an hour. She's pretty shook-up."

Chad tried to get up. "I'll talk to her."

Marco put his hand on her shoulder, stopping her. "She's fine. Rita's been talking to her, I've talked to her, and we're trying to get information on Jason. Seems she is a little worried about the asshole who sold her out."

"Well, she's a soft heart," Reagan said, letting everyone know she was still in the room.

"Yes, she is and she'll make a wonderful first lady." Chad patted Reagan's hand. "Okay everyone, make sure everything is stowed, the equipment is cleaned, and we are ready to have customs board when we hit stateside. Marco, alert Mr. Allegany of our arrival time and brace yourselves, I assume the welcome wagon will be news media from around the world when they find out we're coming home."

"We can go to information blackout protocol, if you want?" Marco said, tapping the screen. "Forget it, they've already announced where we'll be landing." Marco turned the screen towards Chad.

"Well." She looked down at her watch and rubbed the blood off the face. "We've got a few hours before we get home. Everyone get some rest. You're going to need it." Chad swung her leg up on the bed, leaving one foot on the floor and leaning back against the wall. "Thanks everyone, you kicked ass out there."

They'd survived another job. The relief that flooded the room was palpable. Chad suspected her phone would ring off the hook for the next few weeks with job offers and government goons wanting to take her statement. As she saw it, she was due another vacation and said as much.

"When we get back, everyone is on mandatory down time for two weeks."

"Sweet." Someone said outside the door.

"With pay." Yelps and hoots went through the plane. Chad smiled and looked at Reagan. "Now, where were we? I think I nodded off when you were saying something." Chad gathered Reagan up in her arms and hugged her tight.

Reagan looked up at Chad smiled and started, "I was just going to say–"

Chad's lips covered hers before she could finish. She already knew what was in her heart, now she just needed time to recon what her heart was telling her head and make a place for Reagan in her life. One was easier than the other, but she had no doubt it would happen. If she could just survive Reagan.

About the Author

Isabella lives on the central coast with her wife, and three sons. She teaches college and in her spare time, which there seems to be little of lately, she is working on her writers retreat in the Sierra foothills. She is a GLCS award winner for Always Faithful and a finalist for Scarlet Masquerade. She also finaled in the International National Book awards and has two honorable mentions in the Rainbow Awards.

She also writes under the nom de plume - Jett Abbott. A darker, rogue who's a motorcycle enthusiast and loves people watching.

Like her fan page for the latest in news on readings, appearances and books.

https://www.facebook.com/isabella.sapphirebooks

or

www.sapphirebooks.com/isabella.html

Other Isabella titles available at Sapphire Books

Award winning novel - Always Faithful
ISBN - 978-0-9828608-0-9

Major Nichol "Nic" Caldwell is the only survivor of her helicopter crash in Iraq. She is left alone to wonder why she and she alone. Survivor's guilt has nothing on the young Major as she is forced to deal with the scars, both physical and mental, left from her ordeal overseas. Before the accident, she couldn't think of doing anything else in her life.

Claire Monroe is your average military wife, with a loving husband and a little girl. She is used to the time apart from her husband. In fact, it was one of the reasons she married him. Then, one day, her life is turned upside down when she gets a visit from the Marine Corps.

Can these two women come to terms with the past and finally find happiness, or will their shared sense of honor keep them apart?

Broken Shield
ISBN - 978-0-9828608-2-3

Tyler Jackson, former paramedic now firefighter, has seen her share of death up close. The death of her wife caused Tyler to rethink her career choices, but the death of her mother two weeks later cemented her return to the ranks of firefighter. Her path of self-destruction and womanizing is just a front to hide the heartbreak and devastation she lives with every day. Tyler's given up on finding love and having the family she's always wanted. When tragedy strikes her life for a second time she finds something she thought she lost.

Ashley Henderson loves her job. Ignoring her mother's advice, she opts for a career in law enforcement. But, Ashley hides a secret that soon turns her life upside down. Shame, guilt and fear keep Ashley from venturing forward and finding the love she so desperately craves. Her life comes crashing down around her in one swift moment forcing her to come clean about her secrets and her life.

Can two women thrust together by one traumatic event survive and find love together, or will their past force them apart?

American Yakuza
ISBN - 978-0-9828608-3-0

Luce Potter straddles three cultures as she strives to live with the ideals of family, honor, and duty. When her grandfather passes the family business to her, Luce finds out that power, responsibility and justice come with a price. Is it a price she's willing to die for?

Brooke Erickson lives the fast-paced life of an investigative journalist living on the edge until it all comes crashing down around her one night in Europe. Stateside, Brooke learns to deal with a new reality when she goes to work at a financial magazine and finds out things aren't always as they seem.

Can two women find enough common ground for love or will their two different worlds and cultures keep them apart?

Executive Disclosure
ISBN - 978-0-9828608-3-0

When a life is threatened, it takes a special breed of person to step in front of a bullet. Chad Morgan's job has put her life on the line more times that she can count. Getting close to the client is expected; getting too close could be deadly for Chad. Reagan Reynolds wants the top job at Reynolds Holdings and knows how to play the game like "the boys". She's not above using her beauty and body as currency to get what she wants. Shocked to find out someone wants her dead, Reagan isn't thrilled at the prospect of needing protection as she tries to convince the board she's the right woman for a man's job. How far will a killer go to get what they want? Secrets and deception twist the rules of the game as a killer closes in. How far will Chad go to protect her beautiful, but challenging client?

American Yakuza II - The Lies that Bind
ISBN - 978-10939062-20-8

Luce Potter runs her life and her business with an iron fist and complete control until lies and deception unravel her world. The shadow of betrayal consumes Luce, threatening to destroy the most precious thing in her life, Brooke Erickson.

Brooke Erickson finds herself on the outside of Luce's life looking in. As events spiral out of control Brooke can only watch as the woman she loves pushes her further away. Suddenly, devastated and alone, Brooke refuses to let go without an explanation.

Colby Water, a federal agent investigating the ever-elusive Luce Potter, discovers someone from her past is front and center in her investigation of the Yakuza crime leader. Before she can put the crime boss in prison, she must confront the ultimate deception in her professional life.

When worlds collide, betrayal, dishonor and death are inevitable. Can Luce and Brooke survive the explosion?

Scarlet Assassin
ISBN 978-1-939062-36-9

Selene Hightower is a killer for hire. A vampire who walks in both the light and the darkness, but lately darkness has a stronger pull. Her unfinished business could cost her the ability to live in the light, throwing her permanently back into the black ink of evil.

Doctor Francesca Swartz led a boring life filled with test tubes, blood trials, and work. One exploratory night, in a world of leather and torture, she is intrigued by a dark and solitary soul. She surrenders to temptation and the desire to experience something new, only to discover that it might alter her life forever.

Will Selene allow the light to win over the darkness threatening the edges of her life? Two women wonder if they can co-exist despite vast differences, as worlds collide and threaten to destroy any hope of happiness. Who will win?

Writing as Jett Abbott

Scarlet Masquerade
ISBN - 978-0-982860-81-6

What do you say to the woman you thought died over a century ago? Will time heal all wounds or does it just allow them to fester and grow? A.J. Locke has lived over two centuries and works like a demon, both figuratively and literally. As the owner of a successful pharmaceutical company that specializes in blood research, she has changed the way she can live her life. Wanting for nothing, she has smartly compartmentalized her life so that when she needs to, she can pick up and start all over again, which happens every twenty years or so. Love is not an emotion A.J. spends much time on. Since losing the love of her life to the plague one hundred fifty years ago, she vowed to never travel down that road again. That isn't to say she doesn't have women when she wants them, she just wants them on her terms and that doesn't involve a long term commitment.

A.J.'s cool veneer is peeled back when she sees the love of her life in a lesbian bar, in the same town, in the same day and time in which she lives. Is her mind playing tricks on her? If not, how did Clarissa survive the plague when she had made A.J. promise never to change her?

Clarissa Graham is a university professor who has lived an obscure life teaching English literature. She has made it a point to stay off the radar and never become involved with anything that resembles her past life. Every once in a while Clarissa has an itch that needs to be scratched, so she finds an out of the way location to scratch it. She keeps her personal life separate from her professional one, and in doing so she is able to keep her secrets to herself. Suddenly, her life is turned upside down when someone tries to kill her. She finds herself in the middle of an assassination plot with no idea who wants her dead

www.ingramcontent.com/pod-product-compliance
Lightning Source LLC
Chambersburg PA
CBHW021218220726
48287CB00015B/1693